Crush

Crush

by
Jane Futcher

Boston ♦ Alyson Publications, Inc.

Typeset and printed in the United States of America.

An AlyCat Book, published by Alyson Publications, Inc.,
40 Plympton Street, Boston, Massachusetts 02118.

First AlyCat edition: January 1995
First Alyson edition: September 1988
Originally published by Little, Brown and Company, 1981.

ISBN 1-55583-602-X (previously 1-55583-139-7)

5   4   3   2   1

All characters in this book are fictitious. Any resemblance to real persons, living or dead, is strictly coincidental.

For Catherine, with love

OUR FRIENDSHIP BEGAN ON A CLEAR, CRISP October afternoon one month after the start of senior year. The Warren Commission had just announced that a single gunman, not a conspiracy, had assassinated John Fitzgerald Kennedy. In Jackson, Mississippi, the public schools were integrated without violence. And in a few weeks, the names Barry Goldwater and Lyndon Baines Johnson would be posted in every polling booth in America. But at Huntington Hill, it was the day before the second hockey game of the season, and they had put me back on the team.

They put me back on because Maddy Hansen's mother married an Englishman and sailed off to England on a honeymoon, taking Maddy with her. Maddy's leaving had been something of a scandal because of a strictly enforced Huntington Hill rule prohibiting parents from withdrawing their children after term began. Nonetheless, for that very rich woman Randolph Nicholson, the new headmaster, waived a rule that had never been broken during the tranquil 35-year reign of Miss Dunning and Miss Kroll.

Scandal or not, Maddy's sudden departure made me very happy because they played me in her old position. Actually, center forward had been my position until Maddy had decided she wanted it, and beat me out. Hockey was about the only thing that made boarding at Huntington Hill bearable. I loved playing with the team, working out in the cool fall afternoons, completing a perfect series of passes with the forward line. I was playing well that year, with the wild, loose energy of an

7

animal released from captivity. The ease with which I dodged past the defense, led the forwards down the field, and flicked hot shots over the goalie's stick amazed me as well as the coaches.

The school felt different that fall. I guess it was a beautiful place — thirty acres of green, forested land nestled in the Appalachian foothills near Harrisburg, Pennsylvania. Several of the dorms were white clapboard houses left from the days when the land was a dairy farm. On the left, by the Hill Road entrance, were the lower pastures where the school's horses grazed. On the right were the white-fenced riding rings. Beyond them was the forest, carved with hundreds of rambling, winding trails. Farther along the drive were the dorms, and at the end was the parking lot, shaded by tall elms and bordered by a cluster of other buildings: the brown shingled gym, the small school theater, and Century House, the massive white mansion that had once been the manor house and was now the center of campus life.

This year the school buildings seemed to radiate a quiet, classical elegance. The grass looked greener, like fresh paint oozing from a tube. The other students weren't as snobby and self-satisfied. Or maybe their attitude didn't bother me as much because I was playing hockey again and I knew in nine months I'd be graduating. I had almost convinced my parents that it was all right for me to go to art school instead of Vassar, and I was beginning to talk them out of my being a debutante in June. I still hadn't gotten them to explain why, when they were always talking about equality and civil rights, they sent me to a school that didn't admit Negroes, Jews, Italians, or anyone not listed in the *Social Register*, but I hadn't abandoned the project entirely.

For the first time, life in the dorm was fun. I stopped worrying about clothes and dates and rules. From the time we entered Huntington our lives were determined by rules. Rules about hair length, skirt length, sock length, signing in, signing out, waking up, going to sleep, chewing gum, posture, promptness, and so on. The school was infested with rules that startled you like cockroaches crawling in a dark summer kitchen. Sometimes, during my first two years, I would wake up in a cold sweat, terrified that in the course of the day, I had accidentally broken a rule.

My new roommate, Miggin Henry, was much easier to live with than last year's, Elizabeth Knight, who was full of stormy moods and sarcastic remarks. If Elizabeth was a thunderhead, Miggin was a light, wispy cirrus cloud. She had gold-red hair and a shining, freckled face. Senior year was going to be different, I knew it. My hunch proved correct.

On the day Lexie and I became friends, there were orange and red and yellow leaves beginning to cover the ground. I remember the grass — still thick and green — and its sweet, aromatic smell as the workmen mowed the playing field in preparation for the game. I could hear the distant hum of their mowers and the exuberant laughter of the children in the Lower School yard as they played tag. When I passed the door of study hall and saw the rows of students poring silently over their books, I didn't feel the usual anxiety that made me automatically review my list of approaching quizzes, papers due, pages unread in history, biology, French, and English classes. I was easy and relaxed.

A blast of warm air, rich with the smell of paint and turpentine, rushed into my face as I opened the door of the art studio. A Purcell horn sonata exploded from the speakers of the stereo. The pink afternoon sun slanted through the west windows, bathing the room in hot, rosy light. It was a generous room, filled with easels and workbenches, overlooking a pasture that rolled upward to a dairy farm. The ceiling angled sharply down on the

9

far side, giving the impression of an artist's loft. From two to five every afternoon the studio belonged to students working on independent projects. Most of the regulars were already there.

Nora Grange, the small, blonde cheerleader from Atlanta, was drawing animal cartoons as usual, an orange-and-gray-striped scarf from a boys' prep school wrapped loosely around her neck. Jeepers, a junior from Philadelphia, looked up and smiled, then returned to her huge sketchbook. Jeepers always wore jeans and a blue work shirt, with a Philadelphia Phillies baseball cap on her head, visor turned backward, to keep her hair out of her eyes. She was my favorite of the regulars. Spread out on a workbench were Helen and Christine, two sophomores, who were painting a giant mural for the dining room. Then there was Elizabeth, standing by her easel in the far right corner. Over the summer, Elizabeth had developed some strange affectations. She had taken to wearing a French smock and beret, and she talked in a peculiar English accent, which I think she'd picked up on Cape Cod from her summer dates, who'd picked it up at Harvard.

"Ready for tomorrow's game, Jinx?" called Jeepers as I pulled my easel away from the wall.

"Guess so," I said. "Ready as I'll ever be. You coming?"

"You bet," grinned Jeepers.

"'You bet,'" mimicked Elizabeth from the corner. "Wouldn't miss it for all the shin guards in Siberia."

"Shut up, Elizabeth," drawled Nora Grange. "Just because Miss Pennebaker's not here doesn't give you the right to mouth off."

"Well, ah nevah thawt a Georgiah peeech could be sa fuzzy," replied Elizabeth.

"Where *is* Miss Pennebaker?" I said. Miss Pennebaker was young and jolly and she usually hung around the studio in the afternoon. When she wasn't there, we talked too much and didn't work as hard.

"She's at a faculty meeting," said Elizabeth, pulling her beret down over her right eye. "I believe they're discussing the Maddy Hansen affair."

"Still fighting over that?" said Jeepers.

My confidence slipped a notch. "Is Maddy coming back or something?" I said quietly.

Elizabeth shrugged. "Who knows? Frankly, I think Mr. Nicholson handled the whole thing most improperly."

"No one cares what you think," said Nora Grange, stalking over to Elizabeth's corner. "Would you *pulleese* shut up."

For a while we all did shut up and the studio was quiet. I sighed. Since the summer I'd been painting from old photographs I'd found in a box in my folks' house in Washington, D.C. I liked the pictures. They were all black and white. Most of them were taken before I was born. There were snapshots of my mother as a girl, at summer camp in Wisconsin, arms draped around her bunkmates; shots of her when she lived in New York. She was dressed in long, midcalf-length skirts and huge, wide-brimmed hats. Her hair was blonde and curly and she often posed on the running board of an old Packard, in front of her building on East Sixty-eighth Street. There were pictures of my father too, in college, sailing in Maine, looking young and happy, his collar unbuttoned, arms firmly guiding the tiller. There were others, of people I didn't know — women walking arm in arm on Fifth Avenue, men dressed in army uniforms, drinking whiskey at stylish New York bars. There were a few pictures of me, too, and I studied them carefully. In one, I was wearing a pinafore and Mary Jane patent leathers. I stood stiffly against the wall of our house in Washington — a prisoner in front of a firing squad. It looked like I might cry.

I pieced together the family history like an archeologist with pots and shards. Who were those people with their fine city clothes and big smiles? When had my mother changed from an impish kid to a grown-up woman escorted by grown-up men? What about my father? Was he as serious and worried then as he seemed now? Did he know, as he sailed that boat, that he would become a law professor, an expert on maritime trade agreements? And why was I always so sad? So uncomfortable? Where was *my* smile? Sometimes I felt like a detective. I was solving a mystery, but I wasn't sure what the crime was — or if a crime had even been committed.

If I'd been drawing myself the way I looked in that studio at school, the picture would have shown a tall, thin girl with skinny legs, light brown hair, and shoulders raised in a perpetual, self-conscious shrug. Skin pale, eyes retreating behind large, round cheeks, and an expression at once questioning and defensive. But I wasn't painting a self-portrait. I was painting from a photograph taken in 1929 — a picture of the All-County Girls' Basketball Team of Aretha County, Tennessee. All the girls were white, and they stood on the steps of a high school gym wearing dark bloomer shorts and woolen tops. They looked very serious except for one girl, the captain, who stood on the bottom step grinning and holding a basketball on which the words "Aretha County" were painted in white letters. She was shorter than the others but she had a sureness and style I liked. That smiling girl was my mother. I was working that day on her expression. The expressions were hard because they were so subtle, and the colors were hard because I was painting everything in shades of gray, to create the same flat, ghostly quality as the photograph.

I was working on my mother's smile when someone came crashing into the studio. Without looking up, we all knew it wasn't a regular. Regulars tried to enter quietly.

The door slammed and a pile of books thudded to the floor.

"Shut up," hissed Elizabeth.

"Screw you," came the voice. And there was Lexie—Alexis Nicole Genevieve Yves. She was out of breath. Her hair was mussed and slightly orange from a summer peroxide job. She wore a rumpled raincoat over her blue school uniform and her navy knee socks had fallen to her ankles. Lexie stared at us like a child peering at animals in the zoo.

"Ah, *mon Dieu*," she laughed. "I've interrupted *les artistes. Je vous démande pardon.*"

"What on earth are you doing here?" said Elizabeth. Since ninth grade, when they'd roomed together, Elizabeth and Lexie had carried on a vendetta. They were both from New York City, both theatrical, and both sarcastic. But Lexie was a school celebrity, a success. Her sharp tongue had a lovable side; her grades were always better than Elizabeth's; and her popularity with boys was a legend at Huntington Hill. So was her family's wealth. Although Lexie was seventeen, the same age as all the seniors, there was something *older* about her. Her body seemed fuller and more mysterious, her dark eyes more discerning, her attitudes more sophisticated.

"I need a poster for Music Club," said Lexie, who was roaming the studio, looking over everyone's shoulder.

"Stay away from me," screamed Elizabeth.

"You're painting nuns again, Elizabeth," said Lexie, holding both hands on her hips. "You shouldn't be painting nuns. Your mother paints nuns."

"Dammit, who asked you?" Elizabeth turned her back to Lexie and pulled up the collar of her smock.

Lexie persisted. "Elizabeth, it's not at all original to paint the same thing your mother paints. It shows a failure of imagination." Lexie scanned the room to see if she'd missed anyone.

"Ah, Mademoiselle Tuckwell, great star *du hockey. Qu'est-ce que tu fais?*" Without waiting for an answer, Lexie approached, squinting. I hated people to look at my paintings before they were finished. I was afraid that Lexie might sabotage my self-confidence with one quick remark. But instead, she stood quietly beside me, weight sunk into her right hip, carefully examining each member of the All-County Girls' Basketball Team of Aretha County, Tennessee. The smell of Jean Naté Friction pour le Bain filled my nostrils.

"What is this, Tuckwell?" Lexie's eyes were fixed on the painting. My eyes were fixed on her.

"It's the 1929 All-County Girls' Basketball Team of Aretha County, Tennessee." I pointed to the figure at the bottom. "That's my mother."

Lexie moved closer. She sighed. "I don't know what to say. It's very ... unorthodox."

"It's not finished," I said. I was flattered by Lexie's interest. She was a star — sparkling and sophisticated. I never thought she'd waste her time on me.

"I don't care if it's not finished," she said, distracted. "It's a ... it's a fine painting. It's very moving." She pulled a Kleenex from her pocket and blew her nose. Then she looked up at me. "My mother died when I was born and my father died when I was six. I have a guardian and a cousin ... Philip." She closed her eyes. For a moment, she disappeared into another world. The color left her cheeks. Then she opened her eyes. "Philip's an ass," she said quickly. "So's Eleanor." She held my arm. "You're lucky to know your mother, Jinx." Lexie pushed her hair off her forehead.

"Elizabeth," she yelled, in a colder voice. "Come over here and look at this painting."

Elizabeth didn't answer. She dabbed black paint on her nun's habit. "*You* didn't discover Jinx," she said finally.

I was surprised. Elizabeth usually criticized every-thing I did — from my choice of subjects to the way I mixed paint.

Lexie cleared her throat. "Tuckwell," she said loudly, "I would like *you* to make my Music Club poster."

Elizabeth cackled. "Do your own dirty work, Alexis Yves. Tuckwell has better things to do."

"You keep out of this." Lexie turned to me and held my arm. Her eyes were wide and hopeful. "Jinx, will you help me? I need to announce new-girl tryouts."

Elizabeth hurried to my corner of the room. "She's a con artist, Jinx. Don't let her take advantage of you."

I looked at Lexie.

"When do you need the poster?" I said.

"Don't, Tuckwell."

"Shut up, Elizabeth." Lexie gazed at me. I felt as if her brown eyes might swallow me. "Actually, I need it today — right now, in fact!"

I shrugged. What was there to lose? It wouldn't take me long. "Okay, I'll do it."

"Tuckwell, you've been had." Elizabeth retreated to her corner.

With Lexie leaning over my shoulder, her perfume floating by me, I hand-lettered the poster. It wasn't easy, with so much to distract me, but I did it. I even did something extra — a little drawing of a man and a woman, in 1930s clothes, dancing — Fred Astaire and Ginger Rogers. The woman was leaning backward in a daring arch. The man's arm supported her.

"It's beautiful," said Lexie. She slipped her arms around me. "The new girls will think Music Club is hot stuff."

"Jesus," grumbled Elizabeth, eyeing us suspiciously.

"Know something, Jinx?" said Lexie quietly. "You don't breathe when you paint. I was watching you."

"She's actually a fish," called Elizabeth. "She only breathes underwater."

"Really, Jinx. You don't breathe. Here, feel me." Lexie placed my hand on her stomach. She breathed slowly, her abdomen rising and falling under my hand. "You see, I'm really breathing," she said. "You should be breathing this way when you paint. In and out, in and out." Her hands were on top of mine. "When I breathe, my whole diaphragm contracts. Feel?"

"What are you doing to Tuckwell?" Elizabeth was staring at us. Jeepers and Nora and the sophomores were staring too.

"Never mind them, Jinx. Do you feel?"

I nodded.

"You're white as a sheet, Jinx," said Elizabeth.

"The point is," continued Lexie, "if you hold your breath when you paint, you can't paint as freely. You can't do *anything* as well."

"Like sex, right, Lexie?" Elizabeth frowned.

Lexie laughed. "Well, of course, sex is *one* thing."

I looked at Lexie. My face was red. I could feel it. "Should I take my hand away?" I whispered.

"Listen to your voice, now, Tuck. It's way up here." She drew a line across her neck with her finger and spoke in a falsetto.

"There's nothing wrong with her voice," fumed Elizabeth. "What do you know about her voice? Nothing. You're crazy."

"I've had three years of voice at Juilliard, you creep," said Lexie. "Jinx, I'll give you breathing lessons."

"Listen to her," growled Elizabeth to Jeepers and Nora, who were still watching us intently.

"In ... in six lessons, I'll have you breathing and painting at the same time." Lexie's gaze was direct. "I like you, Jinx," she said softly. "I'd like to help you."

I shivered. Lexie was standing close to me. Her body and her voice seemed to be melting into me. Or maybe I was melting into her.

"Are you sure you have time?" I wasn't sure *I* did.

Her hand brushed my cheek. "It won't be difficult, Jinx."

I gulped. "Okay."

"Jesus," muttered Elizabeth again.

Lexie buttoned her trench coat and picked up her books. "In six lessons, Jinx. I promise. Meet me on Tuesday, Practice Room D." Lexie grabbed the poster, wrinkling the edges, and banged out of the studio.

"So much for art," mused Elizabeth.

I laughed. That was the beginning of Lexie and me.

When the studio had emptied, I stood at the sink washing my brushes, warm water splashing over the black bristles and gurgling down the drain. Usually, the cleanup ritual relaxed me, but today I felt nervous; I couldn't stop thinking about Lexie and the sudden strength of my feelings about her. My legs were trembling. What was happening to me? What was it about Lexie that reminded me of last summer and that conversation with my mother? It was the day that I told her I didn't want to go to college, that I wanted to go to art school, in New York.

Mother had looked up from the newspaper. "New York?" she said in her Tennessee drawl. "New York is a rough city." My mother had lived in New York for eight years before she married my father. "You'd get swallowed up, Jinx, coming from a school like Huntington Hill."

"I might not get swallowed up," I said tentatively.

My mother folded the newspaper. "People at art school aren't very attractive." She was crazy about *attractive* people.

"What's wrong with art school people? Aren't they like anybody else?"

Mother stood up nervously and carefully dropped a handful of peppercorns into the silver pepper grinder. "They won't be from the same *background* as you, Jinx. You've lived a very sheltered life. You're too high-strung. People go off the *deep end* in New York. Particularly at *art* school."

The deep end. There was that expression. Mother used it a lot. She seemed to have a special, secret meaning for it.

"What exactly do you mean by 'deep end'?" I said casually. "If I'm going off it, I ought to know what it is."

"Jinx, I didn't say you would go off the deep end." Mother's hands shook as she poured particles of Calgonite detergent into the dishwasher. "I was thinking of Clarence Brown, Uncle Dick's roommate at Yale. He went to art school in New York. I met some of his friends. They were kooks. New York is full of kooks."

"Did Clarence go off the deep end?"

"Jinx!" Mother's face was red. She sat back down in her chair.

"Mother, how come you could live in New York with all those kooks and not go off the deep end, but you think I will?"

"I need to order a cord of wood," said my mother suddenly, whipping out the Yellow Pages.

"But it's summer..."

"New York was different then, Jinx. I lived on East Sixty-eighth Street with my sister and her two roommates from Vassar and we knew lots of attractive men."

"Did Aunt Connie know Clarence Brown?" I asked.

"*Everyone* knew Clarence Brown." Mother's finger moved down a column in the Yellow Pages. "Clarence Brown was from Greenwich and he was very *old* Greenwich."

beneath the collars of her carefully laundered cotton blouses. Her curly auburn hair was neatly cropped and her thin legs were planted firmly on the ground; on her feet were polished leather Weejuns. The only events affecting Woodie's dress were Parents' Weekend and graduation. On those occasions, two red spots of rouge appeared on her cheeks, and instead of a wool skirt, she wore a lavender linen dress, with a gold circle pin fastened near the collar.

I looked from the photographs of Woodie to the woman herself, as she looped a navy sash around Scottie Ellis's waist.

"Don't let their forwards pull you out of position," Woodie growled. Scottie's Campbell Soup cheeks turned pinker. "They did it last week," continued Woodie. "Stay alert this time."

"Okay, Woodie," mumbled Scottie, head lowered.

"Yes, Miss Woodruff," corrected the coach.

"Yes, Miss Woodruff." Scottie's face was deep red.

Woodie's arms extended around Scottie's backside as she patted her behind. Behind-patting was part of the ritual. The laying on of hands. Woodie's last contact before sending us to battle.

I watched Woodie's face, as she began on the next player. Her scowl seemed to have deepened over the summer. There was less warmth in her gruffness. She was more severe. I wondered if Randolph Nicholson's presence had deepened her gloom. Of the entire faculty, Woodie was most affected by his arrival, and by the retirement of Miss Dunning and Miss Kroll, whom she'd worked with for thirty years. Under the two headmistresses, Woodie ran the school. She enforced the rules; she approved weekend permission requests; she coached every sport and supervised the athletic program. Woodie was the one who stood up each week in morning assembly and called for greater attention to dress, more order in study hall, better manners in the dining room. Woodie set the school's moral tone.

But moral tone, I guess, had not been the board of directors' priority when they replaced the headmistresses. The new principal was supposed to bring the school up to date, modernize the curriculum, increase endowments. Miss Dunning and Miss Kroll, they said, were terrible financial managers. Tuition bills were always late, and parents were "on their honor" to pay if they never received their bills at all. Money earmarked for outside speakers and current events was instead used for the Saturday night school movies, usually featuring Doris Day and Cary Grant.

Randolph Nicholson was the man chosen by the board of directors to guide the school into the twentieth century. Nicholson was thirty-four years old and had six years of service in the Marine Corps and three years' experience as an English teacher at a boys' school in West Virginia. He was the first man to work at Huntington Hill since Louis the bus driver and Joe the handyman joined the staff in 1949.

During the transition it was to Woodie that we'd looked for continuity and for the assurance that the school would not change overnight into the junior Marines, or something worse. Woodie had borne the role stoically, without complaint. She never discussed Randolph Nicholson with anyone. Only her scowl had deepened.

"Jean." Woodie motioned to me. I stepped forward. Jean was my real name, but no one called me that. I held my breath as her bony hands wrapped the sash around my waist.

"Hey, kiddo, relax," she said, flicking her ashes into an ashtray beside her knee. "That's your problem, Tuck. You're too nervous. Do you think we'd have you playing if we thought you couldn't do it?"

"I ... I don't know..."

"And for Pete's sake, use your dodges. Understand?"

"Yes..."

"Get going," she said, standing up slowly. A pained smile crossed her face. She looked over the group and called for silence.

Izzie Rogers, the tan, beautifully proportioned half-back who had played on so many varsity teams that her blazer pocket was covered in letters and stars, raised her hand.

"Would you hurry, Woodie? I've got to pee."

The players laughed. "Wait one minute, Rogers," snapped Woodie. She scanned the room, her eyes connecting with each of us, and spoke in a low, sober voice.

"Ladies," she sighed. "You take a lot for granted. You're used to having things come easy. You're spoiled." She paused, letting her words sink in. "You won last week, so you think this week will be easy. If you win today, you'll get uppity about the next game. Well, don't, ladies." She ground her cigarette into an ashtray. "Don't take *anything* for granted. You must enter every game with new energy, as if you're about to face the toughest team you've ever played. Do you understand?" She scanned the room.

Scottie Ellis looked at me and whispered, "She's mad today."

"But that won't work," Woodie continued. "If you intend to be sloppy, don't come down to the field. We don't practice all week so you can forget your plays in the game." She looked at Izzie Rogers, who was winding a rubber band around her long blonde braids. "Do you understand, Miss Rogers?"

"Yes, Woodie."

"Yes, Miss Woodruff."

"Yes, Miss Woodruff."

"Ladies..." Woodie cleared her throat. "You represent this school when you're out on the field, and your conduct reflects upon all of us. I want to see skill, I want to see teamwork. I want to see fair play. Miss Spense, do you have anything to add?" Woodie looked down at the young assistant coach who stood grimly beside her. Miss Spense had taught at Huntington Hill for only two years, but she'd picked up Woodie's mannerisms — her somber voice, her mannish gestures, her dowdy clothes. Miss Spense's best friend was Miss Gibbons, the American History teacher. The year before, a ninth grader claimed she'd seen them making out in Century House. Everyone was shocked, but no one really believed it, because it was just *too* disgusting. Besides, Miss Gibbons had a boyfriend.

"I think you've said it all, Woodie," intoned Miss Spense soberly. She looked down at her clipboard, fingered the silver whistle on her plastic lanyard, and craned forward. "Ladies, you know what you have to do — now get out there and do it."

That was it. The ritual was over. With relief, we picked up our gear and hurried out the front hall of Century House, our cleated rubber sneakers squeaking on the hardwood floor. Outside, the school grounds looked green and manicured, as usual. The brown shingled classroom buildings were empty now, except for the maids who were sweeping and cleaning for Monday. On the front porch of Century House a group of seniors sat tanning their legs, socks rolled to their ankles as they waited for the game.

Scottie and I walked down to the field.

Scottie always smelled of Noxema. "Am I crazy, Jinx, or is Woodie meaner this year?"

"I don't know. Maybe she's meaner. Why?"

Scottie shrugged. She never worried much or analyzed other people's behavior. "Woodie's getting old, I guess. She's been around a long time."

I looked down at the field. Students, dressed in blue uniforms and blazers, were beginning to fill the grandstands, and the cheerleaders, in white sweaters and blue skirts, were scurrying along the sidelines handing out words to the school songs.

"I think Nicholson upsets her," I said slowly.

Scottie bumped me as she walked. "She's a teacher, Jinx. Teachers aren't like us. They don't fight all the time."

"Well, Nicky's not just another teacher. He's a man, and he's the headmaster."

Scottie touched my arm. Standing by the grandstand in his gray slacks and navy blazer, hair sleeked off his forehead, was Randolph Nicholson. His arms were folded in front of him — a general waiting for his troops to parade.

"Hi, Mr. Nicholson," said Scottie, grabbing a practice ball from the bag near his feet.

"Hello, Scottie. Best of luck." He grinned. Scottie looked at me with a smirk.

"Girl Scout!" I whispered.

"Stick with me, Jinx," she laughed, flicking a ball onto the field.

As we dribbled, I watched Nicholson from the corner of my eye. He was a short man — about five feet seven, with a muscular, mesomorph's body beginning to soften at the waist. I had liked him when he first came last year. He had hired some good teachers and the school seemed to be losing some of its stodginess. But even Nicholson never talked about the outer world — about politics or war or civil rights. He seemed more interested in who won the cup races between the *Eagle* and the *Constellation* than in who won the presidential election. There was something phony about Mr. Nicholson. He smiled all the time, even when you were talking seriously with him.

Now, as he waited for the game to start, he was flashing his Colgate teeth at all the girls and shaking hands with everyone who walked by.

On close inspection, there was something sleazy about him. Maybe it was his body hair. He had a lot of it. Even at nine o'clock, at morning assembly, there was a blue shadow on his jaws. And his beard didn't stop at his chin; it grew all down his neck, so he had to shave as far as his collar. When he rolled up his sleeves in his office, you could see little tufts of hair on his wrists, and some hair caught underneath his watchband. He sweated a lot too, and kept a handkerchief folded in his pocket to dab off perspiration from his lips and forehead. I once read in a book that people who sweat a lot are hiding something. It's a sign that the person is keeping a secret. I guess the school's board of directors didn't know that theory when they hired him.

The referees were ready to start the game. They blew their whistles and called the captains to the center of the field. The grandstands were full and the cheerleaders from both schools were prancing along the sidelines, leaping and cartwheeling in energetic spurts. I stood next to Scottie in the huddle. We felt uneasy after Woodie's talk in the Trophy Room. Something funny was going on. And we were all aware of Nicholson's presence on the sidelines.

Across the lawn, up toward Senior House, I could see a student walking slowly down the hill licking an ice cream cone. She moved with an air of nonchalance, as if she didn't care if the game had started or not. On the sidelines I saw Nicky greet her, extend his hand, and help her to a place beside him in the bleachers. It was Lexie.

The image of Lexie and Nicholson sitting side by side in the grandstands stayed with me throughout the game. It didn't keep me from playing well. In fact, knowing that Lexie was there made me try harder, I ran faster and used more dodges. But why was she sitting with him? Why was she talking to him? Did Lexie usually come to hockey games? I tried to remember. Had she come to see me play? Had she planned to meet Nicholson and sit with him? Hockey was a big deal at Huntington Hill. There were hockey teas and award dinners, hockey sweaters, bake sales, and charm bracelets. Hockey players were used to a lot of attention. That's why the competition for varsity was so intense. But now I felt myself wanting more than the school's attention. I wanted Lexie's attention. I wanted *her* to be watching me. And on that day, I played for Lexie.

IT WAS RAINING HARD THE DAY OF MY FIRST VOICE lesson. Hockey practice was canceled and the spell of clear days was broken. The school had the cold, dreary feeling of an army camp digging in for a long, slow siege. Winter was approaching. In Saigon, Buddhist monks were commemorating the death of the priest who'd immolated himself the year before to protest foreign intervention in Vietnam. U.S. troops were still in Vietnam and in one week America would choose between two presidential candidates who were prepared to send even more.

I walked the long way around Knowlton to get to the basement music rooms. I didn't want to run into Thelma Anne Mosbey, the housemother, who had a suite on the ground floor. Thelma Anne was fifty-nine years old, wore spike heels and baby blue, glitter-flecked glasses, and grew up in Roanoke, Virginia. At some point in her life Thelma Anne had taught English literature at Randolph-Macon Women's College, and she never let her students forget that in better days she had shaped the hearts and minds of the South's finest *college* women. Huntington Hill, she made it quite clear, was exile for her, a painful compromise; and each time she mentioned Randolph-Macon, she lifted her eyes toward heaven and drew a peach-scented Kleenex from her sleeve. Her mouth, held in a strained half-smile, would quiver, as she silently pined for the Old South and the days of well-mannered ladies and honey-throated gentlemen.

Thelma Anne did not appear. Practice Room D was a small, dark cell with two small windows close to the ceiling and no furniture except for the piano. The room

28

was empty. I sat at the piano, found middle C on the keyboard, and tapped it lightly. I looked at the door — no sign of Lexie — and touched the keyboard again, slowly playing "Swaying Silver Birches," which I had learned in third grade. "Whatever you do," Mrs. Manson, my music teacher, had said, "don't stop when you make a mistake. Keep right on going as if nothing's wrong."

"Shit." The door swung open and there stood Lexie, face flushed, trench coat sopping, a pile of music books in her arms. "I'm wet," she said, dropping her load onto the piano bench. "How are you, Jinx?" The smell of Jean Naté filled the room as she sat down beside me, her blue uniform clinging to her body, skirt rising above her knees. Drops of rain still glistened on her cheeks.

"Christ, it's hot in here," she said, opening a window. "Don't you want to take your coat off?"

For some reason I was embarrassed to take my coat off in front of Lexie. "I get cold easy," I said.

Lexie shrugged. "Suit yourself." She ran her hands through her wet hair and took a deep breath. "Where shall we start?" Her brown eyes rested on mine. "By the way," she said. "Great game on Friday. You were terrific. I couldn't take my eyes off you."

I stared at her.

"Hockey game? Remember? You played St. Luke's on Friday?" Lexie snapped her fingers. "You there, Tuckwell? This is Lexie Yves. Tune in."

"You came?" I said finally.

"Yes, idiot." She poked my ribs. "That's what I said."

I smiled. "Did you ... was that *you* with Nicky?"

Lexie frowned. "God, he's a creep. He wanted to discuss the Music Club show. I think he's a lecheria." Lexie leaned over and pulled up her falling knee socks.

"Do you think Nicky's a creep?" I said.

Lexie looked at me. "Of course he's a creep. What's your problem today, Tuck? Are you here?"

"I'm here."

"Okay, let's start." Lexie inhaled deeply. I tried to focus on her eyes, but that made me embarrassed, so I just stared in her general direction. "What we want to do," she began, "is start you breathing easily when you paint, so that the air's going all the way down, deep into your lungs, and you're really using your diaphragm. Do you know where that is?" Lexie squeezed the space just under her ribs. I blushed. The word *diaphragm* always reminded me of sex, and the drawer holding a box of rubber bags and tubes and birth control devices I had once found in my parents' bathroom.

"Now," continued Lexie, "what keeps you from breathing correctly is tension. Are you ever aware of tension?" She looked at me quizzically. "Maybe we'll start just by having a little conversation in our normal voices. Just talk a little bit and remember to take deep breaths, like this." Lexie inhaled, and as she did, her breasts rose and pressed against her cotton uniform. "Okay, start talking, Jinx. Talk about anything. Talk about the hockey game; I don't care."

I took a breath. I could hear my voice — high and tight. "The hockey game last Friday was with St. Luke's and we played pretty well. We scored and..." I stopped. I realized that if I talked about the game, I might start saying that I'd thought about Lexie through the whole game.

"What's the matter?"

"Maybe I'll talk about something else. I'll tell you about the time Thelma Anne Mosbey grounded me for brewing hard cider."

Lexie laughed. "I'd forgotten that."

"I put the cider out on our windowsill and forgot about it. When it got hard, Scottie passed it around, and

Thelma found out and told Woodie I was keeping alcohol in the dorm. She wanted to expel me."

"That's ridiculous," said Lexie.

"Woodie told her it was a mistake."

Lexie smiled. "Tuckwell, here's what you're doing wrong. You're cutting off your own voice — here" — she put her hands just above her waist — "because you're not breathing deeply. And here" — she brushed her hands across her throat — "so that the sound doesn't come out."

"That's bad."

"It's not so bad," said Lexie. "Okay." She reached for my hand and placed it on her stomach. I could feel her nylon slip beneath her uniform. "Now, feel my abdomen rise and fall as I breathe. Feel it?"

"Yep," I gulped.

"Okay, now," she said, "lie on the floor."

I looked at her.

"Don't worry, just lie down and breathe. It'll be easier from the floor."

I stared at her.

"Here, I'll show you," she said, sliding off the bench and stretching out on the linoleum. Her skirt rose up past her knees. Gingerly, I sat down with her.

"Now," she said in a soothing voice, "just breathe slowly, in and out, in and out, in and out." The room was quiet except for our breathing, the gurgle of the radiator, and the distant sound of piano scales in another practice room. Lexie's torso, next to mine, rose and fell. I tried to imitate her, but I couldn't relax.

She sat up slowly. Her brown eyes looked down at mine. Her hair was still wet and matted like straw. She placed one hand on my stomach, like a doctor. I could feel a tingling in my legs. "Now," she said, "let's see if you can talk and breathe at the same time."

I started to get up.

"No, stay there," she said. "Try saying, 'Do you know May?'"

"What?"

"'Do you know May?' It's a nonsense phrase."

It was very hard to say, "Do you know May?" Something about the name May embarrassed me. I had never known anyone named May. I tried to say it.

"That's good," said Lexie. Her hand was still on my stomach. I thought I might pass out. Maybe it was from all the breathing — hyperventilation or something.

Suddenly, there was a sharp knock on the door.

Lexie squinted. "Who is it?"

The door opened slowly. "Hello?" came a small voice. A freshman in a shiny red rain hat peeked through the door and looked down at us. We were still on the floor. Lexie's hand rested on my stomach.

"What is it?" Lexie said irritably. "We're in the middle of a lesson."

"I'm looking for Music Club auditions. Is this the right room?" The new girl's voice was uncertain.

"Shit." Lexie jumped up. "This is the right room. Come in. I'm Lexie Yves."

"I'm Flora," said the new girl. She looked at me apprehensively.

"We're having a voice lesson," said Lexie. "Don't worry, you won't have to lie on the floor."

Lexie helped me to my feet. "Your hands are cold, Tuck," she said.

"I guess."

"For the next time, Jinx, practice 'Do you know May?' in front of a mirror." Lexie was back on the piano bench now, flipping through a music book. The chords she played filled the room with rich, warm vibrations. The freshman sat beside her. Without interrupting the tune, Lexie looked up from the piano and winked at me.

THE ROOM I SHARED WITH MIGGIN HENRY WAS on the back side of Senior House, a sprawling wooden farmhouse, shaped like a collapsible Girl Scout cup extending chaotically out across the lawn in segments of decreasing size. Senior House was the only dormitory on the north portion of the campus; it was a short walk from the art studio and study hall, from McAllister — the classroom building — and from Century, where we ate. It faced the long, rolling lawns that sloped down to the playing fields. The back side overlooked the same hilly pasture as the studio.

Miggin and I had been lucky to draw our room in the lottery the spring before. The private bathroom was a luxury; so was the view of the pasture. The room was on the ground floor, separated from the other rooms by a short corridor. At night, through open windows, we could smell the grassy pasture and hear the chatter of crickets and katydids. Because we were removed from the rest of the dorm, fewer people stopped around to talk, and we were out of range of sock hops, beauty pageants, and burping contests. I loved the privacy, and Miggin loved the bathroom mirror, which she could use to roll her hair each night.

All the rooms in Senior House were a pale, washed-out green, furnished with chairs and desks that had been painted so many times their surfaces were crusted with thick scabs of enamel. The floors were bare and gray, and gave the rooms a dry, dusty smell. Bedspreads were regulation blue and so were the curtains. The school permitted a single expression of individual taste — we

33

could hang *one* picture on the wall. Miggin's choice was a huge color poster of Steve McQueen, leather jacket spattered with mud, blue eyes tormented as he reared into the air on a motorcycle. It was a shot from Miggin's favorite movie, *The Great Escape*. My choice was a photograph of Richard Burton, dressed in black, skull in hands, playing *Hamlet*. It wasn't that I liked Burton so much; I liked his wife, Elizabeth Taylor. But I was embarrassed to hang a poster of her. The tiny plastic glow-stars on the ceiling were our private joke. Miggin had ordered them from the back of *True Confessions* magazine and we'd glued them up there in September. They were illegal, of course, but no one knew they were there, because you could only see them at night, with the lights out.

Miggin was a good roommate. She was not stuck-up, even though she was one of the most popular girls in the school and one of the most beautiful. Part of her charm was that she didn't think she was beautiful. She thought she was plain and stupid, and she constantly atoned for her unseen sins by signing up for every good-works project the school offered. Twice a week she visited brain-damaged children at a nearby hospital; every fall she collected for Red Cross and Community Fund; and for three years she'd served on the service committee of the Chapel Club. One year she had tried to start a school debating team, but when the girls found out the club wouldn't be debating any boys' schools they stopped coming to meetings. Miggin had accumulated dozens of awards for her contributions to the school, but her confidence did not increase as quickly as her collection of prizes.

Miggin seemed perfect to me. She was everything the school valued and more. She was pretty, well dressed, and bright; she was a cheerleader, student governor, and club president; her parents were rich and owned half the state of Colorado.

Unlike Miggin's, my deficiencies were glaring: I had pale white skin that never tanned, and blue eyes sunken behind puffy cheeks. I was clumsy and tall and swayed uncertainly when I walked. My wardrobe was a motley collection of skirts and sweaters that never seemed to match or give me the bouncy, color-coordinated look Huntington Hill girls strived for. Although I was an athlete, my career of late had been spotty, and my interest in art simply meant I made good posters for other people's clubs.

Miggin and I used to argue over which of us was more awful and insecure.

"But, Jinx," she would say, standing at the bathroom mirror twisting her hair around her bristly rollers, "everyone in my family except me is brilliant and intellectual and beautiful."

"But, Miggin," I would say, braiding the fringe of her tasseled pillow, "you *are* beautiful. And you're kind and smart and generous. You're much better than me."

"You? You?" said Miggin. "You're wonderful. You have your painting and your hockey and everyone loves you."

"But everyone loves *you,* Miggin. And look at all your awards."

She would slam the door of the medicine cabinet and begin brushing her teeth. "Awards, phooey. They don't mean anything. I'm a selfish person, deep down. I'm spoiled. My parents gave me everything and I'm not even grateful. In fact, I hate them."

"Your parents are okay, Miggin."

"Jinx, your parents are *wonderful*. Your father's for Johnson, and he believes in equality."

"Why does he send me here, then, Miggin? My parents are as snobby as yours. They're just not as rich."

Miggin would shake her head, walk slowly to her bed in her red University of Colorado nightshirt, and kneel down, placing her hands on the mattress. She would pray for at least fifteen minutes. I was curious about her prayers. I had prayed a few times, but it was usually to ask God to help me fit in and be popular. But Miggin couldn't be praying about that. Boys were always inviting her to dances and weekends, and once a week she wrote this guy Peter, in Colorado, although she said he was only a friend.

I thought about telling Miggin about feeling queasy and breathless around Lexie, but I didn't. I thought she would think I was weird. But I was thinking about Lexie more and more. Sometimes I dreamed of her brown eyes and her warm body as she lay next to me breathing in the practice room. I felt the tingling in my legs when I remembered the way she touched my diaphragm or whatever it was. I could smell her cologne and see the little drops of rain on her cheeks. Between classes now, I was always on the lookout for Lexie, and at meals I watched to see who she was talking to. And, of course, I began to practice my voice lessons — not when Miggin was around, because I was embarrassed, but at night, after study hall, when she was at cheerleading. I would stand in the bathroom, by the mirror, and enunciate carefully, "Do you know May?" I would begin quietly, building to a deep, resonant declamation.

"Do you know May? Do you know May?" I repeated, searching for variety of inflection.

One night, Miggin stood quizzically at the door, her eyes wide. "What are you doing, Jinx?"

I stepped away from the mirror. "What?"

"What are you doing?" Miggin's tone was diplomatic, as always. With her pigtails and pink cheeks, she reminded me of Heidi or a member of the Austrian Olympic ski team.

"I'm not doing anything, really." I began to leaf through Miggin's *Mademoiselle*. She sat down beside me. She smelled of cinnamon — her soap, I guess.

"Jinx, you were standing in the mirror talking about May somebody. Who is May? What were you doing?"

I looked at her sheepishly. "Practicing."

Miggin's hands were outstretched, prepared to strangle me in frustration. "Practicing what? Your imitation of a wacko?"

"My voice," I gulped. "My breathing and my voice."

Miggin looked at me closely. "You're taking singing lessons?"

"Voice lessons," I said in a monotone. "Voice and breathing lessons."

Miggin kicked off her sneakers and started to undress. "What's wrong with your voice?" She stood in front of me in her bra and underpants.

"I don't breathe right," I said. "So my voice is high and little."

Miggin stared at me. "Who's your teacher?"

"Lexie."

Miggin laughed. "Lexie?"

"She says it'll help me paint better."

Miggin went to the bathroom, slipped on her nightshirt, and began to roll her hair in the big curlers. "And Lexie thinks you don't breathe right?" she called, cautiously, trying not to hurt my feelings.

"My breathing's shallow."

Miggin turned away from the mirror. "Jinx, I like your voice. It's *you*."

"Thank you."

"I mean it. I wouldn't want you to … to…" She paused. "I wouldn't want you to sound like Lexie."

I sat up. "What's wrong with Lexie?"

"Nothing. She just sounds affected sometimes."

"I'm never going to sound like Lexie," I said.

Miggin turned on the spigots and splashed water on her face. "Hey, have you heard?" she yelled.

"Heard what?"

"Nicholson is meeting with every senior to discuss college applications. They posted the appointment list this afternoon. Guess who has the first appointment?"

"Who?"

"You," she said.

"Me?" The thought of talking with Nicholson in his office made my hands cold. What was there to say? I'd made up my mind about art school.

"I don't like Nicholson," I said.

"Me neither." Miggin began her toe-touching exercises. Cheerleaders had to stay in shape. "But he likes *you*, because you're on the hockey team."

Miggin stood by my bed. She looked adorable in her nightshirt. Her body was neat and compact. She had perfectly shaped calves and round, all-American breasts, like a model from *Mademoiselle*. I blushed. "Do you ... um ... does Nicky..."

"Take a breath or something, Jinx."

"Do you know May?" I said finally.

"This is where I came in," she laughed. Then she knelt down by her bed and started to pray.

Mrs. Gaylord Grant, Nicholson's secretary, sat at a desk that commanded a view of the entire administration office as well as Nicky's inner sanctum. Mrs. Grant was a tall woman with a tight jaw, a horsy smile, and the superficial friendliness of a Philadelphia socialite. She was a Huntington Hill alumna who had come back to work at the school after her divorce. I was sure that the interesting graduates, the ones who had gone off to New York to study acting or moved to New Mexico to make pottery, never returned. The ones who did often seemed stuck in a time warp, as if they had never left the school.

"I'm Jinx Tuckwell," I mumbled to Mrs. Grant. She tapped two extraordinarily sharp pencils on her extraordinarily neat desk and flipped open her appointment book. "He's expecting you, Jean. Go right in."

Nicholson did not look up when I entered. He was reading. His jacket hung on his chair and his shirtsleeves were rolled up his forearms. It was a rule at Huntington Hill that, in the presence of faculty, students had to stand until they were given permission to be seated. So I waited uncomfortably in the middle of the room, looking around his office. He had changed it drastically since taking over from Miss Dunning and Miss Kroll. They had nested like two pigeons in a comfortable clutter of books, papers, and overstuffed chairs. He had transformed their hideaway into a sleek executive suite with thick wall-to-wall carpeting, a huge leather couch, and director's chairs made of leather and chrome. The bookshelves, once spilling over with the novels of Jane Austen (Miss Dunning) and Peterson's *Field Guides* (Miss Kroll), had been removed. The only books in the office now were private school guides and college entrance manuals. There was just one *personal* item in the office — a tarnished silver trophy of a baseball player, and beside it, a green cap with a Dartmouth "D" stitched on the front.

"Memorabilia," said Nicholson, reaching out to shake my hand. He flashed the inevitable smile. "I was an athlete, too, Jean. Won't you sit down?"

Nicky sank back in his swivel chair, pushed up his horn-rimmed glasses, and raised his arms behind his head, revealing two large, dark spots beneath the armpits.

"Think we'll have an undefeated season, sport?"

The big couch squeaked as I sat on it. "I hope so."

"I hope so, too. It's a helluva lotta fun and it's good for business, too."

I stared at him.

"The old grads appreciate a winning season, Jeannie. It's true at the boys' schools, and in spite of the, uh, the

39

basic biological differences, God bless them, the figures appear to hold up at Huntington Hill."

"Figures?"

"Numbers, Jean. Dollars. Endowments."

Did I understand him? Was he suggesting that good seasons increased endowments? I had never thought of playing hockey for that reason.

"Don't worry about it, kid," he said, pinching a nostril. "Doesn't concern you directly; although" — he lowered his voice — "I'm sure you want your school to thrive, even after you're gone."

"I guess," I said. I had never thought much about the school after I was gone. I just wanted to get out.

"Well, Jean, let's get on to the matter at hand." He loosened his tie and wiped a handkerchief across his upper lip. "We're here to talk about college." He lit a cigarette. "I see from your record that you're only applying to art school. Why is that?"

"Why do I want to go to art school?" I said uncertainly. "Did you read my essay?"

Nicholson leafed through my folder. "Righto." He squinted. "You want to be a painter?"

"Yes."

He leaned forward on his elbows and looked hard at me. "Jean, I'll be quite frank with you. I'm against art school." He paused. "I've looked at your file carefully. You've got a very solid record. High B average, several extracurrics, two varsity teams, and strong recommendations. Miss ... uh ... Miss Jonas here says you were one of the best students she's ever had." The tight smile returned. "Jeannie, I'm sure I can get you into one of the Seven Sisters. You're a natural for Holyoke or Vassar. Smith, if we really reach. Art school ... well, art school's another ball game."

"Vassar and Holyoke don't have art programs," I said. "Only art history."

"Jean," interrupted Nicholson, "I think you may be suffering from what we call the 'big fish in a small pond' syndrome. Here at Huntington Hill your work is very good. Undeniably you're quite creative. But..." — he lowered his voice — "it's a big world out there."

I looked at him. I could feel the tears building in my eyes. I had already been through this with my parents and the college counselor.

Nicholson glanced at his watch. "Jean, I'm sure you'll be happier in a women's college where there'll be more sports, more ... more girls like yourself."

"I don't want to be around 'girls like myself.'"

Nicholson frowned. "You're a bright girl, but you take yourself too seriously. And aren't you being a little selfish? Consider the generations of seniors who come after you. Think of the *other* girls."

"Other girls?" I whispered.

"Jean, if you do well at Vassar, it's that much easier for other girls to be accepted there in future years. And if I can get you into Vassar, I want you in Vassar, not in the Philadelphia College of Playdough. Do you understand?"

I opened my mouth. "But I don't want to go to Vassar." The tears began to fall, slowly, silently.

Nicholson closed my file and flashed his toothy smile. "Jean," he said. "Perhaps I've been more candid with you than I should have. Please, consider it a compliment that I confide these thoughts to you." He stood up. "You don't have to make a decision today. Stew it over and get back to me. Meantime..." He walked to his office door. "Mrs. Grant, will you have those applications ready for Jeannie?"

I stood up. My knees were shaking.

"By the way, Jean, Maddy Hansen is coming back. Spoke to her mother today." He smiled. "You're playing her position, aren't you?"

My voice stuck. Nicholson shook his head. "I certainly wish she had varsity hockey on *her* college applications. Her record's not as strong as yours."

"But, she's ... she's been on other teams."

"In her case, it could be the deciding factor. And I'm sure *art* schools won't care one way or the other if *you're* a varsity player. Well," he laughed, "don't worry. Until my mind's made up, your position is secure." He shook my hand. "Nice getting to know you, kid. You'll get those applications from Mrs. Grant."

A week passed. I did not pick up the applications from Mrs. Grant. Whatever Nicholson meant about my position on the hockey team, I was not going to apply to Vassar or Mount Holyoke or anything else he cooked up. It wasn't that I didn't want to finish the hockey season. I wanted to very much. I wanted to finish with my teammates. I loved them. I loved the excitement and the pleasure of playing with the team. And I wanted my parents to see me in the last game. But it was crazy to go to a school I didn't want to go to just because Nicholson had some idea it was going to help another generation. Maybe another generation wouldn't want to go to Vassar. And suppose I filled out the applications. And suppose I got accepted? Maybe he would try some new trick in the spring to make me go. It was crazy. It was some kind of blackmail. Did he do it to everybody? What about Emmy Gaines? She wanted to go to acting school. Would he make her go to Vassar? What about Helen Gates, who didn't want to go to college at all? Or was it just me? I didn't know.

What I did know was that my hockey game began falling to pieces. At practice I missed easy shots, bumbled bullies, fumbled passes.

"Hustle, Tuckwell," Woodie would yell.

"Move it, Jinx," prodded Miss Spense. "Concentrate."

They took turns hounding me, and I simply tightened more, moving in stiff, breathless spurts. There were only two more games to go — one with St. Margaret's the following week, and the last over Parents' Weekend, with Cliff School, our arch rival. The team's spirits rose as the possibility of an undefeated season increased, but my spirits sank. I kept looking toward the upper driveway, waiting for Mrs. Hansen's gray Mercedes to drive up, drop Maddy off at the field, and move on to Nicky's office. There were rumors that Mrs. Hansen had bought Maddy's way back into school by making a colossal donation. And Maddy, people said, had been playing hockey at a boarding school in England. She was better than ever. It was all over for me. I was sure of it.

At the end of practice, Woodie called out a list of girls whom she wanted to talk to. My time had come. I sat on the bleachers and pulled my blazer close to me. It was a cool afternoon and the sun was slowly disappearing behind the campus. To the south, along Middlesex Road, I could see two horses and their riders trotting toward the stables, hurrying in before sundown. Before me, on the sidelines, Woodie coached two JV players; a third practiced roll-ins from the alley.

"Okay, ladies, that's it." Woodie waved to me. "Jean!" I scrambled down and waited while she filled a bag with balls.

"What's wrong, Tuckwell?" she said, without looking up.

I glanced at her brown eyes, set deep behind her brows, and her tan, weathered face. "I've been kind of nervous."

"What about?" She was gruff.

I swallowed. "Everyone says Maddy Hansen's coming back."

"Yes.

"I figure when she does I won't be playing."

43

She tightened the string around the top of the ball bag. "How do you figure that?"

"I've been playing lousy. Maddy's coming back. I'm in her position ... I figured..."

"You've had a few bad days, Tuckwell. You're entitled. Do you think we'd take you off with two games to go?"

I stared at the ground. "It was something Nicky said."

Woodie looked up. "Nicky?"

"Mr. Nicholson. He seems to think that Maddy is ... Maddy's record..."

Her face reddened. "Mr. Nicholson talked to you about Maddy's record?" Woodie moved closer. I could smell cigarettes on her breath.

"Yes."

Her lips puckered forward and she stared over my shoulder, up toward McAllister, where Nicky's office was. "This is a serious matter, Jinx."

I looked at her.

"Whatever he said to you, it's no excuse for you to let your game go. A good player sticks with it. She doesn't give up. Do you understand?"

"I didn't give up. I thought..."

"Don't explain. I don't want explanations." She looked at her watch and swung the ball bag over her shoulder. "Tuckwell, get going. Don't be late for study hall."

I turned to go. Woodie walked a few steps, then stopped. "*I'm* the coach of the hockey team, Tuckwell. *I* decide who plays and who doesn't. Do you understand?"

"Yes, Miss Woodruff."

"It should not have been discussed with you. I'm sorry."

She strode off toward the gym, neck craned forward, jaw clenched, eyes staring ahead. She was mad as hell. I probably should have kept quiet.

I SAT OUTSIDE PRACTICE ROOM D, BACK PROPPED against the door, taking long, slow breaths. Lexie was inside playing the piano — a Chopin waltz — and the notes sounded far away, muffled by the corkboard that lined the room. I had come early, and instead of interrupting her, I sat and listened, my legs stretched across the corridor of Clayton. Sometimes Lexie made mistakes, hit the wrong notes, then paused, and began again. There was one part of the piece that was more difficult than the rest, and each time she came to it she faltered, stopped, and started over. I felt like I shouldn't be listening, but it was interesting to hear Lexie make mistakes, to know that she couldn't do everything perfectly. Even Lexie, who sang so beautifully, who knew so much about everything, wasn't perfect.

Suddenly, the door opened and Lexie stood over me, hands on her hips, surprised. "How long have you been here?"

I rose quickly, embarrassed to have been discovered. "It sounded nice. Don't stop."

Lexie frowned. "It sounds lousy. I hate practicing. I want to be good without working at it. Practicing is so boring."

"It sounded good to me. I don't know much about music, but..."

"But you know what you like, right?" Lexie laughed and sat down on the bench. She was wearing faded blue jeans, a red V-neck sweater, and loafers. Her hair was black now, not orange, after a new dye job she'd given herself to correct the old one, and strands of hair, shocked

45

from all the treatments, stood out from her head. I looked down at Lexie's waist; the top button of her blue jeans, which clung tightly to her hips, was unfastened. Lexie caught my glance, and quickly covered her stomach with her hands.

"I know I'm fat. Dammit, Tuckwell, I like to eat. I adore mint—chocolate-chip ice cream. I can't starve myself like Lucy and Oakie. I can't eat *carrots* all the time."

I shrugged. "You look good to me."

Lexie smiled. "Look how skinny you are. You have the most beautiful body. You probably eat whatever you want."

I blushed. I didn't want to talk about my body. "Is Eleanor coming for Parents' Weekend?" I said quickly.

"Christ, don't ask." Lexie pushed the sleeves of her sweater up her forearms. Her skin, like mine, was very pale. "Eleanor *is* coming. In time for the Glee Club concert Friday night." She paused and touched my arm. "Did I tell you I have a solo? Well, I do, and she's bringing Philip, my cousin. Jinx, I told her, 'For Christ's sake, don't bring Philip; he's a bad influence on me.' She thought I was joking. Philip loves to drive her around in the rental cars and he tunes in WBZ, so she's bringing him. Do you know what that means?"

"What's WBZ?"

"A radio station. She heard it once in Boston at a bridge tournament and she liked it so much she won't listen to anything else. Jinx, she's sixty-three years old, and she listens to rock and roll, and she is bringing Philip, which means I'll be a nervous wreck the entire weekend, because the three of us are totally incompatible."

"Philip's your cousin?"

She paused and sighed. "Well, yes and no. He's Eleanor's nephew, but since Eleanor's not my real mother, Philip's not my real cousin." Lexie lifted my wrist and

46

looked at my watch. "What time is it? I'm supposed to call her today. We should start."

"Okay," I said. I wasn't looking forward to the lesson.

"Did you practice 'May'? Did you practice breathing?" She was more serious now.

"Yeah, but Miggin thought I was crazy when she heard me."

Lexie shrugged. "Screw Miggin. She'll get used to it. Okay, try some 'May's."

I began slowly, in a tiny voice. "Do you know May? Do you know May?"

"Not much conviction there, Tuckwell. And breathe."

I began again, gulping a breath first, and spoke louder.

"That's better." Lexie put her hand on my stomach. "Are you breathing? Okay, Tuck, who's May?"

I stopped.

"Make something up; tell me a story about May. Talk naturally and remember to breathe."

I looked at her. "Uh, May. May is, let's see, a junior who lives in Briggs."

"That's good. Keep going."

"Uh, May is ... I don't like May very much. She's ... she's conceited and she talks about people behind their backs." I was warming up now. "May is vicious, she looks in people's drawers and snoops, and she steals your food from..."

"Charming," said Lexie. "Now talk loud. Get mad if you want."

"She steals food from the kitchen and she's a Girl Scout. She flatters teachers and—"

"Jinx..."

"What?"

"You're not breathing."

"I'm sorry."

"Don't apologize. Okay, let's stop a minute and just breathe." Lexie looked at me. Our eyes met and we

47

began to breathe at the same rate — in and out, in and out. It was strange. I didn't want to take my eyes away from hers, but it felt so intimate, so close, that I was afraid.

Lexie sat up abruptly. "Do you ever get angry at people?"

"What?"

"I mean, do you ever yell at people? When you get mad, do you ever let someone have it? Just to blow off steam?"

"Uh..." I looked down at the piano pedals. There were only two. It must be an English piano, I thought. American pianos have three pedals. I read that somewhere.

"Jinx?"

"No, I don't yell too much."

Lexie rolled up the sleeves of her sweater. "I'm going to show you something, Tuckwell. It's an exercise."

Suddenly Lexie's voice filled the room. She yelled at the top of her lungs, "Goddammit, May, you're a lousy, no-good bitch. You..." She turned to face the window. "You're filthy. You go in people's rooms and you take the things they care most about and, May, I hate you!"

I felt a pain in my chest and I thought my head might explode. Why was she screaming? Was she mad at me? Surely Thelma Anne Mosbey was going to rush in any minute with the police.

"Lexie..."

"It doesn't matter who the hell wants me to shut up," roared Lexie. "I'm not going to. I have a right to my feelings. I have a right to my voice no matter how many crummy demerits I get. They can't take my voice away; I won't let them." Then, abruptly, Lexie stopped, exhaled, sat down beside me on the bench, and smiled.

"Lexie..." I was crying. I wrapped my arms around my stomach. Lexie's screaming had touched a dark, scared place inside me ... a place I kept covered up with jokes and shrugs and quick exits.

She slipped on her loafers. "Want to take a walk?" she said, wrapping my coat around my shoulders.

"Suppose they see me?"

"You haven't done anything wrong, idiot. You can cry if you want to."

We walked across the back parking lot and followed the path down past the stables toward the lower playing field. Side by side, we continued on, hands deep in our pockets, heads down. There was no gym class playing on the lower field, and the wooden bench, built around the huge elm tree near the field, was empty. We both sat down, resting our backs against the enormous trunk. Our shoulders touched as we looked out at the green riding fields and the line of pines that buffered the campus from the Huntington road. The cool air helped.

"Wish I had a cigarette," said Lexie.

"Me too."

"I've never seen you smoke."

"I smoke," I said. I could hear my self-consciousness.

Lexie turned and squinted at me. Her cheeks were pink from the cold. "What happened, Jinx?"

I looked down at my black hockey sneakers, then up at the field on the right. "You scared me."

Lexie touched my sleeve with her hand. "I wasn't yelling at you. You know that, don't you?"

"It felt like you were yelling at me." I tossed small twigs onto the ground.

"Jinx, I wanted to show you how frightened you are of anger, of loud voices, of your own voice." She pulled both legs onto the bench, cradled her knees in her arms, and looked at me. "Is anything wrong?"

I paused. Could I trust Lexie? Could I talk to her? "Nicky may take me off the team," I said softly.

Lexie sat up.

"It's weird," I said, staring out at the pasture. Two riders cantered along the edge of the field. "He thinks if I go to a women's college it'll increase endowments."

"But you want to go to art school..."

"I know."

"Well, it's none of his business."

I looked at her. I could feel the tears again. "He's going to put Maddy in when she gets back."

"Jinx..."

"Because it'll help future generations and Maddy needs the varsity credit."

"Well, screw Nicky!" Lexie kicked her heels against the trunk. "When did this happen?"

"A few days ago."

"That's shitty," said Lexie. "What are you going to do about it?"

I looked at her. "What *can* I do?"

Lexie held her chin in her hand. "No wonder you're angry."

"I'm not angry."

"Well, you *should* be."

I shrugged. Suddenly, I felt very tired. Maybe it was the crying or the cold air. I just felt tired.

"Jinx..."

"I feel like going to sleep," I said wearily.

Lexie put her arm around me. Her hand brushed my bangs off my forehead. For a moment, the cars passing on the Huntington road sounded like ocean waves.

"Jinx? Will you have dinner with my family on Parents' Weekend? You and your parents?" I smiled at Lexie. She seemed soft and caring — a friendly stray dog in her trench coat and jeans, her hair wild and unnaturally black from the rinse. I was flattered by her invitation.

"Miggin's going to be with us. Her folks aren't coming from Colorado."

"Miggin can come too. Philip will love her."

"I'll ask my folks. It's nice of you."

"Jinx, I'm not being nice." Lexie's gaze grew more intense. "I *want* you to come." Her body was close to mine.

"Thank you," I said. I could hear my voice. It was small and tinny.

Maddy Hansen came back that night. I saw her in the common room, after evening study hall. She was sitting on the couch in jeans and a t-shirt, laughing and talking with people about England. She looked relaxed and self-assured, not at all embarrassed about being the cause of a scandal at school. Her green eyes sparkled; her short brown hair was newly cut; her tan, sinewy body was perfectly composed. I turned away so I wouldn't have to speak to her.

"Jinx!" a voice called. My heart sank. It was Elizabeth. She had seen me. "Look who's back, Jinxie."

"You're back," I said, trying to smile at Maddy.

"Isn't it fantastic?" she beamed. "Yesterday I was in London. Today I'm back at school. It's like I never left."

"You're a jet-setter," I mumbled. What was I supposed to say?

"Jinx has been playing center forward," piped Elizabeth.

Maddy's smile faded. There was a sudden silence in the room. "I played in England," said Maddy uncomfortably. "You should see their fields. They're smooth as putting greens. The ball never takes a bad bounce."

"Did you meet the Beatles, Maddy?" yelled Dawson Clay, jumping in her seat.

"What about your weekend in Cambridge? Tell us about it. Was your date terribly attractive?" Nora Grange always wanted to hear about boys.

It was safe to leave now. I had said hello. Outside in the hallway, Elizabeth caught my arm.

"Isn't it awful, Jinxie? After all that and she behaves as if she owns the school. It's hideous."

"Why did you do that, Elizabeth?"

Elizabeth flicked her long black hair behind her shoulders and looked at me with calculated innocence. Her bony shoulders rose like hackles. "Tuckwell," she said turning to go, "it's not my fault that Maddy's back. If you're jealous, don't take it out on me." With that, she hurried off to the common room.

I lay on my bed staring up at the glow-stars on the ceiling. I tried not to think about Maddy and Elizabeth and hockey, but I couldn't help it. I wanted to pack up my bags, take a taxi to the Harrisburg station, and go back to Washington. Leave them all, with no message, no parting words, just an empty room, the bed stripped, mattress bare and exposed. Stupid, snobby school. Let them have Goldwater for president. Let them have their fox hunts and cup races. Some day the rest of the world would get back at them. Some day Martin Luther King, Jr., would be president; Malcolm X would be secretary of state. And they'd be sorry. Spoiled rich kids. It was a lousy school. A rotten, screwed-up place. It wasn't worth the energy. I'd just go, run away. Who really cared if I stayed or not?

"Jinx..." The door opened. Miggin stood beside my bed. She reached over to turn on a lamp. "Why are you lying in the dark?" I could smell her cinnamon. "What's the matter?" Her hand touched my shoulder. "What's wrong?"

"Nothing."

"Jinx, stop it." I heard the concern in her voice.

"Maddy's back," I said finally.

"We knew she was coming. Woodie told you not to worry." Miggin stroked my hair. "Maybe you *are* more insecure than me. I thought I had the prize." She poked my rib cage and tickled under my arms. "You're just a helpless little baby," she giggled. "You're just lying in the dark feeling sorry for yourself."

"Stop!" I laughed, squirming under her grip. She pinned my shoulders to the pillow.

"Jinx is a baby. Jinx is a baby," she teased.

"You're going to get it." I tried to sit up, but the tickling made me weak and I sank down into the mattress.

"I've got you now," said Miggin, crawling on top of me. Her red hair dangled in my face.

"Hello?" Someone stood in the doorway. We pulled quickly apart.

"I'll come back later."

I jumped up. It was Lexie. "Don't go. We were just—"

"Changing Jinx's diaper," laughed Miggin, shutting the bathroom door behind her.

"Hi," I said to Lexie. The blood rushed to my face.

She stepped self-consciously into the room. It wasn't like her to be embarrassed. "I came to see how you were feeling." She sat down beside me. "I know Maddy's back. Are you okay?"

"I'm okay."

She looked at me closely. "I'm not kidding about Parents' Weekend, Jinx. I want you and your folks and Miggin to have dinner with me and Eleanor and Philip."

"I'll ask my parents. And I know Miggin would enjoy it."

"Enjoy what?" said Miggin, emerging from the bathroom with a layer of cold cream smeared on her face.

"Parents' Weekend," I said. "Lexie's invited all of us to dinner with Eleanor and Philip."

"That'll be nice," said Miggin mildly, dumping her curlers onto the bed.

"Don't be too charming around Philip, Miggin," said Lexie. "He's a lecheria."

"Me? Charming? Are you kidding?" Miggin never thought she was charming at all. She was always surprised when boys asked her out.

Lexie stood up. "I should go." She turned, stopped, then turned again. "Good night, you all," she said finally.

"Lexie likes you," said Miggin, dabbing white shoe polish onto her sneakers. Cheerleaders had to have very white sneakers.

"Do you think so?" I said casually.

Miggin continued polishing. "She doesn't like many people," she said thoughtfully. "She thinks I'm an idiot."

"That's not true."

Miggin looked at me. "That's okay, Jinx. I'm not a big fan of Lexie's anyway." Miggin walked into the bathroom.

"I think she's funny and smart," I said loudly, so she could hear me over the gurgle of water.

"You don't know her," said Miggin, closing the door.

LEXIE PASSED ME THE NOTE BETWEEN BIOLOGY and Ancient History. It was the day of the school's mock election and Goldwater posters were all over the place. Between classes, when everyone was giving me Goldwater leaflets because they knew I was for Johnson, Lexie handed me a folded piece of paper from her looseleaf.

"Voilà, chérie," she whispered, staring up at me with her big brown eyes. The press of bodies in the hallway forced us to one side, right against the wall.

"Is this a personal plea for Goldwater?" I laughed, sticking the note in my blazer pocket. I couldn't help noticing the tendons of Lexie's neck beneath her open collar.

"I can't be bothered with those tired old men." Lexie's fingers stroked her neck, where I'd been looking. The hall was emptying as second-period classes began, but I felt rooted there. Lexie brushed a hair off my lapel. "I'll save a seat for you at lunch."

Every time Mrs. Kelbow turned to write something on the board in Ancient History, I opened another fold of Lexie's note. *"Ma chère Jinx,"* it began, in her large, loose script, *"Tu es ma plus chère amie. Pourquoi?* You're cute. Also you have a nice bod. See you at lunch. Love, Lexie. P.S. I voted for Johnson."

"What's that?" Miggin looked over my shoulder.

I put the note away quickly. "A note."

"In French?"

"It's—"

"Jean..." Miss Kelbow was staring at me.

"Do you have something you wish to share with the rest of the class?"

I blushed. "No. No, thank you."

"Then refrain from talking." Kelbow continued her description of the Roman aqueducts, and I began a reply to Lexie. "Dear Lexie, My French isn't too hot. I like being your most *chère amie*. You are a good voice teacher too. Miggin says you think she's an idiot. Lady Bird and I thank you for your support of LBJ. Bye, Jinx."

I handed Lexie the note between Ancient History and French. At lunchtime Lexie sat by me, but most of the time she talked to Oakie about some boy they knew from Hotchkiss. But her knee was touching my knee under the table, and there was plenty of room.

"Miggin's not an idiot," said Lexie abruptly, when we were almost finished eating. "She's just dumb."

"No, she's not."

"There, there, defend your roommate like a good girl." Lexie patted my hand. "You're cute. Will you eat with me every day?"

I laughed. "Well, um, I guess so. I ... I..."

"Breathe, Jinx," said Lexie, standing up. Then she hurried out.

At Huntington Hill, Goldwater won in a landslide. But the next day in the real world he lost. His supporters at HH recovered quickly from the blow, because Parents' Weekend, which was approaching quickly, seemed far more important than a presidential election in the outer world. The Glee Club was rehearsing for the Friday night concert, the Drama Club was preparing a one-act play, and the Faculty Welcome Committee was organizing the Faculty-Parents' Tea on Saturday. In the dorms, the pay phones rang constantly as students arranged weekend plans with their parents and confirmed motel reservations in Huntington and Harrisburg. Everyone was excited and apprehensive. With parents around, anything could go wrong. Suppose they drank too much at dinner? What if they announced they were getting divorced? Or remarried? What if no one had anything to say at all?

Lexie and I were writing notes all the time and eating lunch together every day. She had decided she wanted to be a poet, and she brought me paperback books of William Blake and Theodore Roethke and Baudelaire. Then she wrote me poems — half in French, half in English. Usually they were about flowers and autumn leaves and sunsets with *frissons*. Her poetic surge made me work harder on my paintings. And the afternoons in the studio were a relief from the excitement of being Lexie's *plus chère amie*.

"Who's your favorite artist, Jinx?" said Lexie one day, following me into the studio.

"Pierre Bonnard, I guess. Then Matisse."

The next day she arrived with a huge book — a collection of Bonnard paintings. We pored over them, our arms and shoulders touching whenever we turned a page. It felt very intimate.

"He understands women, don't you think?" said Lexie, tracing the form of a naked woman lying in a bathtub. The woman's skin was pink, her shape elongated by the water.

"He paints a lot of nudes," I said uncertainly.

"Not always." Lexie turned to a painting of a tea party with ladies sitting stiffly around a table.

"They're not talking to each other," I said.

"That happens a lot in life," said Lexie, twisting a strand of hair in her fingers. "People aren't honest with each other."

"Yeah."

Lexie took my hand. "Are you honest with *me?*"

"I guess," I said. "I try." Sitting beside her was the most exciting thing I had ever felt. I was afraid to move or breathe. I might melt into a pool of water on the floor.

"You better be honest." Lexie stood up and looked around the room — at the easels, the tubes of paint, the windows overlooking the pasture. "I like this place."

"Maybe you should be a painter instead of a poet."

"Jamais," she replied. *"Je suis poète."*

My folks were scheduled to arrive from Washington on Friday afternoon of Parents' Weekend. My father changed his teaching schedule so that he could see the hockey game. But the way things looked, I wouldn't be playing. Nicky had come to practice every day. He stood grimly near the bleachers, back stiff, arms folded, blue-shadowed chin jutting forward. His smile was gone, and he was unusually quiet as he followed the scrimmage. Woodie ran the practice as if he weren't there, making only one change in her usual routine — she coached from the far sidelines, away from the bleachers ... and Nicky.

The day before the game, midway through the practice, Nicholson walked onto the field and stopped at the fifty-yard line, where Maddy and I were lining up for a bully. He stared at Woodie, who watched him silently, lips pinched around her whistle.

"I'd like Maddy to play with the varsity," he called loudly.

I took off my number. Woodie scowled.

"Stay where you are, Tuckwell. Maddy, give Jinx back her number." No one moved. Woodie mumbled something to Nicholson and marched to the sidelines. He followed her slowly.

"Miss Spense, take over," ordered Woodie.

Spense, as baffled as we were, squared her shoulders, looked quizzically at Nicky and Woodie, now walking silently up to McAllister, and blew her whistle. "All right, ladies," she barked, "back to your places."

Maddy glared at her. "Who's playing center?"

Spense hesitated, puffed her cheeks with air, and exhaled. "Tuckwell's playing varsity, you're with the JV."

"Damn," said Maddy Hansen under her breath. We leaned in to bully, and for the next fifteen minutes, we played for blood, not stopping to joke during roll-ins, not gossiping when we lined up for corners.

"What's going on?" whispered Scottie when we got in place for a bully on the twenty-five. I looked at her pink cheeks and hopeful eyes.

"Politics," I said.

Scottie cocked her head to one side. She didn't understand.

When practice was over, Spense fumbled with her clipboard and scratched her head uncertainly. Finally, she cleared her throat, and buried her hands in the pockets of her Bermuda shorts.

"Ladies, we've, there's ... we're having a little change in our routine today. Uh ... as you can see, Woodie's not here, and, uh ... I ... I won't be reading off the roster for tomorrow. I think you all know" — she stood up straight and craned her head forward — "that tomorrow's game with Cliff School is the most important one you'll play this season. Now, we've been over and over our dodges, we've drilled corners, roll-ins, tackles, the works. We've spent nine weeks together as a team and tomorrow will be the culmination of your efforts. A win will mean an undefeated season." She looked down at the ground. "Are there any questions?"

Silence. On the bottom row, a hand went up.

"Scottie?" said Spense apprehensively.

"Will ... um ... Miss Spense, will we be playing with the usual lineup? Will ... are there going to be changes?"

Scottie had asked the question we had all wanted to ask. The group listened attentively; we could hear the screams of Lower School children as their study hall let out.

Spense looked soberly at Scottie. "Not as far as I know; no changes as far as I know." She kicked her sneaker against the grandstand. "Any other questions? Then you're excused. Ladies, good luck tomorrow." We clattered down the bleachers and went back to our dorms.

BY NINE THE NEXT MORNING, THE LAWNS AND driveways were lined with cars. The parents — nervous, eager, and overdressed — were arriving. Mothers in bright tweeds and chunky gold bracelets hugged and giggled with their daughters, while fathers scrutinized the grounds and buildings — investors analyzing the quality of their property. The noise level in study hall was slowly rising as parents shared desks with us, waiting for assembly to begin. The cheerleaders and Glee Club members trotted in and out gathering last-minute props for their skits, and even the faculty was loud as they lined up in the annex for their entrance during the processional. The whole room smelled of perfume.

I sat at my desk looking over the study hall. Until Woodie read out the roster, I could not be sure if I was playing. Parents' Weekend was beginning to be a nightmare.

"In a way, it's easier for me without my parents," Miggin had said before breakfast. "I get to have all the fun and none of the worries." She winked. "Just don't desert me at dinner tonight."

"Are you kidding?" I said, but I knew she wasn't. It might be awkward for her to get through the evening with my family and Lexie's.

Although the study hall filled, Lexie's desk was empty. She was probably practicing her solo in Knowlton, rehearsing one more time before the concert. Miggin was still outside with the cheerleaders. On my right, I saw Elizabeth Knight's mother, the only parent who didn't look like she was dressed for a garden club luncheon. She was wearing a black Guatemalan cape stitched in bold, colorful embroidery; long silver earrings dangled below her curly brown hair. She gazed around the room with an impish smile on her face.

"Jinx," she called when she saw me. I liked Elizabeth's mother. She was an artist, and always looked at my paintings when she visited. She waved excitedly to me.

"Stop it, Mother." Elizabeth pulled her down on to the seat. I knew Elizabeth wished her mother were more reserved. She would probably have preferred having Maddy Hansen's mother, who was seated next to Maddy now, jaw clenched, blonde hair pulled back off her forehead with a gold headband, face tan, hands placed carefully on the desk where her new engagement ring, a cluster of diamonds the size of a walnut, could be viewed from all angles.

Suddenly, the room was quiet. Mr. Nicholson opened the annex door, strode down the center aisle of study hall, and mounted the front platform. He announced the page number of the processional hymn. "All Things Bright and Beautiful" was the day's choice. How appropriate. The faculty walked in slowly, taking their places on the benches by the wall. There was Miss Cummings, the angular French teacher; Mrs. Dolby, the sexy math teacher, wearing a particularly tight turtleneck sweater; Mrs. Stall, the pale-faced Latin teacher. Finally, at the end of the line, came Thelma Anne Mosbey, dressed to kill in a powder blue scoop-necked dress. After a pause, Miss Woodruff entered soberly, followed by Miss Spense.

When the hymn was over and the unwieldy group was finally seated, Mr. Nicholson smiled — a minister pleased to find that his flock is exceptionally well turned out.

"Good morning, ladies and gentlemen. Welcome to Huntington Hill. For those of you who don't know me, my name is Randolph Nicholson and I am headmaster." He nodded warmly to some parents in the front and continued, "For many of you, this is your first Parents' Weekend, and I'm sure you look forward to it with as much anticipation as I do. For many of you, this is a familiar event. A few of you have been through Parents' Weekend as students. You have taken the same courses, studied with the same teachers as your daughters, and have watched, with the same sense of sadness and respect, the retirement of our two headmistresses — Miss Dunning and Miss Kroll."

That last line was aimed for the heart, a real tearjerker. Endowments, I thought. Future generations. He's already counting the money.

"Parents," concluded Nicholson with wrenching sincerity, "we will all have to work hard to continue the tradition of excellence fostered by Miss Dunning and Miss Kroll. We must work with the same dedication for the principles of truth, justice, and honor. It is only with your support that we can continue; and it is *upon* your support that the future of our children depends. To each of you here today, I extend a special, heartfelt thanks, and a warm, warm — welcome." I nearly retched. The parents burst into applause.

It was not until the very end of assembly, not until Lexie had performed her Glee Club solo, and Miggin had sung off-key with the cheerleaders, that Spense and Woodie stood up to read the starting lineup for the game. Woodie was in a dress today, for the parents, and wore the two spots of rouge on her cheeks. But she looked tired. She did not try to woo the parents or promote the hockey field as the battleground of truth and honor.

"The starting lineup for today's game…," she began. I gripped my chair, looked at Miggin, then Lexie. They were watching me.

"...which will be played today," continued Woodie, "against Cliff School, will be as follows: left wing, Alice Goodrich; left inner, Ann Powell; center forward, Maddy Hansen..." She kept reading, but I no longer heard. That was it. I was out, Maddy was in. They listed me as a substitute.

NICKY CAME TO SASH TYING BEFORE THE GAME. A slow, knotting spasm of tension ran through the players. Woodie, for the first time anyone could remember, refused to tie the sashes. She sat alone on the sofa, back hunched, elbows on her knees, hands holding her jaw, while Spense tried awkwardly to give the kind of frank advice that Woodie was known for. Nicky stood in one corner, arms folded, eyes narrowed, watching the procedure. He shouldn't have been there. His presence at our ritual was draining.

"What's *he* doing here?" whispered Scottie. The other players shifted uncomfortably, stealing glances at him. Spense knelt on the floor mumbling advice. Nicky spoke quietly to Maddy Hansen, who stood near him, jubilant and cocky. She was the only player enjoying the unexpected turn of events. Maddy's giggles fell heavily on the room.

We moved out of Century House like a funeral procession, each of us walking slowly down the long hill to the field. Our mood clashed with the festive spirit in the grandstands. Parents and children who had come early for good seats were laughing loudly; their conversation was animated. Above the field, cars were parked in the driveway and on the lawns near Senior House and McAllister. The Cliff School bus arrived; their team, cheerleaders, and fans ran down to the visitors' grandstand.

Before the warm-up, I looked up at the driveway. My parents' Chevrolet was stopped near the stands. I could see Mother scanning the crowd.

She jumped from the car when she saw me. "Baby," she yelled, throwing her arms around me. "How are you? It's grand to see you." It always amazed me that my mother was so cute and bubbly — so much smaller and bouncier than I was. She wore a rust-colored suit and a rust-colored blouse and a gold bracelet jingling with charms my father had given her.

She squeezed my hand. "We were so afraid we'd be late for the game. I told Daddy please to hurry, but he got a call from Bill Dudley at Harvard. You know, the professor of international law."

"Mother—"

"Frederick!" she called to my father. "Aren't you getting out of the car?"

"Hello there, Jinxie." My father waved. "I can't leave the car here, Helen. You go on and save me a seat."

Mother smiled at me. "We're so excited about the game. When was the last time? It must have been two years ago."

"Mother—"

"'Course, Daddy's the one who's really excited. Last night he found an old hockey rule book in your room and read it to me at dinner. I didn't understand a word, but we're so proud of you."

"I'm not playing," I said quietly.

"I was afraid we'd be late. Imagine Bill Dudley calling—"

"I'm not playing," I repeated.

"What?"

"They took me off, Ma. I'm a substitute." I looked down at the field. The forward line, led by Maddy Hansen, was practicing a play near the circle.

Mother looked at me sadly. "Jinxie, I'm sorry." She turned around. "Where's Daddy? I can't bear it. He'll be so disappointed."

66

"Ma, I've got to go. I'll see you after the game." I turned.

"We love you, Jinx," said Mother. "We love you whether you play or not."

Whatever Maddy Hansen had learned in England, it wasn't teamwork. She held onto the ball for the whole first half, never passing, never using the wings, never looking up to see if other players were open. She was determined to do everything herself. The Cliff School defense caught on; they took the ball from her — once, twice, three times. And they scored. The audience watched, stunned and subdued. Cliff School pushed by our defense every time they got the ball.

"Rack 'em up, stack 'em up, boom!" shouted our cheerleaders hopefully. Woodie sat silently, watching each play grimly. At halftime she strode onto the field to the huddle. I went with her. We were down 3–0. The faces of the players were tired. Their lungs heaved as they sucked orange slices from the kitchen.

"Gooooo, HH," screamed our cheerleaders, leaping incongruously on the sidelines. Woodie squatted on her haunches, clipboard in hand. She picked up a twig and broke it in two.

"What the heck is going on?" she growled, looking at each player ominously. She read down her list of comments, then stopped. "What's going on?" she repeated.

Silence. Slowly, from the sidelines, Randolph Nicholson, arms folded, walked deliberately toward the huddle. Scottie Ellis raised her hand.

"Woodie, we're not used to playing without Jinx. How do you expect—"

"Scottie's right," piped Izzie. "Tuckwell's part of us." She looked at me. "We're not the same without her."

Woodie straightened up. "Ladies, you'll play with the team we've assigned. *We* pick the players, not you."

Nicholson coughed. "Put Tuckwell in," he said. Maddy Hansen jumped up.

"But, Mr. Nicholson..."

"Tuckwell plays," he said again. Maddy started for the gym.

"Hansen," ordered Woodie, "you'll sit with the subs through the second half. Tuckwell, take her number."

Scottie squeezed my arm. The crowd cheered when they saw me tie on my number.

"Go, Tuckwell," Miggin screamed, leaping on the sidelines.

Lexie threw a red rose down from the stands.

"Whoopee," cried Scottie, waving her stick in the air. "We've got Tuckwell back."

As we lined up on the fifty, my skin felt the cool of the air; my eyes registered the deep green of the grass and the blue of the fall sky. Just before the bully, I scanned the field. Dawson and Briggs were inner and wing to my right, Goodrich and Powell to the left. Izzie Rogers, center half, was behind me, flanked by Rouse and Webster. At fullback were Scottie and Ross, and behind them, in the goal cage, Sandy Adams. They were all there. My teammates, my friends — classmates I had played with all season, who would be graduating with me in June. We were ready to fight Cliff School. We would win this game. We would win it to show Nicky he was a lousy bastard. We would win it to show Mrs. Hansen what we thought of her money. We would win it; we would win it, not for endowments, but for ourselves.

The whistle blew. A push pass to Dawson started us off. She flicked the ball across to wing, and the forwards moved as one toward the Cliff School goal. At the twenty-five, Briggs stopped the ball dead, scooped it over the fullback's stick, then dribbled to the circle. In a long, lovely drive, she angled the ball into the corner of the cage. It was a goal. The spectators went wild. The cheerleaders clapped and leaped and tossed their pom-poms.

Cliff School took their time lining up for the bully. The more time they used up, the less time we'd have to score. Their center forward ambled toward me. "Nice goal," she said pleasantly. Her easy style disappeared when the whistle blew. She wedged her stick between me and the ball and tore off down the field. But she held on too long. Izzie caught up with her, lunged, and knocked the ball to Powell at inner. Powell dribbled to the fifty, passed to Dawson, who dodged their left halfback and drove the ball back to Powell. Just as their goalie positioned herself for a shot from Powell, Powell turned, pushed the ball back to me, and I flicked it into the far side of the cage. Whistles and whoops and Huntington Hill pennants went up in the bleachers. I looked at the referee. Was anyone off-side? Any penalties? No. It was a goal.

"Nice work, Tuckwell," yelled Woodie. "Tie it up now, girls." Spense stood beside her, both fists raised triumphantly in the air. Nicky chain-smoked.

This time, Cliff's center looked worried when we lined up for the bully. She took forever adjusting her shin guards. "Let's go, center," grumbled the referee.

There were five minutes left when Cliff's left half tripped Scottie with her stick and the referee called a foul.

"You're wrong," hissed the halfback. Cliff's entire team converged on our goal cage. The referee blew her whistle again. "Is Huntington Hill paying you?" spat the halfback.

The referee only glanced at her. "You're out of the game."

I looked at Scottie. In three years, I'd never seen anyone thrown out. Suddenly, all the coaches were on the field. Time was called. Cliff's coach was chewing out the referee. Woodie put her hand on my shoulder. "Get the ball to Dawson," she whispered. "They're leaving her wide open."

Woodie was right. We got the ball to Dawson, and with a minute to go, Dawson tied the game 3–3.

I glanced back at Izzie as we lined up at the fifty. She looked at me oddly. The whistle blew and we leaned into the bully. Instead of lunging for the ball, I took a chance and lifted up my stick. Cliff's center, unopposed, knocked the ball directly into Izzie's waiting stick. Izzie aimed a perfect pass to Briggs at right wing and the forward took off. Moving with long, smooth strides, Briggs switched places with Dawson and dodged past Cliff School's center half. She was inside the circle with one fullback and the goalie between her and the goal. Just as the fullback approached, she tripped and fell. But from the ground, she pushed a pass to me. I stopped the ball, and scooped it over the goalie's stick. It was a goal. The clock ran out.

Parents, students, and cheerleaders flooded onto the field. Sandy, in her goalie pads, waddled up from the cage to join the huddle. We had won the game! An arm pulled the back of my tunic. Miggin, face shining, held my shoulders. Behind her, Lexie, hair wild and rumpled, reached out with her hand. In a moving, undifferentiated mass, we walked up to Century House. Scottie, Izzie, and I found ourselves together, side by side. The three of us linked arms.

"That's it," I said.

Scottie and Izzie looked at me. There were tears in their eyes.

"You played, Tuck," said Scottie.

"Almost didn't," I whispered.

The three of us climbed up to the Century House porch. Dawson, Briggs, and Powell joined us. Everyone was crying. It was over. We would never play together again. I would never play hockey again. Not at art school. I had made the choice. We stood, looking down over the groups of parents climbing slowly up the hill, looking at the green grass, the bright, neat school buildings, the pink-orange glow of the afternoon light. A solitary figure climbed the Century House steps and stopped.

"Ladies," growled Woodie, "where are your manners? The Cliff School is waiting inside for you."

I stood in the Century lounge, punch cup in hand, making conversation with the Cliff School center. The sounds of girls' voices drifted around me; there was the clink of cups and china, the laughter of cheerleaders, voices of children yelling, somewhere in the distance. In a daze, I walked next door to the Trophy Room, where it was quiet. My eyes rested on a series of photographs hanging on the far wall. They were the "mother-daughter" alumnae shots of smiling, suntanned mothers and daughters holding hockey sticks and tennis rackets. Beneath them were captions like "Two generations of varsity tennis at Huntington Hill — Mary Bliss Jones ('40) and Lisa Bliss Jones ('63)."

I shivered. Why did the mothers look so pleased with themselves? Why were they always smiling? The photographs puzzled me. Did the mothers ever drop their smiles long enough to *look* at the school, to think about what their children were being taught? Would they ever look close enough to discover that the headmaster was forcing students to apply to colleges they didn't want to attend, close enough to hear the hypocrisy in the lyrics of the alma mater praising truth and fairness and freedom?

"Jinx?"

Miggin moved toward me. "It was a beautiful game."

Something inside me trembled. I wrapped my arms around her. "Miggin…"

71

"I know, Jinx. It's been hard." She was crying too.

"Hey, idiots, what's your problem?" Izzie approached us and pulled something out from behind her back. A glass of pink punch. "Want some?" Before I could answer, she poured the sticky pink liquid over my head. I wiped it off.

Izzie giggled. "Don't bother." The Cliff School team staring from the doorway, she emptied the rest of the bowl on my head.

MIGGIN AND I SANK INTO THE BACKSEAT OF MY parents' Chevrolet. We were on our way to the Holiday Inn. While the folks had hurried off to my grandmother's to drop their suitcases and dress for dinner, I had showered and changed. In Senior House, waiting, I'd felt strange, distant, detached from the excitement now building again as parents picked up their kids and took them off to dinner.

Something had happened today. Something more than being taken off the team and put back on at halftime, with the score 3–0. The *real* world had broken through the protected bubble of Huntington Hill. The power struggles and politics, the maneuverings I thought only happened "out there," were happening here. Nicholson himself had used his power to take me off the team, because I wouldn't apply to Vassar, because Maddy Hansen's mother had the money and connections to put Maddy back on. Woodie's opinion, my opinion didn't matter.

I didn't want to believe it. I wanted to live in my private world, sink into my dreams of being a painter, of being Lexie's *plus chère amie*. But if I pretended it hadn't happened I'd be just like everybody else at Huntington Hill, like the teachers and students and alumnae mothers who smiled their big smiles and passed the lies on to the next generation. I kept waiting for them to stand up and shout out the truth, to admit that corruption and injustice weren't just in Washington and Saigon, weren't just stories we read in *Newsweek* and *Time*. They happened wherever somebody had more power or money than somebody else. The discovery made me sad ... and sleepy.

73

Mother turned around, gripping the seat with her arm. She was happy again, ready to be sociable. I had made two goals in the second half and all was well.

"You're awfully quiet, Jinx," said Mother. "Anything wrong? And how are you doing, Miggin?"

"Great," said Miggin enthusiastically. "Wasn't Jinx terrific in the game?" Miggin sat forward in the seat. Her red hair shone, even in the darkness, and as usual she smelled of cinnamon.

"Now, Jinx," said Mother, suddenly distracted, "what's Lexie's mother's name? It's not the same as hers, is it? I don't want to mix it up."

I reminded her that Lexie's last name was Yves, her "mother's" last name was Dennis, and her "cousin's" name was Keaton.

"Everyone has a different name," she said, shaking her head. "Now, who is Philip?"

I sighed. Maybe I was more used to the varied last names and marital arrangements of Huntington Hill parents. Many of them had divorced and remarried and divorced again. My classmates had handfuls of step-relatives, all with different names.

"Mrs. Dennis isn't Lexie's mother," I said. "Her parents are dead. Mrs. Dennis is her guardian and Philip is Mrs. Dennis's nephew."

"Complicated," said Mother to herself. "Well, I'm sure we'll have a marvelous time." We drove the rest of the way in silence.

The Huntington Holiday Inn towered over the Interstate like a plastic castle. The residents of the carefully zoned Huntington Valley had never entirely recovered from the shock of the inn's presence in their horsy paradise. But it was one of the only places out-of-towners could stay when they visited the valley.

Muzak and blinking orange lights greeted us as we entered the front vestibule, where we were nearly trampled by a group of Shriners wearing fezzes and smoking cigars.

"What's the room number?" demanded Mother.

"One twenty-seven," I said.

"One twenty-seven, Fred," repeated Mother.

"Mother..."

"I think," said my father deliberately, "we should call Mrs. Dennis on the house phones."

"Don't be silly, Fred. This is a motel. They don't have house phones. Furthermore, we're expected." Mother snagged the arm of a motel employee wearing black slacks and an ocher nylon vest.

"Where's room one twenty-seven?"

"I'm only the bartender." He pivoted around her.

My father patted down his pockets. "I'll ask at the desk."

"Oh, come on, Fred. We'll find it," said Mother, pulling Miggin and me with her. The three of us entered a long, dimly lit corridor carpeted with orange Astro-Turf. At room 127, Mother paused.

"We *are* expected, aren't we, Jinx?"

"I spoke to Lexie this afternoon. She *said* six."

Mother looked at her watch. "Well, it's six-fifteen." She rapped loudly on the door. There was no answer. We could hear a phone ringing in the room.

"That's probably your father calling," grumbled Mother. She turned to me, fussed with my collar, and shook her head. "This Philip, Jinx. Does he have a room?"

Miggin, who had been waiting patiently for the little drama to be resolved, offered to check at the reception desk. Mother insisted we all go with her.

Halfway down the hall, a voice called us from behind. "Hello. Hello there." A tiny woman with wild white hair stood in stocking feet, looking confused and disarrayed. Her slip dangled an inch below her dress.

"That's Mrs. Dennis," whispered Miggin.

"Hello there," she called again. "Are you Lexie's friends?"

"Mrs. Dennis?" Mother charged back down the hall.

"Come on," said the woman, who waited for us by the door, then limped slowly into the room, which smelled like whiskey.

"Alcohol," whispered Mother, after the introductions were made. As Mrs. Dennis closed the door, my father appeared.

"Frederick Tuckwell," he said eagerly, with his Boy Scout smile. Mrs. Dennis shook his hand, then fumbled with a light switch by her bed.

"I'll get that," said Miggin. Mother was inspecting the room; I knew she would approve of Mrs. Dennis's Vuitton luggage and her unmistakably WASP assortment of clothes, but in general I knew she was not impressed with the initial stage of the evening I had arranged.

"Where's Lexie?" she said suddenly.

"Alexis?" Mrs. Dennis scratched her head. "She's ... she's with Philip."

"Should we call her?" It was more of a command than a question, and Mrs. Dennis became a flutter of activity, picking up the phone, searching for her glasses, then abandoning the project to offer us drinks.

"I *am* sorry," she said. "I'll call room service. What would you like?"

"Why don't I take orders and run to the bar?" volunteered my father, eager to leave our intimate gathering.

"Fred..." My mother shook her head. "Mrs. Dennis has a bottle here, I see..."

"That's so dreary," said Mrs. Dennis. "I'll have a dry Rob Roy, and Mrs...."

"Tuckwell," said Mother.

76

"Tuckwell, yes, of course. What will you have?"

"A Manhattan," said Mother, disapproving. She was thinking of the bar bill, I know. When my father had gone, Mother, finding the situation too unstructured for her taste, took control.

"Jinx, you call Lexie. Mrs. Dennis can't find her glasses."

"Is Lexie there?" I said to the sleepy male voice that answered the phone, having first dropped the receiver onto the floor. I heard Lexie take it from him.

"It's Jinx," I said.

Lexie swore. "Jesus, Jinx, I'm sorry. We were watching TV and lost track of the time. Be right there."

I put down the phone. Miggin, Mother, and Mrs. Dennis were staring at me. "They were watching TV and lost track of time," I repeated mechanically.

"Lost track of time?" Mother was incredulous.

Mrs. Dennis jumped up. "Playing bridge, I'll bet."

"You play bridge, Mrs. Dennis?" said my father, entering the room with a tray of drinks. For the next few minutes, the grown-ups carried on a polite, disconnected conversation about New York, bridge, and WBZ Radio. It was not one of those irresistibly charismatic encounters in which everyone feels, after only a few minutes, that they've known each other for years. Mrs. Dennis didn't know any of Mother's New York friends, nor did she have any friends in Washington. This was frustrating for Mother, since "Do you know" was the backbone of her conversation in these encounters. When the door burst open and Lexie appeared, with Philip, we were all relieved.

Lexie looked beautiful. She wore a black V-neck dress and black heels; her hair was unusually neat, arranged in a kind of bouffant. Her dark eyes were exquisitely made up, her eyeliner accenting their brightness. Behind her stood Philip, tall, immaculately dressed in a navy blue suit and silk tie. His hair was brushed off his face, European style, showing his high forehead and pale green eyes.

"Why, you're a grown man," exclaimed Mother, examining Philip, whose eyes were already fixed upon Miggin. My father headed for Lexie, who sat down on one of the twin beds and lit a cigarette. I sat on her other side opposite Mrs. Dennis, who chewed distractedly on the potato chips my father had brought from the bar.

"Why, Lexie," said Mother, "Jinx has talked so much about you." She seated herself quickly between Lexie and my father. "It's such a pleasure, Lexie. And how pretty you look."

Lexie smiled and looked at me, pleased to be meeting this new perspective on my personality. "Your mother's accent is so strong," she whispered. "She talks like a maid." I winced. Lexie turned to Mother. "It's a pleasure to meet *you*, Mrs. Tuckwell. I'm so happy that Jinx will be going to art school. Mother and I want her to stay with us when she goes to New York for interviews. Don't we, Mother?"

My mother's smile vanished.

"Interviews?" said Mrs. Dennis, who had been trying to find her station on the radio.

"Art school interviews," said Lexie. "When Jinx visits New York, she'll stay with us, won't she?"

"I'm sure that's perfectly fine," said Mrs. Dennis, emptying the last of the Scotch into her glass. "I'll have to ask Juliet, of course. She's gotten so difficult."

"Hard to get good help," said Mother sympathetically.

Lexie rolled her eyes and moved closer to me. Was she making fun of Mother?

"We'd sure like Jinxie to stay with us," Lexie said with a trace of a southern accent.

"Well," said Mother, "that's the nicest thing I ever heard of, Lexie. Of course, I usually go with her when she visits colleges..."

"Oh, we'll take good care of her." Lexie put her arm around my waist. "We're crazy about little Jinxie."

"Well, we're crazy about her, too," said Mother, looking dubiously at Lexie's arm.

Mother whispered to me as we approached the Holiday Inn restaurant. "Lexie's very grown-up."

"What?"

"She's — she's very mature for her age. She's practically ... practically a *woman*," said Mother, as if that were the most unlikely thing in the world for a seventeen-year-old to be. "She's not like you and Miggin," said Mother. "It's night and day. You two are schoolgirls. You act your age. You ... you..." Mother could not quite put words to her thoughts, an unusual occurrence.

"I think it's very odd," she said, recovering, "that she was in the room watching television with Philip. He's a grown man. It's not at all attractive."

"I think Lexie's great."

"Well, don't be angry at me. She's very fond of you and that's fine," concluded Mother, as we entered the dining room.

The restaurant was a large, noisy room covered with more orange Astro-Turf and bug-repellent lanterns. Waitresses in black nylon uniforms hurried from table to table serving platters of overcooked roast beef and red plastic baskets of fried chicken. Huntington Hill parents and daughters were all over the place.

Lexie sat next to me at dinner. "Do I look okay?" she whispered, touching my hand.

"You look good," I gulped. "Really."

"God, I dressed in five minutes. I'm amazed I'm here at all. Philip ... detained me." She laughed loudly. I pretended not to hear.

"What'd you think of the election?" said Mother to the ever-distracted Mrs. Dennis.

"I'm sorry?" Mrs. Dennis pointed to a waitress carrying a tray of food. "Lexie, aren't those little baskets of chicken cute?"

"Eleanor, Mrs. Tuckwell asked what you thought of the election. You know, Goldwater and Johnson? Did you vote, Eleanor?"

Mrs. Dennis hunched over the menu. "Terrible. Just terrible."

Mother sat up straight. "Of course, Fred and I are Democrats..."

"Lexie, why don't you get that basket of chicken?"

"Jesus," sighed Lexie.

The folks gave up on Mrs. Dennis. My father told Miggin about his college camping trips to Colorado and Mother entertained Lexie and Philip with tales of her days in New York.

"Now, Lexie," said Mother, whose respect for Lexie's worldliness was increasing, "what do you think of this Mr. Nicholson?"

Lexie laughed. "He's a bastard. Furthermore, he took Jinx off the team and he should be dismembered for that."

"For goodness sakes." Mother frowned.

"He can be charming when he wants but deep down he's a bastard..."

"You seem to know a lot about him," said Mother.

Lexie plunged her fork into a tomato. "I talk to him a lot. He appointed himself faculty advisor to Music Club because I'm the president."

"I see," said Mother.

Suddenly, Lexie looked at her watch and jumped up. "Philip," she said, "get your coat on. You've got to take me back to school. Our rehearsal's in five minutes." Philip stood up deliberately.

"Eleanor." Lexie pulled on her coat. "You can ride with the Tuckwells." We all stared at Lexie. Having insisted on dinner together, she had arrived late and was leaving before we had finished.

"Lexie," said Mrs. Dennis, finally realizing that something was happening, "you haven't eaten your dinner." By the looks of it, Mrs. Dennis planned to drink her dinner.

"That's showbiz." Lexie laughed and hurried out.

"Where did Lexie go?" said Mrs. Dennis.

"Back to school," comforted Miggin, in loud, careful syllables, as if addressing her retarded children. "She has to be there early."

"She hasn't eaten her dinner."

"Never ate before a concert in *my* glee club days," said my father cheerfully.

"My husband went to St. Paul's," said Mother, still hoping to spark a conversation.

"Lexie told me not to bring Philip," mused Mrs. Dennis. "They used to get on famously."

Mother cleared her throat. "They seem to get on well enough."

"Philip won't work. Says jobs bore him," continued Mrs. Dennis, to no one in particular.

"He has a private income?" queried Mother.

"I should think so," replied Mrs. Dennis vaguely.

Mother made one last attempt with Mrs. Dennis. "You know, Jinxie's on the hockey team. Made the winning goal today."

"Waitress, I'll have another Scorch and a doggie bag for the young lady's dinner." Mrs. Dennis's head trembled slightly.

The waitress returned with the Scotch and the doggie bag, which she handed to Mrs. Dennis, and the check, which she handed to my father. Mrs. Dennis did not reach for the check, and Mother looked nervously at my father. "I thought we were *her* guests," she whispered. My father smiled uncomfortably; Mrs. Dennis, oblivious, drank her Scotch.

81

"What do you think of Philip?" I said to Miggin as we drove back to school.

She shrugged. "He's handsome."

"He's a creep," I said glumly.

The auditorium was bursting with people, all very jolly after dinner and drinks. Parents introduced themselves to other parents, glancing proudly at their children as they talked. Philip had saved seats for us in the front row, and my parents, disappointed with Mrs. Dennis and Philip, looked around eagerly for familiar faces. They were gratified by the sudden appearance of Emily Jonas, a favorite teacher of mine the year before. Her usually pale face was flushed and animated as she introduced my parents to a tall, bearded man who stood uncomfortably beside her. She turned to me.

"How are you, Jinx? How's the weekend going?"

"We had dinner with Lexie's family," I said quickly.

"Lexie's family?" Jonas was surprised.

"She's giving me voice lessons. We're friends." Jonas squinted at me.

"You're very different people," she said, touching my arm. "Lexie's very much ... a performer," continued Jonas. "Of course, she's very bright," she said, as an afterthought. She straightened up and tapped her bearded friend's arm. "David, we should find seats." She waved good-bye to my parents, and headed down a side aisle as the houselights faded.

Lexie's voice was pure and clear, sweet and moving. The audience listened spellbound as she sang her part of a Bach cantata. Many of the girls struggled as they sang, eyes rolling toward the ceiling as they reached for the high notes. Lexie sang effortlessly.

Backstage, a crowd gathered around Lexie. Philip and Miggin led us back; Mrs. Dennis trailed behind, waving the doggie bag.

"Lexie, your dinner," she called when she spied her ward. She tossed the bag to Lexie, who caught it, handed it to someone else, and opened her arms to embrace the approaching headmaster.

"Let's go," I said to the folks. "That's Nicholson."

"But we haven't congratulated Lexie," said my father.

"Fred, he took Jinx off the team," said Mother protectively.

"I'm sure he had a reason." Daddy was determined to speak to Lexie.

"Who's that man?" said Mrs. Dennis, pointing to Nicholson.

"That's the headmaster," said Miggin politely.

"Piggy little man," muttered Mrs. Dennis.

That night I lay in bed, staring at the glow-stars Miggin and I had glued to the ceiling our first week of school. I was exhausted, but I couldn't fall asleep.

"Miggin?" I whispered. "Are you asleep?"

"No," she said sleepily. Her covers rustled.

"What'd you think of the evening?"

"It was fun. Your parents are nice. Your father talked to me about Colorado."

I paused. "What about Mother?"

"I like her. You get sort of quiet around her. You're probably afraid she's going to embarrass you. I'm the same way with my folks."

"What about Lexie?"

"What about her?"

"She was good, wasn't she?"

"Yeah."

"She sang well, right?"

"Jinx, I don't feel the way you do about Lexie."

I sat up. "What do you mean?"

"You know what I mean. You think she's wonderful. 'Course," laughed Miggin, "if you knew her better, you probably wouldn't like her so much."

"What?"

"Jinx, Lexie can be a bitch. She tortures Elizabeth all the time."

"*Elizabeth* can be pretty awful," I said.

"Don't worry, Tuckwell. Lexie likes you. She won't torture *you*. Not yet, anyway. And maybe I'm jealous."

"What?"

"Never mind."

An hour later, I was still awake.

"Are you awake?" I said.

"I am now."

"Do you think..."

Miggin turned on the light. "Jinx, why don't you come over here if you want to talk."

"I should come to your bed?"

"Sure."

I tiptoed to Miggin's bed and sank into the cinnamon-scented sheets. "Was it odd," I said, "that Lexie was with Philip when we got to the motel?"

"She was watching TV." Miggin's toes bumped mine. "Cripes, Tuck, your feet are cold. I'll warm them up." She twisted her feet around mine.

"I used to sleep with my parents after I wet the bed," I said suddenly.

"Well, don't wet mine."

"Miggin, Lexie and Philip *weren't* watching TV. They were asleep."

"They were asleep?" said Miggin.

"Is that odd?"

Miggin thought for a minute. "Maybe they were making out."

I shivered. "That's a funny time to make out — when everybody's waiting for you."

Miggin laughed. "I guess if you get the urge, you get the urge."

"Yech."

"Lexie's reputation isn't lily white, Jinx. Are your feet warmer now?" She squeezed my toes.

"Yeah. I should go back to bed."

Miggin reached over the pillow and touched my hair. "It's cozy with you here."

"I should go back to my bed."

"You can stay."

"I ... I'm pretty tired."

"I wish you would stay." She lifted my arm around her head and suddenly I felt the cloud of bright hair against my collarbone. Could that be her lips against my neck? I stared at the ceiling until the glow-stars blinked orange as the lights of the Holiday Inn. My shoulder tingled from the weight of her head, but I didn't dare move until I heard her soft, slow breathing.

"'Night, Miggin." I kissed her cheek and climbed quickly out of her warm bed.

THE NEXT MORNING, I WOKE UP WORRYING. First, there was Nicky and Woodie and the hockey game. Then there was Lexie, sleeping in that room with Philip, doing something, being "detained," whatever that meant. And her comment about my mother sounding like a maid. Then there was my father, always so distant and hard to talk to. And Jonas. Why did she say Lexie and I were "very different people"? And Miggin, last night, in bed, wanting me to sleep with her. I liked feeling close to her, but did it mean something? Did she want something sexy to happen?

Other people didn't seem to be so easily disturbed by things. My worry mechanism went into effect at the slightest provocation. And I didn't worry nearly so much about the important things, about nuclear bombs or the Negroes in the South, although sometimes I could get a pretty good worry up about those things, too.

Here it was, a beautiful fall morning, sun shining brightly on the pasture behind us, sky blue, air cool and fresh, and I was worried about a stupid conversation at dinner. Maybe I would just try to fake it, just act like an ordinary schoolgirl flying through Parents' Weekend on cloud nine, whatever that was. Could it hurt to try?

I sat up suddenly. "Hey, Miggin," I said to the inert pile of covers on her bed. "Wake up. It's Saturday."

Miggin rolled over and squinted. "Has the bell rung?"

I pulled off her covers. She was wearing a flannel nightgown covered with pink and yellow teddy bears, and she looked like a little kid. No curlers this morning. "Get up," I said. "It's beautiful today." I pulled on my blue jeans and an old gray sweater, then dashed to the bathroom. Miggin was up now, standing in a daze, hair falling in her face.

"Jinx, what are you doing?" Her voice was still thick with sleep.

I splashed my face with cold water.

"Miggin, it's a new me, it's a happy-go-lucky me. I'm not going to worry anymore."

She looked at me thoughtfully. If I was really serious, her social worker's nature didn't want to discourage this sudden change. She decided to go along with me.

It was good while it lasted, and it lasted two hours. We ran to the lower field and back, then we played Frisbee on the lawn by Senior House. Scottie saw us from her window and came out to join us, and then Oakie, the school president, came too, and pretty soon about fifteen of us were playing. The students waiting in line for breakfast laughed at us. But it was good. At breakfast the morning light poured in the south window of Century and the dining room seemed warmer than usual. There was the smell of coffee and bacon and buttered toast. The long blue tables looked cheerful, and the students, excited by parents and families, were more spirited than usual.

At Miss Pennebaker's table, two rows away, I saw Lexie, her makeup gone, face pale but animated. My stomach didn't trip, and I didn't start to worry. I just enjoyed looking at her and thinking of the poise with which she sang her solo last night. I savored my coffee. Jeepers was at my table and we joked about Miss Jonas's new boyfriend. And two freshmen were arguing about whether it was legal to wear leather oxfords with your gym tunic.

"I swear," said one, who was from the South and had a funny, musical accent, "that Miss Woodruff said distinctly you *cannot* wear oxfords with gym clothes."

"Ask Jinx what the rule is," piped Jeepers. "She's a jock. She hangs around with Woodie." Jeepers smiled sheepishly at me; her Philadelphia Phillies baseball cap hung on the back of her chair.

"Well," I said, straight-faced, "as one who hangs around with Woodie, I can assure you that the *precise* rule doesn't matter to her. She wants you to wear whatever makes you happy, whatever footwear is personally meaningful to you." The two freshmen stared at me.

"Are you serious?"

"No," I said.

And then the bell rang.

There were other parents in the studio that morning — they walked through, looked silently at the work, and left. At least my parents reacted.

"That's the 1929 Aretha County basketball team," said Mother. "Why on earth would you want to paint that old photograph?"

"I like the way you look. I like the picture."

Mother peered at the painting, half-pleased, half-disturbed. "Do you see, Fred? She's painted my old basketball team. She's captured my likeness pretty well."

My father's brow rumpled like a loose carpet. "I ... I can see the likeness." But his gaze was now on a painting of him and his college roommate standing arm in arm, holding a huge fish. "Look at this one, Helen," he said, suppressing a laugh. "It's me and Ike Miller in the Rockies. That was a rainbow trout. Must have weighed ten pounds."

"Jinx, I've never seen such things," cried Mother. "I don't know — and here's — Fred, look at this one — here's Jinx in front of our old house in Washington." Mother stood up close to the large, square canvas. "Now *that's* a likeness..." Suddenly, she was quiet. She looked around the room nervously.

"Jinx," she whispered, "do you really think everybody should ... see these?"

"Why not?"

"You probably want to put them away now," she continued. "I think..." She was looking at the painting of me, standing stiffly by the house. "You don't look very happy in that picture, Jinx."

I shrugged.

"Jinx, you look like a poor little orphan. People will think no one loved you." She touched my arm. The corners of her eyes filled with tears.

"Just because I look sad doesn't mean I wasn't loved."

"Oh, no, no, no ... I don't mean that." She stepped back. "I mean ... well, I just can't bear to see you looking so unhappy, and to think people will see that." Mother half stood, half sat on one of the tall wooden stools; she was not sure she liked the art studio. "Jinxie, you worry too much. You think too much and you worry and you dig up the past. You're still a child. You should be having fun, enjoying yourself. Right, Fred?" She looked at my father, who had wandered off to look at a nude on an easel.

"Fred," she called, "tell Jinx not to worry so much. Tell her to have fun."

My father cleared his throat. He tucked his chin close to his chest. "Self-expression is important, Jinxie," he began, "but one wouldn't want to forget the more objective disciplines — science, economics, the law. And" — he pinched a nostril — "can one *support* oneself with painting? Can one—"

"Fred," fumed Mother, "listen to me. Jinx doesn't have to support herself yet." She stood up. "The point is, she's dredged up these ancient old photographs — where she found them, I don't know — when she should be having fun."

My father stroked his jaw. "It's an excellent likeness of Ike Miller, Helen."

Suddenly, the art room door swung open. Mrs. Knight's brightly colored Guatemalan cape swished through the room.

"Jinxie," she called. "How wonderful to see you." She approached us with the erratic movements of a swallow darting after a fly; her brown eyes sparkled mischievously. "And Mr. and Mrs. Tuckwell," she cried, shaking my father's hand vigorously. "How good to see you." She turned toward the door. "Elizabeth, come say hello to the Tuckwells."

Elizabeth stood silently in her corner of the room, assembling her paintings. "Hello," she said perfunctorily.

Mrs. Knight hovered over my paintings, clucking enthusiastically, her small body alive with interest. She looked up, smiled, and enveloped me in her enormous cape. "Jinxie, these are remarkable." She turned to my parents. "You must be very proud. Your daughter's work is intriguing — so much character for one so young."

"Well, I think that's a terribly nice thing to say," said Mother. "If we knew anything about art we—"

"Do you think, Mrs. Knight," began my father, "do you think one can expect to make a living, to support oneself, if one becomes a painter?"

Mrs. Knight stared at him, serious for a moment. "I shouldn't think so. Certainly not right away. Is that really so important now?" She paused, then her merry tone returned. "Of course, it's never easy. But she's much too young and talented; we shouldn't discourage her."

"Mummy!" Elizabeth, shoulders raised, dark hair shining electrically, was impatient. "Are you going to look at *my* paintings?"

Mrs. Knight swept her cape around her and headed for Elizabeth's corner. "Certainly, I am, darling." She turned back to us and whispered gravely, "Lizzie's father has put us all in a terrible mood. He wants her to spend the entire summer in Texas. It's a terrible bore and she's furious with us both. God knows, I can't stand the man. That's why I divorced him."

"Mummy," cried Elizabeth shrilly.

"We'll see you at the party this afternoon," said Mrs. Knight.

Mother and Father looked at her with amazement. "Well, Jinx," whispered Mother finally. "She says you're very talented."

I wanted to see Lexie, right then, right at that moment. I wanted to be alone with her, to have her all to myself, to sit with her, somewhere, and tell her about my parents, about how lonely it felt to be with them. We could never get close. I wanted to be close to someone. I wanted to be with someone who understood about painting and doing something just because you enjoy it, not for any reason like making a living or helping somebody. I could never share anything with my parents. We always seemed to miss. They had these ideas about how people were supposed to behave and what things were supposed to make you happy. Even if you didn't feel happy you were supposed to act happy, which could make you feel worse. It was as if all of us were circumscribed by this thin, narrow band called "acceptable" behavior. Sometimes it seemed like being honest was outside the narrow band. In fact, almost everything new or different was outside the band. Painting was definitely outside it. That's why it made my parents nervous. Anything that challenged the old illusion that everybody's happy all the time was bad.

The narrow band made it hard to talk to Mother and Daddy. If I said anything serious, they told me I worried too much. Gradually, I stopped talking to them, not telling them about myself. And that made me sad.

I wanted to talk to Lexie because with Lexie I could say what I wanted. She didn't worry about the narrow band. She laughed at it. I didn't feel crazy and weird around her.

Before we left school for lunch at my grandmother's, I went up to Lexie's room. She had the only single in Senior House. It was empty. I looked at her poster — Jean-Paul Belmondo, dressed in tight pants, smoking a Gitane. Lexie's clothes were all over the floor and her desk was covered with books and makeup. I found a piece of paper and wrote, "Lexie, I miss you." I folded it up and I put it on her pillow. Just writing the note made me feel better. At my grandmother's, even though lunch was very formal and she was nervous and sick, I had a nice time. Looking at her furniture, at the beautiful, polished antiques, at the rich, dark wood, which smelled of lemons and linseed oil, was comforting. The change from the dorm — from furniture that had been used and abused, painted again and again with thick enamel, tossed and kicked by indifferent students — was a relief.

"I got your note," said Lexie, at the Faculty Tea. There were parents and students and teachers packed into every corner of Century. "I missed you too," she said, her face softening.

"Where's Philip and Mrs. Dennis?" I said. I wanted to tell her how *much* I missed her.

Lexie's face clouded. "They're late. Eleanor got bombed at lunch." She looked past me, distracted. As if on cue, Philip and Eleanor entered the front door of Century. "Jinx," she said, "I want you to come stay with us in New York. Will you ask your parents?" She touched my arm.

"I'll ask my parents."

The folks left for Washington that night, after the Drama Club show. I guess I owed a lot to Miss Jonas, because she talked to them for a long time at the Faculty Tea. She had reassured them about art school and New York and painting. She told them I was happy and not to worry about me and that I had lots of friends. She told them all that stuff last year, but they liked hearing it again.

When I asked them before they left if I could stay with Lexie when I went to Parsons and Cooper Union for interviews, they said it would be okay. My mother was worried — I could see it in her face. She had gone with me on all the other interviews. We'd stayed in motels and eaten pancakes and hamburgers in little chrome-covered diners with jukeboxes. I think she was sorry we wouldn't be having that last trip together. But she knew I wanted to stay with Lexie.

When I said good-bye to the folks, I felt closer to them, because they seemed as if they were trying to understand. As we stood in the darkness by the upper driveway near Senior House with Mother squinting, handbag on her arm, and Daddy nervous because he was saying good-bye, I cried. I wanted to be good. I wanted to make them happy. I wanted to be what they wanted, but maybe I never would be. That made me sad, and I cried as the Chevy moved slowly down the driveway and the red taillights turned onto the Huntington road.

THE ELECTRONIC BUZZ OF THE ALARM CLOCK stabbed through our sleep. Disoriented, hearts pounding, we both lunged to silence it and in doing so, sent the clock crashing to the floor. I switched on the light and sat up. It is December five, I thought slowly. I am going to New York today. I will stay at Lexie's.

Miggin's covers rustled. "What time is it?"

I shivered. The room was cold. It was still dark outside.

"Five-thirty. Go back to sleep."

Miggin plodded to my bed and began to remove the curlers from my hair. The night before, she had set my hair in plastic rollers lined with nylon bristles that had pierced my scalp like tiny needles whenever I moved. Now, most of them were dangling from my head like ornaments on a Christmas tree.

"These things are deadly," I said, pulling one out slowly. Miggin's body was close to mine. I liked feeling her hands touch my hair.

"You must pay the price for beauty," she laughed, gathering the rollers into a huge scarf.

"Why do I have to be beautiful for art school interviews? They're supposed to look at my paintings, not at me."

Miggin frowned. "Don't start that again, Jinx. There is no justice; just shut up and get ready."

"*You* shut up," I said, standing in front of the mirror. Where each roller had been there was a long, looping curl. "I look stupid."

"Be polite, Tuckwell, or I'll never roll your hair again." Gently, she brushed out my curls. We stood side by side in our flannel nightgowns like two grandmothers. "You're nervous, aren't you?" said Miggin.

The funny thing was, I wasn't as nervous about the interviews as I was about staying at Lexie's house for two nights. But I didn't want Miggin to know.

"What are you supposed to say at interviews? My mother always tells them how great I am, but how do I work that into a conversation?"

"You'll do fine." Miggin curled up in my bed and watched me dress. I wore the gray wool suit, my old "weekend" standard. "I'll miss you," said Miggin, absently stroking my blanket. There was a soft knock on the door. Woodie, already dressed in her tweed skirt and blazer, stood stiffly, clipboard in hand.

"Tuckwell, your cab is here."

Miggin grabbed my leather portfolio and walked with us to the door.

"Give me that," said Woodie. "The two of us can manage."

I looked at Miggin, suddenly terrified to be leaving without her. She smiled sweetly and wrapped her arms around me. "Don't worry," she whispered. "Good luck."

"Come on, Tuckwell." Woodie started down the path.

Miggin stood in the doorway of Senior House, nightgown billowing in the cold air. I waved back to her, feeling like a prisoner escaping at dawn while the other inmates slept. An orange taxi, the getaway car, idled in the road, its driver slouched in the seat, cap pulled down over his eyes.

"Do you know where you're going?" said Woodie as we walked.

"Parsons, four-ten East Fifty-fourth Street, at eleven a.m., and Cooper Union, Cooper Square, at two-thirty."

"And when do you meet Lexie?"

"Five p.m., six-ninety Park Avenue."

"Allow time for traffic," mumbled Woodie as she leaned down to speak to the driver. She scowled at his unshaven chin. "Driver, Miss Tuckwell is going to the Harrisburg station. She'll be boarding the seven-o'clock express to New York. Will you help her on?"

"Yes ma'am," he said, straightening up and pushing his cap off his forehead.

Woodie turned. She had not really looked at me since Parents' Weekend. She had never mentioned the game or Maddy Hansen or Nicky. "So you're going to art school, then?" Her face was solemn.

"I think so. If I get in."

She frowned. "No athletics in art school. Not in New York."

"I know."

"You'll miss hockey."

"I'll miss a lot of things."

Woodie sighed and looked over the roof of the taxi, down toward the playing field. "Well, kiddo, get going."

The driver moved the cab cautiously down the front entrance, aware of Woodie's gaze. But once on the road, no longer subject to her scrutiny, he tore off like a gangster.

"Which way do you want to go, miss? The Interstate or Harrisburg Pike?" He peered into the rearview mirror.

"I don't care."

"What's the difference when Daddy's paying, right?"

I didn't answer. Strange voices bleeped on his radio.

At the station, the driver dropped my luggage on the sidewalk. "Sorry, sweetheart. Got a radio call. Find a redcap." He winked. "You can afford it."

The Harrisburg station yawned like a bag lady waking up on a sidewalk grate. Redcaps stood in groups, dwarfed by the huge marble columns supporting the roof, drinking coffee from paper cups and telling jokes. Concessionaires in long white aprons and little hats wiped their counters down with sponges and activated their swirling plastic orange juice tanks. In a tired monotone, the stationmaster announced arrivals and departures. At the far end of the station, close to the stairway, was a game room. Some soldiers leaned over a miniature shooting gallery, firing tiny pellets at circus animals rotating on a tin track.

My heels clicked against the marble floor as I crossed and descended to the gray, windblown track. I didn't mind waiting alone on the deserted platform or struggling onto the train with my luggage. I liked riding trains. I liked the slow, steady motion, the blur of changing landscapes, the low moan of the huge wheels on the tracks. Something about the rhythm, about being *between* places, in limbo, loosened my mind, made me feel free, unattached. I stared out the window, never focusing on anything for long, as if I could see backward, into the past, and forward into the future. A strange kind of dislocation.

Pictures of Lexie flashed into my mind, then disappeared. There was Lexie at my voice lessons, sitting next to me on the stool, moving closer, telling me to breathe, holding my hand against her stomach. There was Lexie at lunch, beside me in the dining room, gripping my arm, a letter from Philip in her lap, tears of anger in her eyes. I could smell the fragrance of her bath oil and feel the warmth of her grasp. There was Lexie at the drugstore in Huntington, sitting opposite me in a cushioned booth, eating hamburgers and french fries. Her black turtleneck matched her dark eyes, deepened their intensity.

It seemed natural that Lexie came from New York City. Only the strong and unconventional could live beneath its mammoth gray skyline. New Yorkers were eccentric and smart. They were writers and actors and artists. Some worked on Wall Street, where machines clicked out financial mysteries on ticker tape. Others worked on Madison Avenue, writing jingles for Alka-Seltzer and Oxydol. In dark, windowless television studios, New Yorkers produced quiz shows and soap operas and Ed Sullivan. On the Lower East Side, Puerto Rican families crammed into long, dark apartments. In Harlem, Negro militants sat on doorsteps reading James Baldwin and LeRoi Jones.

New Yorkers were fast. New York was the place where, as a child I had seen, from a hotel window, a lady undress in her room across the courtyard. Slowly she had removed each garment, piece by piece, until she was completely naked — breasts, crotch, everything, exposed, for anyone to see. She never pulled down the shade. I remembered that. She never pulled down the shade.

Steam shot up from the bowels of the huge locomotive. Soot from the tracks swirled into my eyes. I walked toward the long, narrow escalator. The engines breathed — restless iron monsters. Already I could hear the blaring taxis, the screeching brakes, the twenty-ton trucks pounding up Eighth Avenue. I could feel my metabolism adjusting. I grasped the handle of my portfolio tightly and pushed my shoulder bag beneath my arm.

The stumpy baggage checker smiled broadly, exposing the large black gap between his front teeth. "How long you gonna be, darlin'?" Woodie had told me to check my suitcase until the interviews were over. I looked doubtfully at the baggage area, where suitcases and cardboard boxes were piled haphazardly along the walls. He winked and peeled a ticket from a roll that he drew from the pocket of his smock. "Spending the day in the big city?" He pointed to my portfolio. "Don't you want to check that? You can't shop with it."

"I'm not going to shop."

"No offense, dolly." He pinched my palm as he handed me the claim check. "Have a ball."

The cab lurched uptown, accelerating wildly on Eighth Avenue, turning abruptly on Fifty-fourth. The city looked immense and gray. The skyscrapers were gigantic ice trays rising vertically from the cement; people crowded the sidewalks, their bodies braced to fight the cold December air.

"Where you from?" said the driver as we waited for a light.

"Washington."

"Washington, huh? Your quarterback's having a bad year. Getting older, what? Don't hold a candle to Y.A. Tittle. Not anymore." He laughed heartily to himself, then turned and glanced at me. He was about thirty, I guess. He had a dark complexion and hair wet down with Brylcreem or something. "What's in your case?"

"Paintings," I said.

"You're an artist?" The driver laughed and slapped his hand against the steering wheel. "I knew it. I just knew it. I can always tell an artist. Friend of mine in Queens's an artist — lives in my building. Smart fella; name's Al. He works the Village — on weekends. Sells to the tourists. You know, folks in from Jersey and Ohio — come to see the beatniks and, you know, the pansies." He glanced around at me. "You see this guy, Al, he gives the tourists a whole line of garbage about being a starving artist. Wears this beret and smokes the French cigarettes. Whadayacallem? Gauloises. Yeah. That's it." The driver slammed on the brakes, then swerved past a car double-parked on Fifty-fourth Street. "To show you how smart this Al is — he don't even paint the things himself. His partner in Brooklyn paints 'em, and this Al, he has a deal where he sells them. He must clear a grand a week, easy." The driver turned around. "Lady, if you can do something like that, I'll take my hat off to you." He laughed again. "Some artist, ha, ha, ha. Clears over a grand a week."

The cab stopped in front of a large warehouse. A long banner hung from it like a shroud. "Parsons," it said, in huge white letters. I handed him the money and climbed out.

"Ciao, lady," he called. "Nice gettin' to know ya."

Parsons was about as far over as you could go in Manhattan without falling into the East River. It wasn't built as a school; it was an old factory in a neighborhood of old factories that had been converted into offices and studios. Inside, nobody was dressed like me at all. None of the girls were wearing little gray suits and pump heels and white blouses with bows at the top. The girls in the lobby wore dark capes and colorful scarves and black stockings; they had long, silky hair and cool, worldly exteriors.

"What floor do you want?" said a tall boy in a red fireman's hat, who was standing in the elevator when the doors opened.

"Admissions," I said.

"That's four," he said, pushing the button. He looked at me with curiosity. "You have an interview?"

"Yeah."

He scratched his beard. "Who with?"

"I'm not sure. They didn't tell me."

"Hope it's not Dean Housman," he said, as the elevator opened on four. I looked back at him doubtfully.

"Good luck," he called.

I walked down a long corridor, covered on both sides with posters, announcements, and ads for roommates, furniture, and apartments. As far as I could see, there was no reception lounge, just an empty desk and several chairs at the end of the hall. Parsons didn't look like the girls' colleges I had visited with my mother. Those admission offices were quiet, cushioned rooms, where the silence was interrupted only by the modulated voice of the receptionist and the discreet clatter of the typewriter. When you entered, they smiled and handed you catalogues and slick brochures and copies of the school newspaper. Not here. Here, there wasn't even anybody around. I sat down at the far end of the hall. The elevator doors opened and a slim, neatly dressed man in a gray flannel suit clipped down the hall carrying a cup of coffee in one hand and a briefcase in the other.

"Mrs. Meyers? Mrs. Meyers?" he called, looking at the empty desk near me. "Have you seen Mrs. Meyers?"

"No ... I don't think so."

He shook his head. "Third time in two weeks." He glanced at his watch. "Eleven-ten. Not bad. The E train was forty minutes late." He turned down another corridor and disappeared into an office. I waited.

Silence. Then the man reappeared. "Do you have an appointment this morning?"

"Yes."

"I'm Dean Housman," he said. "Follow me."

His office was a small, cluttered cubicle piled high with books and papers. On his walls were announcements of art shows and openings. He sat down in a swivel chair, leaned back, and flipped through a folder.

"You're Jean Tuckwell?" He glanced at me. "You're a senior at Huntington Hill School in Huntington, Pennsylvania. And you want to go to Parsons because...?" He looked at me expectantly. "You want to go to Parsons because...?"

I realized he was waiting for me to finish the sentence. "I'd like ... I think I would like to be a painter."

Dean Housman sighed. He pursed his lips. "Miss Tuckwell, I had hoped that you already *were* a painter."

"Oh, yes, well, I am, really. I mean, I paint, I like to paint. I guess I'm just not sure I would call myself a painter."

"You've read the catalogue?" He did not look up from his notes.

"I'm never quite sure how to read a catalogue. I think I know which courses I can take."

"Miss Tuckwell, I suggest you *learn* to read the catalogue. If you'd read the catalogue you'd know that Parsons is primarily a school for commercial artists. We take only six painters a year. Most of their courses are in other departments — graphic arts, design, illustration."

"I know that."

Mr. Housman cleared his throat and stroked his black moustache. "Miss Tuckwell, we get a number of private-school girls applying to Parsons each year. For some reason, they seem to think Parsons is a finishing school where they can dabble around until they get married. Most of them drop out. You understand?"

"They drop out?"

"They drop out because they have no real intention of completing the program. Miss Tuckwell, what are *your* career plans? How do you see yourself in five, ten years?" His small, dark eyes bulged like an insect's.

I looked at him hopefully. "Painting is very important to me. I enjoy it, I like to express myself ... visually."

Mr. Housman looked glumly at his desk and sighed. "Enjoying art, Miss Tuckwell, has very little to do with what Parsons is about. We're a professional school. We train artists to make their living in a highly competitive business world." He looked at me disdainfully. "If you expect to be supported by your parents ... if, if you don't *need* to make a living, then Parsons is not the place for you. Pleasure, enjoyment of one's work ... these are not things we emphasize. We leave that to ... the dilettantes. You understand?"

I looked at him. I could feel the tears building. Maybe I should have brought my mother ... or Miggin.

"I'd say, Miss Tuckwell, that in the ten years I've been here, only half a dozen girls like you have pursued a career. Do you think, Miss Tuckwell, that you are one of the half dozen who will stick it out?" He watched me.

"I want to be a painter," I began, in a whisper. "I've never really thought about my life ten years from now. That seems very far away. It's hard, sometimes, just getting from week to week."

"What amazes me," said Mr. Housman abruptly, "is how certain you private-school girls are of your own opinions. You assume a lot. There's an arrogance, there's ... well..." He looked at his watch. "I have another appointment at eleven forty-five. Your portfolio?"

I slid the large case over to him. He unzipped it, turned over the pictures quickly, and straightened his tie.

"You know that applicants are required to show at least ten pieces? I see only six here."

"I brought my sketchbook."

"Sketches are not considered finished work."

"I came up today on the train. I have more. That's all I could carry. I can send—"

He stood up. "I'm afraid you'll *have* to send more. Slides, photographs; it doesn't matter." He zipped my case. "Your work does show a certain ... definition." He paused. "I see a ... a glimmer. But this is not enough to make a decision."

"I'll send more."

"Indeed. Well, yes..." The phone rang. Housman picked it up, then cupped his hand over the mouthpiece. "Yes, dear, keep in touch," he said to me. "Let's hear from you soon, Miss ... Miss..."

"Tuckwell," I said, and turned away.

It was eleven-forty. The interview had taken twenty minutes. I stood on the street, cold and scared. My appointment at Cooper Union was not until two-thirty. Usually, the schools gave you a tour or something. But Mr. Housman hadn't said anything about that. I had almost three hours to kill. Slowly, eyes on the ground, I walked toward First Avenue. I had messed up. The dean had rattled me. I hadn't had a chance to tell him how great I was. That's what you were supposed to do. That's what my mother always said.

At Fifty-third and First I sat down at a pay phone, twisted my case inside the booth, and found a dime.

"It's Jinx Tuckwell," I said to the voice that answered.

"Jinxie!" cried Mrs. Knight. "Where are you? Do you need a place to stay?"

"I'm in New York," I said. "I had an interview."

"Will you have lunch with me?"

"I'd like that."

"Come on up. Right now."

Elizabeth's mother wore loosely fitting khaki pants and a faded worksheet, open at the collar. Her brown hair was wild and uncoiled. When she hugged me, I could smell paint and perfume on her clothes. The apartment on East Eighty-sixth Street was huge and bright; color splashed out of every corner. Brilliant hand-woven rugs hung on the walls and leafy green plants were suspended from the ceiling. The dining room, which was also her studio, was crowded with paintings, piled three and four deep against the walls.

"How are you, Jinx?" Mrs. Knight pulled back from her embrace to look at me. I opened my mouth to speak. Tears came before words. "Come, sit down, love," she said, guiding me to the sprawling wicker sofa in the living room. "So," she said — she flicked my bangs off my forehead — "you had an interview at art school and it was awful. You look exhausted."

I smiled. "Parsons. I—"

Mrs. Knight jumped up. "Wait one second. Don't say a word. I'll get some tea." She disappeared into the kitchen. I held my breath. If I could stop worrying, I would enjoy being here. The apartment wasn't at all like Elizabeth. It wasn't the formal, fancy East Side place I'd expected Elizabeth to live in. It was warm and simple.

Mrs. Knight returned with a plate of sandwiches and a pot of tea. In the sunlight I could see tiny, delicate wrinkles, running out from the corners of her eyes — crow's-feet, they call them. When she was seated again beside me I told her about the interview at Parsons.

"What was his name?" she said, indignant at the treatment I'd received.

"Dean Housman," I said. "His office was on four."

Mrs. Knight stared out the window, toward the high-rise on Eighty-sixth Street. "Housman? Housman?" she mumbled. "Don't think I know him. Could be a commercial artist, Jinx. Bitter about kids who don't want to do commercial work. Probably a painter himself once."

I laughed. "He said he saw a glimmer in my work. What do you think a glimmer is?"

Mrs. Knight leaned back against the sofa and kicked off her shoes. She touched my shoulder. "Kid, you're going to have to grow thicker skin in New York. Most of us are not the least bit kind or likable. We'll gobble you up if you give us the chance."

"Mother says I'll go off the deep end here. Maybe she's right."

"We mothers are all alike," laughed Mrs. Knight. "We worry too much about our chickabiddies. The best thing for you right now is to relax and hope that your interview at Cooper Union will be better. Now." She sipped her tea and swallowed. "How is school?"

"School's okay. Elizabeth is good. She told me to call you."

"And you did. How obedient." Mrs. Knight leaned closer. "You know, of course, that Elizabeth is furious with you."

"Me?" In a corner of the living room I saw a painting of a nun, on a bicycle.

"She tells me you've dropped her for Alexis Yves."

I sank into the sofa. Lexie was right. Elizabeth's nun paintings *were* like her mother's. "She didn't tell me she was mad."

"Well, of course Elizabeth didn't tell you that. She never tells anybody anything to their face. My own daughter..." Mrs. Knight smiled impishly, then looked more serious. "God help us if she doesn't get in Bryn Mawr. She insists that's the only place she'll go and she hasn't applied anywhere else." Mrs. Knight stopped herself. "Here I go, like a mother again." She touched my hand. "Jinx, how are you? Oh, shy and quiet one."

I sat up. "I'm not so quiet."

She winked. "Quiet on the surface, wild underneath. All sorts of awful things go on in your head." Mrs. Knight laughed and straightened my collar. "I've seen your work, Jinx. You're very talented."

I looked away. Why didn't I ever know what to say?

"Forgive me, Jinx. I'm too serious today." Mrs. Knight tapped her bare feet against the rug. "So," she said. "Will you stay here tonight? I've got lots of room."

"Thank you. I'm staying with Lexie. She took the weekend too."

Mrs. Knight held my hand between hers. "Well, dear girl," she said, tracing my palm with the tips of her fingers, "you must be on your way. Now, you show the people at Cooper how very exceptional you are. You must not let them terrify you. I won't have it."

We stood together in the hall. Mrs. Knight looked at my face and opened her arms. I would have loved to stay there, swallowed up in her warmth, breathing the smell of paint and perfume on her clothes. "You must run, Jinxie," she said. "Do call me when you've finished at Cooper."

She waited with me by the elevator. Her eyes looked wistful. "I don't think Elizabeth will be a painter," said Mrs. Knight suddenly, as the elevator doors closed around me.

On the street, I glanced down at my hands and feet. It was still me; I was still there, wearing my gray suit and black pump heels. I was still in one piece. And I found a cab.

Two hours later, I called Mrs. Knight from a pay phone at Penn Station. If she'd answered I'd have told her that the interview was good. I would have told her about Annette Dorfsman, the small, pale woman with long gray hair pulled back off her head in a chignon, who smoked cigarettes and talked to me about the school and took me around to all the studios. I would have told Mrs. Knight about the soft, respectful way Annette Dorfsman looked through my paintings and my sketchbook, and about her remark that, after painting for twenty years, she still wondered sometimes if *she* were an artist. I would have told her what Annette said about New York, about the art shows and galleries and theater, about the people and restaurants and museums, about the fact that New York was the perfect place for an artist to live. I would have told her that Annette Dorfsman walked me to the street, and stood, waiting, without her coat, arms clutched around her, while I found a cab. She had said, as she closed the door behind me, that my chances for acceptance at Cooper were very, very good. But Mrs. Knight was not home.

"Spend all your money, darlin'?" The baggage-check man winked at me.

"No," I said, handing him my ticket.

"Don't get snippy with me. You're no smarter than the next one," he grumbled.

"Screw you" is what Lexie would have said. But I walked away in silence.

I HELD MY BREATH AS THE POLISHED DOORS OF THE elevator opened onto the small, private vestibule. There was no long corridor of numbered doors and fluorescent lights, just Eleanor's apartment, protected by a wrought-iron gate. I stepped out, while the elevator man, who was wearing a dark red morning coat, watched me. I still remember the smell of that vestibule — burnt rubber; I guess because the black-and-white tile floor, which looked like marble, was really linoleum. Beyond the gate, I could see another, longer hallway, lined with dark wood paneling.

"Ring the bell, miss," said the red-faced man. He pointed to the button by the gate. I pressed it, and instantly a light-skinned Negro woman in a gray uniform appeared, smiling.

"Miss Tuckwell?" she said, taking my suitcase. "I'm Juliet, the maid. I'm afraid Miss Alexis isn't here yet, but I'll take you in to see Mrs. Dennis."

I followed Juliet past an immense formal living room with tall windows overlooking Park Avenue, past a formal dining room and down another hallway, to a small, lighted room. The place was like a museum — all it needed was a guard standing by the paintings and little gold cords looped across the arms of the chairs.

Mrs. Dennis was hunched over a card table, blanket covering her knees, her hair a shiny blue color. Her skin was ghostlike under the light of the lamp. Flames from the fireplace cast shadows onto the wall behind her. The room was like the library of an English men's club or a Victorian novel. It smelled of wood and leather and liquor. The walls were lined with books and etchings. In a corner, near Mrs. Dennis, a large portable radio blared, *"Baby, baby, your lovin' makes me feel so good."*

Juliet entered first. "Mrs. Dennis," she said quietly, "Miss Alexis's friend is here."

Mrs. Dennis, absorbed in the playing cards lined in front of her, did not answer.

"Mrs. Dennis?"

She jerked up. "These are the Suprettes, Juliet. They're *your* people."

Juliet disregarded Mrs. Dennis's observation and sat down beside her on the leather sofa. "This is Miss Alexis's friend. She's going to stay with us this weekend."

"I'm Jinx Tuckwell." I stepped forward to shake hands.

Mrs. Dennis peered at me. "Where's Alexis?"

"She'll be here shortly," Juliet replied. "They came separately."

Mrs. Dennis looked at me foggily. "Does she know where she's staying?"

"I'll show her now. She'll be sharing with Miss Alexis." Mrs. Dennis nodded and Juliet led me out.

"You'll want to wash up, Miss Tuckwell," called Mrs. Dennis. "Then come have a drink with me."

Lexie's room was small for an apartment so enormous, cozier than the rest of the place. It was modern, decorated like a movie star's dressing room — in pink, red, and white. Thick white carpeting covered the floor; red satin comforters were folded like layered French pastries on the ends of the twin beds. Along the left side of the room was a wall-to-wall mirror, encircled by powder pink light-bulbs. The white formica dressing table was covered with lipsticks, perfumes, and mascara bottles. Opposite the door were two windows overlooking a dark court-yard. Thin white curtains hung limply across the windows, framed on the sides by heavy red brocade draperies.

I put down my portfolio and sat on the bed nearer the door. The room had the same unlived-in feeling as my room at home. Her important things were with her at school. The belongings that remained were Lexie's leftovers — a faded jewelry box, a tray of discarded curlers. The clock by Lexie's bed said six o'clock. She was late.

Lexie had her own bathroom. The sink and tub were white porcelain, with large brass faucets and spigots. On the floor was an intricate geometric tile design. I wanted to take off my clothes — my garter belt and stockings, my gray suit and white blouse — and soothe myself under a long, hot shower. Only hot, rushing water could make the fear go away. But what if Lexie found me naked? Suppose she saw my pale, exposed skin, my small breasts? I looked at my face in the mirror. My eyes seemed to have sunk behind my white cheeks; my skin was almost gray. My expression was a sort of blank, empty stare that I knew well — it was fear.

Mrs. Dennis was trying to stay sober. She fiddled with the radio, poked the fire with a long black stick, and rattled the ice in her empty glass. Finally she sat back on the sofa.

"Alexis wants to go to Bennington," she said, staring at the fire.

"I'm sure she'll get in." *"Don't mess with Bill,"* sang the Marvelettes on the huge portable.

"Oh, she'll get in. She's a bright girl."

"Oh, she'll get in," I echoed nervously.

"Won't be happy in Vermont. She's a city girl. Not interested in the outdoors." Mrs. Dennis rocked in her seat. "Never swims or rides in Easthampton. Just sits on the beach with her friends. Won't even play bridge." The tiny woman shook her head. "If she went to Juilliard, she'd continue singing. That's what she's best at. She says she's bored with singing..." The fire crackled and a spark popped against the screen and fizzled out quickly.

"She could always transfer," I said hopefully.

"Doomed from the start," Mrs. Dennis turned the dial of her radio.

"I guess she doesn't see it that way. Can I help you with that?"

"Alexis does what she likes." Mrs. Dennis squinted at the dial. "Never pays any attention to my advice. I'm too old, she says. Don't understand. Just give her the money. That's what I do, too."

"WBZ, Boston, playing solid gold. Don't touch that dial."

"Children aren't very nice," I said.

Her gray eyes fixed on me. "I remember you now. I had dinner with you and your parents."

"That's right. At the Holiday Inn."

"You're a nice girl," continued Mrs. Dennis. "I'm glad Alexis has a nice friend. Polite." She looked toward the doorway. "She's never obeyed me. But you don't seem a rebel."

I swallowed. "Well, sometimes I—"

"I wish Alexis would live in New York. I'd be so happy."

"Well, *I* would be extremely unhappy, Eleanor." Lexie, cheeks pink, fur coat slipping off her shoulders, stood at the door. She shook her head.

"Alexis!" Mrs. Dennis limped toward her.

"Guess what, Eleanor? We've picked the spring show for Music Club. Want to know what it is?"

Mrs. Dennis clutched Lexie's arm. "Where have you been?"

"Guess what the show is, Eleanor?" Lexie threw off her coat and opened her pocketbook. "I've got the script. Guess what it is?"

"How can I guess? You know I don't go to shows. Never cared for them, I..."

Lexie's smile faded. "Sorry I'm late, Jinxie. Oakie and I shared a cab uptown. Traffic was horrible." Mrs. Dennis stood eagerly beside her, waiting for a hug. Lexie hugged *me*. "How are you, Tuck?"

"I'm okay. Mrs. Dennis and I were having a talk."

"Alexis, I was telling Miss Tuckwell..."

Lexie scowled. "Eleanor, her name is Jinx. She's not an old lady."

"Yes, quite right. My apologies..."

"I don't mind."

"I do," said Lexie, scooping a hunk of cheese from the table by the sofa. "When's dinner? I'm starved."

"We've been waiting for you." Mrs. Dennis limped toward the door. "I'll tell Juliet we're ready."

"I'll tell her, Eleanor," said Lexie. "You sit down. Jinx, keep me company while I change."

I followed Lexie down the hall. "Should you talk to Mrs. Dennis for a minute?"

Lexie looked at me. "What for?" She dropped her coat on a chair in her bedroom. *"You* can talk to Eleanor if you want to. I'm sure she'd prefer talking to you." She studied her room for an instant, then began to peel off her clothes — black dress, silk slip, panty girdle. She threw them all into the middle of the floor.

"There goes my small ass," she laughed, kicking her girdle. "Does Miss Congeniality want to go talk to Eleanor?"

I looked at Lexie's soft pale skin and her breasts, which were pushed up like spheres by the rims of the bra. She saw me looking.

"This is my French whore's bra. Got it last year at Bonwit's." Lexie cupped her hands under her breasts. *"Très sexy, n'est-ce pas?"* She leaned over the bathroom sink and tossed water on her face. "Oakie asked us for lunch tomorrow," she called. "Want to go?" I could see her ass and her knees, bent slightly as she washed.

"I'd rather spend the time with you."

Lexie wiped her face with a pink towel. "That's what I figured. I told her you'd never been to New York and we couldn't waste our precious time with her."

"I've been to New York."

Lexie slipped a long white caftan over her head. Her black mascara was smeared from the water.

"I know you've been to New York," she laughed. "I was being uncharacteristically diplomatic." She frowned at herself in the mirror. "Do you like my room?"

The red curtains were drawn now.

"It's like a movie star's or something."

"But, of course, dahlink," she laughed with a French accent. She pinched my cheek and opened the door. "Let's eat."

We were three strangers sitting around the long mahogany table, which was set with spotless, shining silver, sparkling crystal, and damask napkins. Juliet popped in and out, neat and efficient, carrying silver serving dishes, water pitchers, and condiment trays. We ate in silence: Lexie brooded; I concentrated on using the right piece of cutlery for each course; Mrs. Dennis stared into space. She had succumbed again to the temptation of the bottle while Lexie and I had been in the bedroom, and she now began to sway precariously.

"Your train, Alexis," she struggled. "Was it … satisfactory?"

Lexie carved her roast beef slowly. "Divine, Eleanor. A real joy. I met a man from the Metropolitan Life Insurance Company. He asked after you."

"After me?" Mrs. Dennis held her napkin to her mouth. Juliet filled her goblet with water.

"Actually, Eleanor, I sat by Paul Newman and we conversed from Philadelphia to Newark." Lexie left the room and returned to the table with a bottle of Coke.

114

"Didn't say *why* he got off at Newark."

"Alexis, Juliet would have gotten that. Where are your manners?"

"My manners are better than yours, Eleanor." She pronged a piece of roast beef with her fork. "At least I'm not drunk."

"Alexis, I won't have that," whispered Mrs. Dennis.

"'I won't have that,'" mimicked Lexie. The portraits on the dining room walls frowned down at us.

"You're very rude, Alexis."

"'You're very rude, Alexis,'" mimicked Lexie, using Mrs. Dennis's inflection.

Mrs. Dennis sat in a daze while Juliet whisked out the dinner plates and brought in dessert.

Lexie turned to me. "What do you want to do tonight?"

"You must be sure to call your cousin Philip," said Mrs. Dennis suddenly. "He wants to see you this weekend."

Lexie glanced quickly at Mrs. Dennis, then dabbed her spoon into the mound of whipped cream on her dessert plate. "Cousin Philip's an asshole."

"Alexis!"

"Alexis!" echoed Lexie.

Mrs. Dennis reddened. She turned to me. "Alexis never sees her cousin and he's so fond of her. I really think—"

"Jinx doesn't care what you think, Eleanor." Lexie pushed her chair away from the table and dropped her napkin into her plate.

I looked at Mrs. Dennis. "I *am* interested, Mrs. Dennis. It's okay. I—"

"It's not okay," hissed Lexie.

Mrs. Dennis sat up. "Miss Tuckwell..."

"Eleanor," shouted Lexie. "Her name is Jinx."

"Miss Tuckwell," continued Mrs. Dennis, eyes red. "Do you play bridge? I thought after dinner we could set up the card table. Of course, we have no fourth, unless Juliet..."

Lexie stood up, staring at Mrs. Dennis in disbelief. Her long white caftan loomed over us. "Eleanor, you can't be serious. Juliet does not play bridge, nor does Jinx, nor do I. Furthermore, we are going to the movies." She looked at her watch. "In fact, we're going right now." She pushed her dark hair away from her eyes. Mrs. Dennis swayed pitifully in her chair.

"Should we wait till everyone is finished?" I said nervously.

"Everyone *is* finished." Lexie disappeared down the hallway. Mrs. Dennis and I sat in silence while Juliet cleared the dishes. Lexie reappeared with our coats.

"Let's go, Jinx. We can make the eight-o'clock show."

I rose awkwardly. "It was a lovely dinner, Mrs. Dennis. Everything was delicious." Mrs. Dennis picked up her purse and limped after us to the elevator.

"Alexis, you didn't tell me you were going out. I really think..."

Lexie opened the gate. "You would have forgotten anyway."

The old woman leaned against the wall. "When will you be back?"

Lexie shrugged. "When we feel like it."

Mrs. Dennis opened her pocketbook. "Well, here's some money." She held out a twenty-dollar bill.

"I've got money." Lexie pushed her hand away.

"Good night, Mrs. Dennis," I called. "Thank you for a wonderful dinner." The elevator doors closed around us. Mrs. Dennis stared hopelessly at us, the twenty-dollar bill still dangling from her hand.

The cold of the streets slapped us like the hand Mrs. Dennis had been afraid to raise. Suddenly, I felt better.

Limousines idled on Park Avenue, their red taillights glowing in the dark. Fancy couples in fur coats and tuxedos glided in and out of restaurants and hotel lobbies. Lexie walked quickly, moving between cars, crossing against the lights.

"Is Mrs. Dennis okay?" I called.

She kept walking.

"She seemed upset," I continued. "I feel sorry for her."

Lexie reeled around. "How do you think *I* feel?" Streetlights lit her eyes. "How do you think I feel when she's drunk and calls you 'Miss Tuckwell' and is totally messed up?"

"Lexie..."

"Why don't you ask if *I'm* okay?" Her eyes were small slits now. Steam from a subway grate blew up beneath her caftan.

"Are you okay?" I said.

"Shit." She walked faster.

"Lexie, she wasn't drunk when I came in. We had a nice conversation."

"Terrific."

"Lexie..." I felt the night creep around my throat. Pedestrians pushed around us. Lexie stopped.

"If Miss Goody Two Shoes would like to go home and play bridge with Eleanor she may do so. I don't give a shit. I'll see you after the movie." She dodged between two taxis and hurried across Madison Avenue. I followed her, panicked — what if I lost her in the crowd? What was the matter with her? What had I done? What was going on?

I caught up with her at the ticket counter and trailed behind her into the dark theater. We seated ourselves without speaking. The movie had already started. It was French and it was hard to follow. Jeanne Moreau and Jean-Paul Belmondo were two crooks planning a heist. Halfway through the movie, Lexie leaned against me.

"You didn't know how obnoxious I can be. I'm quite impressive when I'm in full form."

I looked at her cautiously. If I said the wrong thing she'd get angry. But what was the right thing to say?

She gripped my arm. "It's a little family tension, Tuckwell. Nothing to do with you."

"Shhh." A woman behind us tapped Lexie's shoulder. Lexie turned around. "Screw you."

When the movie was over, we stood on Fifty-sixth Street while Lexie decided if we should walk or take a taxi. An old Negro man in a frayed jacket approached us. "Spare some change?"

"Don't," said Lexie, as I opened my purse. "It doesn't really help them."

"I don't mind, Lexie."

"Jesus, Jinx."

I gave him the money and hurried to catch up with her. Something was bothering me. "Do you ever feel funny around Negroes?" I said after we'd walked a couple blocks.

Lexie squinted at me. "What do you mean?"

"Like that old man. He's old enough to be our father but we have more money than he does."

"He's a drunk, Jinx."

"Maybe that's a bad example. What about Juliet? Do you ever feel funny around her? Having her serve you all the time?"

Lexie laughed. "Jinx, Eleanor *pays* her."

"I know, my mother pays *our* maid. But I feel funny about it. She's a lot older than I am, but she's *my* servant too."

"Juliet *likes* working for Eleanor. The only thing she has to do is keep Eleanor in Scotch."

"Yeah, I guess."

That night, I couldn't fall asleep. All night, I listened to Lexie's breathing in the bed next to mine. I heard cars honking on the street, doors slamming, garbage cans scraping on the sidewalks. An elevator moved on its cables, then stopped. Steam from the radiators hissed and gurgled, and somewhere, maybe in the basement, a hammer or a club banged against the furnace pipes. I was afraid to go to the bathroom, although my bladder began to ache from the need. I didn't want Lexie to wake up, I didn't want her to hear the trickle of my urine into the toilet. I couldn't let go. I had been trying hard all day to say the right thing, to be polite and diplomatic. First art school, then with Mrs. Knight, then with Mrs. Dennis and Juliet and Lexie. Now, when I wanted to stop trying and sleep, I couldn't. If I relaxed, I might accidentally walk to Lexie's bed and touch her, get in with her or something. Maybe if she woke *she* would get in with me. It was crazy. Each time Lexie turned or moved, I held my breath.

Finally I got up and peed. Then slowly, as the street noises grew louder and light filled the dark courtyard, I fell asleep.

The mattress shifted beneath me. I opened my eyes slowly. Lexie, nightgown falling off her shoulder, was sitting on my bed.

"Jinx, are you awake?" she whispered.

"I'm asleep," I said. My eyes burned. I was dizzy from fatigue.

Lexie tucked her feet under her knees. "I'm cold. Can I get in with you?"

I opened my eyes. "What?"

Lexie leaned closer. "You look so cozy. I want to get in with you."

"Now?" I was too tired.

Lexie smiled. Her face was soft again, not like it had been last night. Her eyes were no longer small from anger.

"I'm still sleeping. I didn't sleep too well."

"You can go back to sleep. I won't talk." She lifted the covers.

I rolled against the wall. Our bodies were so close I could feel the heat from her skin and smell her perfume. I shut my eyes, afraid to breathe.

"Jinx?"

My eyes were still closed.

"Will you give me a back rub?" Lexie moved onto her side.

"I thought you said I could sleep." My hands and feet were like ice.

Lexie laughed. "I'll give *you* a back rub then." She inched closer and began to knead my shoulders, squeeze my neck and spine. "Back rubs are wonderful," whispered Lexie. I stared at the wall. Her fingers pressed my scalp, her palms pushed against my forehead.

"How does that feel?" Her hands touched my waist, then my ribs. "God, you're skinny, Jinx," she said. "There's no meat on you."

"There is."

"No, there's not. You should feel me. I'm like a pillow."

I didn't move.

Lexie started to pull me over. "Go ahead. Feel me." Her mouth was inches from mine. She smiled. Even in the darkness her eyes seemed bright.

"My hands are cold," I said.

"I don't care. Go ahead, feel how fat I am."

I touched her shoulder. "You're not fat."

"Touch my stomach. Then you'll really know."

I touched her stomach; her skin was soft and warm. My legs tingled. "You're not fat."

"I am too," she giggled, moving even closer. Her nightgown, silky and sleeveless, grazed my skin. "You're

120

so shy, Jinx," she said. "Don't you and Miggin give each other back rubs?"

"Not too much."

"Well, don't be afraid to rub hard. Here..." She rolled over on her stomach. "Do my back."

I glanced at the door. What would Mrs. Dennis say if she walked in the room now? Suppose she found us in bed together? I knew what *my* mother would say.

"Jinx."

"Okay." I touched Lexie's shoulders.

"Your hands are cold."

"I told you."

"Give them to me." She turned on her side, reached behind, and pulled my arms around her waist, placing my hands on her stomach. I shuddered. My breasts touched her back. Her ass rested against my abdomen; my legs pressed her thighs.

"How far have you gone?" said Lexie suddenly.

"What?"

"How far have you gone with boys?"

I swallowed. "Not too far."

"How far?" Lexie's rear end nestled closer to my stomach.

I took a breath. "I've kissed."

"You're kidding? That's all?" Lexie's fingertips tickled my palms. "What about on dates?"

"I haven't been on many dates. I don't know many boys."

Lexie pulled my hands up her stomach, then placed my hands on her breasts. "Don't you get horny?"

I closed my eyes. I was sweating. "I get horny sometimes."

Lexie turned over. We were breast to breast, stomach to stomach. "How many boys have you kissed?" Her lips were so close that if I moved, *we'd* be kissing.

"This is stupid," I whispered.

"No, it's not. Tell me." Lexie's fingers scampered along my spine.

"I've kissed one boy."

"Such an innocent." Slowly, she slid her breasts back and forth across mine. My skin was wrapped in a filmy gauze. "How far have *you* gone?" My voice cracked.

"That's impertinent."

"I told *you*."

She laughed. "I'm just kidding, Jinx. I'll tell you." She paused. "I have kissed so many boys that it's a miracle I have any lips left." Her hands massaged my scalp. "And I have committed so many other indiscretions that I will be damned to hell forever. What do you think about that, Tuckwell?" Her smile was gone.

"About what?"

"About me," she whispered. "Do you think I'm wild?" I glanced at the door.

"Tuckwell, look at me."

Her eyes were — dark and inviting. She just kept staring at me. I wanted to hold her, hug her, but I was afraid.

The door swung open. Lexie twisted away from me.

Juliet, startled, stood over us.

"What is it?" Lexie squinted.

"Breakfast is ready, Miss Lexie." Juliet closed the door behind her.

LIGHT SLANTED THROUGH THE WINDOWS OF THE dining room, where we sat, once again, in silence. Across Park Avenue, a woman in a black uniform peered out of the window of a high-rise. Juliet, in her uniform, hurried through the swinging kitchen door with a silver platter of scrambled eggs. Was that a scowl on her face? Lexie, expressionless, helped herself; Mrs. Dennis spooned a tiny portion. My hands trembled as I lifted the eggs onto my plate. Juliet moved the serving dish closer.

Lexie was in her bathrobe. Head bowed, she read the *New York Times*, fork moving automatically to her mouth. Mrs. Dennis watched her expectantly. Mrs. Dennis was more composed this morning. Her tiny wrinkles were covered with powder; her eyes were brighter — not as sad and hurt as last night.

"How was the movie, Alexis?" Mrs. Dennis folded her napkin.

Lexie's eyes stayed fixed on the paper. "Tell Eleanor about the movie, Jinx," she said flatly. Mrs. Dennis turned to me.

"It was good," I began, sitting up. "It was in French. Some kind of crime movie. I wasn't sure what was going on."

Lexie glanced at me and smiled, then returned to the newspaper.

Mrs. Dennis wheezed. "Alexis is fluent in French, Miss Tuckwell. Her father was French, but, of course, he died when she was six, and her mother died..."

"Eleanor!"

Mrs. Dennis looked nervously at Lexie and tinkled the silver bell by her plate.

"If you're going to tell Jinx the story of my life, be sure to tell her how I ended up with you. I'm sure she'd enjoy that."

"Alexis, I was..." Juliet stood in the doorway. "We'd like more coffee," sputtered Mrs. Dennis.

Lexie squinted at me. "Eleanor took me in when I was six and we've lived happily ever after, as you can see. Two peas in a pod."

"It's worked out very well." Mrs. Dennis stirred her coffee. "We've had a happy life; we..." Lexie was no longer listening; she was reading the paper again. Mrs. Dennis cleared her throat.

"Alexis, I've made luncheon reservations at the Cos Club today. I would like you and Miss Tuckwell to be my guests."

Lexie glared at her guardian. "Eleanor, Miss Tuckwell and I have other plans. We're not spending the day at an old-ladies' club."

"It's not an old-ladies' club," said Mrs. Dennis. "We've many new members, younger women..."

Lexie rose, pushing her chair away from the table. "Eleanor, why do you do these things? Why do you make these plans? You only get hurt when I say no. Are you a masochist or something?" She moved close to Eleanor. "Do you know what a masochist is?"

Mrs. Dennis trembled. "Of course I do."

"Let's eat at the Cos Club, Lexie." My coffee cup turned over on its side.

"We're *not* eating at the *Cos* Club." Lexie stared out the window. Juliet cleaned up the mess.

"Well, then, where *will* you eat?" said Mrs. Dennis.

Lexie folded her arms. "I don't know. Nedick's if we feel like it."

"Nedick's is a filthy place." Mrs. Dennis gripped the table.

"I like filth."

"Alexis Yves!" Mrs. Dennis stood up, opened and closed her mouth, then turned toward the kitchen. "Will you be home for dinner?"

"Probably."

"I'll tell Juliet. By the way," she said, limping into the kitchen, "your cousin called this morning. He'd like to see you." Lexie glanced at me and left the dining room.

Wind blew the dirt on Fifth Avenue into tiny tornadoes. The warm, pungent smell of roasting chestnuts floated from the carts of sidewalk vendors. Lexie turned up the collar of her black fur coat and linked her arm through mine.

"Look," she said, stopping in front of Cartier's. A wave of diamonds, each suspended by a tiny thread, cascaded down a blue velvet waterfall. On the bottom, a mirror reflected their brilliance and cast specks of light onto the velvet.

Lexie looked at me and smiled. "That's the way I feel when I'm with you."

I blushed.

She brushed her cheek against my shoulder. "Like water sliding into a pool." She paused. "How 'bout you?"

I looked at her pink cheeks and clear, expectant eyes. "Strange," I said.

Lexie laughed and pulled me with her up Fifth Avenue. Then suddenly she stopped. "Do you hate me?"

"What?" I bumped into a pedestrian whose Pekinese was peeing on the sidewalk.

Lexie sighed. "Do you hate me because I'm awful to Eleanor?"

A taxi screeched to a stop at the light on Fifty-fifth.

"Yes, I hate you a little bit. But it's complicated, isn't it?" I said slowly. "I mean, you love her, but she's..." I paused. "She's sort of strange."

"Do you know what it's like to have a mother who's a drunk?" Lexie's eyes searched mine. I kept thinking of this morning. We started to walk again. The wind blew a newspaper down the street. The open pages grabbed my ankle. "Liz Taylor: My Marriage with Burton," said the headline. Beside it was a photograph of a Green Beret pointing a machine gun at a Viet Cong soldier. I kicked the paper away.

At Fifty-ninth Street, Lexie pointed across Fifth Avenue to the Plaza Hotel, with its mansard roof and neat black awnings. "That's where Eloise lives." Black limousines pulled up in front, their drivers huddling by the hotel steps.

"Eloise, what are you doing, doing, doing?" giggled Lexie. "Come in off that ledge, my dear, before we all freeze, freeze, freeze." Lexie squeezed my hand.

"Tuckwell, what goes on in that head of yours?" She pulled me down on a park bench. Her tone became serious. "You're quiet, but I know those cogs are always turning."

"I don't like fighting," I said finally.

"Who's fighting?" Across the street, an old man, back hunched, walked a tiny French poodle, almost as ancient as he was.

"With Eleanor. I feel funny."

Lexie paused. "Do you wish we'd gone to the Cos Club?" She looked at her watch. "If we hurry, we can still make it."

"Maybe you could have said no in a nicer way."

"Jesus, Tuckwell." Lexie slammed her fist on the bench. "A nicer way! Tell you what. You write my speech for me, the *nice* one, and I'll deliver it to Eleanor. How 'bout that?" Lexie elbowed my ribs. "How 'bout that, Goody Two Shoes? That way there'll be no discomfort for little Jinxie."

I should have told her right then that I was afraid I might be queer. That was what was bothering me. I wanted to ask her right then what it had meant in bed, whether what we had done was something she did with everybody, or whether maybe she had a crush, a whopping big crush, like I had on her. A few minutes ago we had touched each other, we had felt so close, but I didn't know how to talk about it. I felt like a stranger, formal and scared.

"You're afraid of me, aren't you?" Lexie's voice was calm.

"Sometimes I think you're going to ... turn on me," I said.

"But I'm not mad at you," Lexie pleaded. "I'm mad at Eleanor. I *love* you."

I cleared my throat. The man with the poodle was walking back down Fifth. Lexie leaned against me. "I enjoy being with you, Jinx. I'm happy with you."

"I'm happy with you," I said slowly.

Lexie stood up and turned toward the park. "Don't say it if you don't mean it."

"I mean it." I stood beside her.

She held my arm. "Do you love me, Jinx?"

"What?"

Lexie squeezed my arm tighter. Two women passed, speaking French. They glanced at Lexie. "Do you love me?"

"Lexie..."

"Tell me."

I cleared my throat. Lexie's eyes were swallowing me. She was smiling.

It came out in my small, constricted voice. "I love you."

Right there by the Plaza, Lexie threw her arms around me. "Oh, shit," she whispered. "I love you, too, Jinx."

Dear God, what is happening? I thought. What is happening? I was in the deep end now. I had jumped, eyes open, right into it. Here was Lexie saying, I love you, and me saying, I love you, and us touching, right by the Plaza Hotel. It was the deep end. I should do something about this. I should stop this craziness right away. I should say, "Now, Lexie, we better behave and cut this stuff out." But suppose Lexie said, "What stuff?" Suppose she hugged and touched all her friends. Suppose she turned around and said, "Why, Jinx, we're pals. Just pals."

"Jinx." I focused my eyes. We were standing in the vestibule of Rizzoli's Bookstore, a plush, brass-fixtured store lined with walls of tall, colorful art books.

"Where are you?" Lexie whispered.

I shook my head. "I don't know."

Slowly, Lexie guided me through stores — in and out of Bonwit's, where she tried on dresses, in and out of Bergdorf's, where she sat at the beauty bar and painted her face with lipstick and eyeshadow and powder. At Saks, she disappeared into a changing booth and came out in a long purple gown. On the ground floor, she ordered monogrammed stationery and bought a leather handbag. I followed her, dazed, wherever she led me.

"I'm hungry," said Lexie in the cold air of Fifth Avenue. She looked at her watch, then ran to the curb, waving her arms. We climbed into the backseat of a taxi. Lexie took off her gloves and held my hand in hers.

"We're going to the Stanhope," she said, leaning back against the seat. I began to wake up. I looked at Lexie.

"Jesus," I said.

"What?"

"You look like a model." Her eyes were huge, black orbs lined with blue dust. Her lipstick glistened wetly on her mouth. Pink powder colored her cheekbones.

Lexie laughed. "Did you just notice?"

I nodded.

"You're crazy."

"Lady…" The cabdriver turned around and saw us holding hands. "Here's the Stanhope."

Lexie paid the man, gathered her packages, and led me toward the lobby of the Stanhope.

"Is it fancy?" I whispered.

Lexie laughed. The doorman greeted us deferentially. "I'll protect you, Tuck."

Every table was covered with a white tablecloth and had a small vase of flowers. The people there were older, gray-haired men in dark suits, women in heavy makeup, like Lexie, in hats and fur coats and silk scarves. The waiters wore black ties and tuxedos and carried napkins over their arms.

Lexie asked me about my interviews at art school. I told her about Dean Housman and Annette Dorfsman. Then I told her about Mrs. Knight.

Lexie was surprised. "You went to see Elizabeth's mother?"

I nodded. "I like her." The waiter brought us salad.

"You amaze me, Jinx. You're supposed to be a shrinking violet. You went to her apartment all by yourself?"

"Yeah. I took a cab."

Lexie frowned. "I'm not too fond of Mrs. Knight. Of course, I wouldn't care for anybody related to Elizabeth."

"I like her. She's a painter. She's the only grown-up painter I know."

We ate our omelets and looked out the window. Across the street people were going into the Metropolitan Museum of Art. "Elizabeth's a phony," said Lexie.

"Maybe 'cause you're both from New York, you compete or something."

Lexie frowned. "Oakie's from New York, and we get along. Ellis is from New York. Dunhill is, too."

Under the table, Lexie's knee rested against mine. I wasn't sure if she intended to touch me, but she *was* touching me.

"Jinx?" Lexie leaned back in her chair. "What about Bennington?"

"What?"

"Why don't you apply to Bennington?"

I stared at her. "I want to go to art school in New York."

"Dessert, ladies?" The waiter hovered over us. Lexie flashed a beguiling smile at him. When he was gone, she leaned forward.

"You can paint your ass off at Bennington. Lots of painters go there."

Across the street, a hansom cab stopped in front of the Metropolitan. "I want to go to school in New York."

"But that's too close to Eleanor," she pouted.

"Well, Eleanor's not my guardian," I said, puzzled.

Lexie's knee pressed mine harder. "If you came to Bennington, we could have so much fun. I could sing and you could paint and we could put on musicals together. We..." Her eyes brightened. "By the way, you're going to design the sets for the Music Club show."

"Me?"

"Why not?" Lexie lit a cigarette and exhaled slowly, staring at me like a cat.

"I've never designed a stage set."

"You'll learn. Alice will help you. I'll help you. Miss Jonas will help you."

"I'm not in the Music Club, Lexie. That would be cronyism or something." Actually, I had always wanted to be in the Music Club, but I'd never thought of working on the set.

"We'll make you an honorary member." The top button of Lexie's silk blouse was unbuttoned, and I could see the pale skin of her neck. "You're the best artist in the school. It makes perfect sense." Lexie leaned forward, her breasts rising. "After you've designed the sets and we've worked together, you'll want to go to Bennington and put on shows there too. You better apply right away."

I stared at her. "I thought you were going to study opera and stuff."

Lexie sighed. "Do you know what my teacher at Juilliard would say if he saw this cigarette?"

"You could *stop* smoking."

"We're not talking about me, we're talking about you coming to Bennington and being my roommate."

The vinaigrette bounced in my stomach. The thought of being Lexie's roommate made me feel dizzy.

Lexie stood up. "Jinx, wait here." Her hand touched my shoulder. "I've got to make a phone call." She hurried out of the dining room. I looked out at the street, at the bare limbs of the trees in Central Park. A cloud crossed the sun, dropping a gray veil over the chic pedestrians, over the hot dog vendors and the museum. An old lady with newspapers wrapped around her feet tapped a stick on the window of the Stanhope and started yelling. I shivered.

It was funny that Lexie wanted me to go to Bennington. I was flattered that she asked me, but it didn't make much sense.

"Anything else, madam?" The waiter bowed. "Coffee? Tea?"

"Coffee, maybe," I said. "My friend will be back soon. She's..." I paused. Did I have to explain? Anyway, I didn't really know *where* she was.

"Of course," said the waiter, removing the remaining dishes. Most of the people in the restaurant were gone now. The waiters were setting up for dinner. Where was Lexie? I looked in my pocketbook. I had just enough to pay the bill if she didn't come back.

"Jinx!" Lexie scowled. "Let's go." She threw some money onto the waiter's silver tray. "Get your coat, Jinx." She slung her own coat over her arm.

I'll talk to her, I thought to myself. I'll talk to her about my crush. It's the only thing to do. Maybe if I tell her about it, the crush will go away — I won't want to touch her, I won't want to hold her again. We'll just be regular friends.

Lexie walked fast.

"Where are we going?"

"Where do you want to go?" She didn't look around.

"I don't know."

Lexie's makeup was smeared. She was crying. "Don't leave everything to me, Jinx. *You're* going to live here. *You* decide."

"Lexie..." She walked on. The streets were cold now, but she still carried her coat on her arm. "Put your coat on, Lexie." I touched her arm. She jerked away.

"Where do you want to go?" she said. "And don't say, 'I don't care.' I'm sick of 'I don't care.' Do you understand?"

"Lexie, what's wrong?" People were looking at us now. It was too cold to be walking without a coat. "Did I do something wrong?"

Lexie stopped. Her eyes were small. "For Christ's sake, Jinx, I'm not mad at you. You're so egocentric. You think everything happens because of you. It doesn't."

"Who are you mad at?" I asked finally.

Lexie wiped her eyes. "Philip."

"Why did you call him?" I tried to sound cheerful.

"I don't want to talk about it." Lexie's face was red and swollen. "I'm going to see him tomorrow."

"What?"

"I'm going to see him tomorrow," she repeated.

I started walking. This time I was mad.

"Jinx..." She caught up with me. "I'm sorry."

That night, we took a cab to Greenwich Village.

"Let's hold hands," said Lexie, when the cab stopped on a small, dark street.

"What?"

"There are addicts down here. And Mafia. If we hold hands, nobody will bother us."

"Why?" I said.

"They won't bother us if they think we're lesbians."

"Lesbians?" I got a mental picture of dark, seamy bars, where women were wearing men's clothes, acting like men.

"Your hand's clammy," said Lexie.

"Really?" I tried to sound casual.

"We're safe this way." Lexie peered into a store window.

"Where are we going?" Not that it mattered, this close to the deep end.

Lexie looked at me. "To a coffeehouse."

Ahead of us was a long street full of nightclubs. "Have you ever been in a coffeehouse?" I said.

Lexie hesitated. "Yes ... well, no."

"How do you know which one to go to?"

"Jesus, how do you know how to do anything, Jinx? How do you know when to blow your nose?"

I touched my nose reflexively. Often, in the cold, my nose ran.

Lexie stopped in front of a brick building, over which a large sign hung. "The Café Bizarre," it said in huge white letters. A hawker man stood in the doorway. "Come on in, girls." He winked. "Two dollars cover and one free drink."

Lexie glanced at me. She paid the man four dollars and we walked down a long, narrow corridor, which opened into a longer, wider room. On the right side was a bar, where some people slouched. They looked at our hands.

"This is silly," I said, letting go.

Lexie shrugged. "Suit yourself."

Under a small spotlight, a man on a platform was singing an Irish sea shanty. He finished just as we sat down. The audience clapped.

The next act was a hypnotist who also performed feats of extrasensory perception. He wore blue jeans and a top hat and he asked people from the audience to volunteer. He guessed people's weight and age and hometown. A sailor and two tourists from Ohio went up.

"He's a fake," said Lexie loudly.

"It's sort of funny," I whispered.

"This is a tourist trap."

"Where are the beatniks?" I asked.

"Let's go."

That night, Lexie didn't mention back rubs or getting in bed with me. She said she had a headache.

"Are you okay?" I wanted to talk to her. I felt strange and nervous. She got into bed without speaking. "Good night," I said, and lay staring into the darkness. I would talk to Lexie on the train tomorrow. I would talk to her and get everything off my chest. I would find out if she had a crush too. Then things would be better.

The ring of the telephone jarred us both awake.

"Hello?" answered Lexie hoarsely. She listened, then hung up and began throwing her clothes into a suitcase.

"What are you doing?"

"Going to Philip's. I'm half an hour late."

"Are you eating breakfast?"

She sat down on my bed. She was wearing her black wool suit and a lavender blouse. Her face was pale, her hair still uncombed.

"I'll eat at Philip's. Juliet will fix you something." Her hand stroked my head distractedly. "Why don't you go to the Guggenheim? Have you been there?"

"No."

Lexie looked at herself in the mirror. She flattened the front of her skirt. "I look awful."

"Do you have to go?"

She picked up her suitcase. "I'll meet you at Penn Station, under the clock, at one. Do you know where the clock is?"

I nodded.

"I'll miss you," she said as she closed the door.

When my bag was packed, I found the envelope I had brought from school and put a ten-dollar bill in it. "Be sure to tip Mrs. Dennis's servants," Mother had told me. I wrote Juliet's name on the envelope and took a deep breath. I had never tipped a servant.

The kitchen door was closed, but I could hear Juliet talking inside. I knocked lightly.

"...and you know how she is when Lexie's here. She's worse this time, 'cause Lexie brought a friend." I froze in the hallway, afraid to move.

"Uh-huh. In the bed together. Bad enough the way she carries on with Philip. No, indeed, I wouldn't tell her mother. That child's caused enough suffering. All right, then, see you Thursday."

I must have stood there for five minutes wondering what to do. Finally, I knocked again.

"You don't need to knock, Miss Jinx." Juliet opened the door. "No one else does."

My knees were trembling. I held the envelope in my hand. "Juliet, I want to thank you for everything you've done." That's what Mother told me to say. "I..."

Juliet frowned and looked at the envelope. "What's that, honey?"

What was I supposed to say? "I ... it's a tip."

Juliet folded her arms beneath her breasts. "Don't worry about this morning. I wouldn't tell her."

"Oh, no, it's not that. I just wanted to thank you for everything you've done."

"Well, that's kind of you, but you keep your money." She glanced at the clock by the icebox. "Better hurry if you want to catch your train."

I left the envelope on Lexie's bureau. I should have done that in the first place.

At twelve-thirty I called Mrs. Knight from a pay phone at Penn Station. I told her about my interview at Cooper Union while the cold, inflectionless voice of the stationmaster called out arrivals and departures.

"Give Elizabeth a hug for me," said Mrs. Knight. "I spoke to her this morning, but hug her anyway."

"I should go, I guess. I'm supposed to stand under the clock." I was nervous. I was going to talk to Lexie.

Mrs. Knight paused. "Are you all right, Jinx?"

"I'm fine," I said. "I'll hug Elizabeth."

At one-fifteen Lexie still hadn't arrived. The announcer had called the train. People hurried down the steps and escalators. A cold draft blew through the station. I kept looking at the clock. One-twenty, one twenty-five. Where was Lexie? What was she doing with Philip? I thought of calling Mrs. Dennis, but Mrs. Dennis might get upset and phone the school or something. If Woodie found out Lexie had disappeared, there'd be trouble.

"Last call for the Harrisburg Express." The announcer spoke with greater urgency. I scanned the soda fountains and newsstands, the ladies' lounge and luggage check. No Lexie. Finally, I descended the staircase. I didn't know what else to do. It was a big deal to miss your train at Huntington Hill, especially since Woodie herself was picking up five of us at the station. Had Lexie called Woodie to tell her she'd missed the train? Should I call Woodie? What was I supposed to do? I had wanted so much to talk to Lexie. Where was she? What was she doing?

I found a seat on the aisle of a stuffy coach. The train moved slowly away from the platform as I hoisted my stuff onto the baggage rack. I sat down and closed my eyes. What would I say to Woodie when she greeted us at the station? I should have called Mrs. Dennis. I could have taken a later train. The prickly upholstery poked through my stockings. The woman next to me lit a cigarette. Curls of smoke rose around me.

At Newark, a hand pressed my shoulder. Oakie, the president of the school, stood beside me, a wax cup of Coke in her hand. She was wearing a red suit and black heels. Oakie wasn't beautiful, but she always looked terrific, even when she was sitting around Senior House in Levi's and a sweatshirt.

"Tuckwell?" She paused. "Why aren't you with Lexie?"

I gulped. "I ... we got screwed up..."

"Couldn't you find two seats together?" Oakie didn't seem suspicious, just curious.

"The train's crowded today."

"Jinx." Oakie lowered her voice. "You should get her out of the club car. You know Woodie hates that."

"Club car?" The train jerked. Oakie grabbed the luggage rack.

"Two cars back."

I sat up. What was she doing there? When had she boarded the train? "I'll get her," I said.

Oakie walked on.

It took all of my strength to pull open the huge steel door of the club car. Cold, dirty air blew up from the tracks. Once I was inside, the smell of alcohol and cigarettes filled my head. I looked down the rows of tables — mostly men, drinking and smoking, reading the Sunday paper. Then I heard a familiar laugh from the far end of the car. I could see Lexie sitting beside a man, legs crossed, skirt above her knees. Her hair was wild, her makeup smeared. The man's hand rested on her shoulder. She smiled at him coyly, a cigarette dangling between her fingers. I trembled. The man was not Philip. He was small and greasy. I wanted to turn away, go back to my seat. If I could just sit down by myself, I could work this thing out. If I spoke to Lexie she might have a tantrum, go all crazy and mad. But Oakie had said to get her out of the club car. I shuddered at the sound of Lexie's thin, flirtatious laugh and the man's hand, now stroking her cheek.

"Lexie?"

She looked up, surprised, as if I were the last person she expected to see on the train to Harrisburg. Maybe she didn't even know she was *on* the train to Harrisburg.

"Jinx, darling," she said, reaching for my hand. "You must meet my friend Tom." She was drunk. Her eyelids were red, swollen. The man grinned self-consciously.

"What are you doing here?" I said flatly.

She laughed. "I'm sitting here with my friend Tom." Tom stiffened.

"Are you okay?" She was going to hate me for this.

"'Are you okay?'" she mimicked, touching Tom's sleeve.

138

"You shouldn't be here," I continued grimly. "Oakie already saw you."

"Well, kiss Oakie's ass."

Tom stood up. "Better get back to my seat." He winked at Lexie. "Pleasure meeting you, Lexie. Look me up when you come to Trenton." He glanced at me. "Nice meeting *you*." He extended his hand. I stared at it. When he was gone, I sat beside Lexie.

"You've got to get out of here. People are watching."

"I feel sick." Lexie raised her hand to her mouth.

"Sick?"

She nodded.

We lurched slowly down the aisle to the ladies' room at the end of the car. It was one of those lounge-type places with a sofa in one room and a toilet in the other. Someone was in the toilet. Just inside the door, Lexie threw up on the floor. The toilet door clicked open and a gray-haired woman stared at us.

"My friend's sick," I said. "She's got flu." I locked the outer door and mopped the floor with paper towels. Lexie sat on the sofa, head in her hands, leaning over the floor.

"Shit," she groaned. "I'm going to die."

"No you're not." I patted her shoulder. People started knocking on the door.

"Just a minute," I called.

There was a sharp rap. "What's going on in there?" It was the conductor.

Lexie looked at me. "Don't open it."

"My friend's not feeling well," I yelled.

"Open the door."

"Don't," begged Lexie. "Let me die in peace."

"He's got a key anyway." I unfastened the lock.

The conductor stood, red-faced, hat pushed off his forehead, eyes narrow. "What's going on in here?" Lexie was bent over the couch.

"My friend's got flu," I said.

"You'll have to get out. Other people need the bath-room."

I looked at Lexie. She was still drunk and helpless. "We couldn't find two seats together," I said.

He rattled the change in his pockets. "Two seats to-gether in the next car. Go on, out!"

We walked through the cold, noisy passage and found the two seats in the car ahead. Lexie sat down, head against her seat, and closed her eyes.

"Where's your suitcase?" I said quietly.

"How the hell should I know?" She held her stomach. "Is it in the club car?"

She nodded. I stood up. "Don't talk to anyone. Keep your eyes closed. Don't talk to Oakie or anyone."

"Who the shit am I going to talk to? I feel like dying."

I started down the aisle.

"Coffee," she called.

"You want coffee?"

She nodded.

It took me twenty minutes to gather our suitcases and get coffee. As I headed back to our car, Oakie stopped me.

"Did you find Lexie?"

I told her yes.

She looked at me with curiosity. "Is she all right?"

"Got the flu," I said.

"I was hoping you two could have lunch yesterday."

"Yeah. Thanks for inviting us."

"I'll come sit with you," said Oakie. "You won't believe the weekend I've had. *Paul* called."

"Oakie." I blinked. "Lexie's asleep and I've got to study."

"On the train?"

"I've got a quiz tomorrow."

Oakie shrugged, then looked at me closely. "Is every-thing okay?"

"Yeah," I said. "Everything's great."

Lexie woke up somewhere between Philadelphia and Harrisburg. She was still drunk and her breath smelled horrible.

"Where's my coffee?" Little red veins popped in her eyes.

I handed her the paper cup I'd gotten earlier.

"It's cold. I can't drink this."

A wave of anger passed over me. I looked at her bleary eyes and wrinkled clothes. What had she been doing with Philip, and Tom, and everybody else she happened to meet?

"You smell like a distillery," I said.

"Get me some more coffee."

I stood up.

"Hurry," she called.

At the snack bar I bought another cup of coffee and some Doublemint.

"What were you drinking?" I said to Lexie.

She glared at me. "I wasn't drinking."

"Next stop, Harrisburg," said the conductor, taking our seat checks.

"You *were* drinking," I said. "You better comb your hair."

She brushed her hair, using the plate glass window as a mirror. It was gray outside. Gray and dirty.

"Chew some gum," I said. "Don't talk to anyone when we get off. Don't let anyone know you're drunk."

"I'm not drunk," she said loudly. A man on our left was watching us.

"You're lying. Don't talk to Oakie or anybody. Just say you don't feel well. They can wait till tomorrow to find out about your weekend."

Lexie buttoned her coat. "I don't like your tone."

I stared at her. "Lexie, do you know what happens if you come back to school drunk? You'll get thrown out. It's not funny. It's not a joke."

"You're cute," she giggled. The train bumped to a stop. The cold tracks of the Harrisburg station waited for us.

I stood up. "You're about to play a great role, Lexie. Biggest role in your career. You're about to play a sober person. Do you understand?" I pulled her up. Passengers pushed by us. "If you lurch or puke, they'll kick you out. Now spit out your gum." I held my hand to her lips.

For an instant, her eyes met mine. "I'm fucked up," she said.

"Right," I said, leading her toward the exit. We followed a line of people onto the tracks. At the steps, Lexie looked at me. "I'm sober, right?"

Woodie didn't meet us at the track. She didn't see the slow, careful steps Lexie took or the inane smile on her face. The other Huntington Hill girls climbed the stairs ahead of us, laughing about their weekends. Nobody but Oakie noticed that Lexie was acting strange, and Oakie didn't say anything. She didn't want to know.

"We'll sit in the back," I said at the curb. The rear seat of the station wagon faced backward.

Woodie waited in the driver's seat while we packed our luggage. "Did you girls have a good weekend?"

Everyone answered cheerfully. Woodie looked in the rearview mirror as she pulled out of the station. "You're awfully quiet, Lexie."

"Lexie's not feeling well," said Oakie. "She got the flu."

Woodie's hands gripped the wheel. "Stop at the infirmary when we get back, Lexie."

"I'm okay, really," said Lexie slowly.

"Stop at the infirmary," repeated Woodie. The subject was not open for discussion.

About halfway to school, Lexie woke up. She realized she was in trouble, that she would have to get out of the car with Woodie watching and register at the infirmary. Lexie squeezed my hand. "What do I tell the nurse?"

My knees were shaking now. The closer we got to school, the more afraid I was. It was dark. Car lights on the Interstate wound behind us like an endless trail of torches. "Tell her you'd feel worse if you stayed in the infirmary."

"She'll never believe me." Her dark eyes smoldered. "Philip's a bastard," she said hoarsely.

"Tell it to the nurse."

"You're my best friend, Jinx," said Lexie quietly.

I shrugged.

Lexie pulled it off. She put on so much Blush-On that her cheeks glowed with health and the nurse didn't bother to examine her that night. She told Lexie to come back in the morning when the doctor would be in. By the morning, she was sober. Her breath didn't smell of puke and she could walk in a straight line. But by morning, I wasn't speaking to her.

SOMETIMES I THOUGHT I WASN'T MEANT TO LIVE IN the world. I wasn't constructed for it. After the trip, I walked around the school in a daze. My body seemed to contract, to fold into itself defensively. Maybe physical withdrawal would keep me out of trouble. I felt cold inside and the fact that it was cold *outside* didn't help. It was December, close to Christmas vacation, and the outer made the inner cold feel worse.

I avoided Lexie. At lunch, I wouldn't sit near her and I never went up to her room anymore. In the corridors, between classes, I hurried by her, pretending not to see her. Of course, I watched her from a distance. I couldn't help doing that. She was very busy casting the Music Club show and rehearsing for the Christmas concert, and she was always running around making announcements. At first she didn't notice that I wasn't speaking. She was too manic and self-centered to notice my withdrawal. She didn't know anything was wrong.

Actually, I wasn't sure what *was* wrong. Then one day in English class we were reading this story, *Billy Budd*, by Herman Melville, and I realized what was wrong. I was furious at Lexie. I wanted to hit her, the way Billy hit Claggart. This thing had happened between us, this opening, this connection, in New York, and the next day she forgot about me. She forgot that I was waiting for her in the station. She went off with Philip and she boarded the train without me, crazy and drunk. I couldn't understand it. How could she do that — after lying in bed, after touching, coming so close? The answer must be that she didn't care, or that she did those things with everybody. I wasn't special. Lexie was affectionate and I just happened to be around one day when she felt like holding a warm body.

I had wanted to talk to her, on the train, about my crush. I wanted to tell her that I felt closer to her than I'd ever felt to anybody, that her intelligence, her warmth, her beauty had swept me away. I wanted to go to her and tell her whatever the consequences, that I loved her, that I was *in love* with her.

Then the train ride stunned me. I couldn't talk to anyone. Miggin asked about the trip. She knew something was wrong, but I said Lexie's place was nice. We saw a movie and we went to a coffeehouse, I said. Miggin was hurt. She didn't understand why I wouldn't talk. She thought I was mad at her. She was more considerate than usual. At breakfast she saved me her bacon, and at night, when we lay in bed, she talked to me about Colorado and her sisters, and Mills College, where she wanted to go to school. Sometimes she'd ask again about what happened in New York. But I kept saying it was okay. Nothing happened.

Miggin left a day early for Christmas vacation. She missed the Christmas concert, starring Lexie and the Glee Club. I went to the concert alone and stared at Lexie as she sang a duet from the *Messiah* with Oakie. It was beautiful — sweet and clear and delicate. Lexie was radiant, her eyes bright and happy. She was the most beautiful person I had ever seen. Afterwards, people clapped and yelled, "Bravo," and pushed backstage to congratulate her. I walked out of the theater and went to the room and lay on my bed.

Then, after what seemed hours, my door opened slowly and Lexie stood beside me in her black dress, a red rose pinned to her chest. Her fingernails were painted red and her lips were red, and her hair was dark and soft. Far away, in the common room, I could hear a sock hop beginning. The faucet dripped in the bathroom.

I smelled Lexie's perfume. She sat down on the bed and crossed her legs. The room was dark, lit by the small lamp on Miggin's bureau.

She touched my shoulder. "Did you come to the concert?"

I nodded.

One of Lexie's heels dropped on the floor. "I sang for you, Jinx." Her brown eyes were fixed on my face. Her breasts rose beneath her black dress.

I turned away.

"Why aren't you speaking to me?" she said softly.

I stood up, turned off the spigot, and sat down again. "I'm speaking." I could hear the flatness of my voice.

Lexie leaned back against the pillow and stretched her legs out on the bed. "Jinx, if it's the train ride, I'm sorry."

"You're not," I said.

She leaned forward. "Jinx, I'm sorry. Please don't be so distant. I miss you. You've just disappeared."

Above us, I could hear the sound of dancing feet.

"Did you ever think how I felt being left in that station — wondering where you were, not knowing what to do?"

"Jinx..."

"Or how I felt when you were drunk in the club car holding some man's arm like ... like..."

Lexie's nostrils flared. She sat up. "Like a whore?"

"Lexie..." I looked at her now, really looked at her for the first time since New York.

Lexie stood up and turned toward the door. "God, you're selfish."

I followed her. "*I'm* selfish?" I laughed a small, tight laugh.

Her cheeks were flushed. "Jinx, I was very upset. I had two glasses of cherry brandy on an empty stomach. Philip..."

"Philip," I repeated with disgust.

Now Lexie's voice was flat, cold. "You never told me you cared if I went to Philip's. I didn't know it meant a flying shit to you. If I'd known..."

"Lexie, you didn't ask me. You *told* me. You left me." She was drawing me into this argument. She was forcing me to fight.

Lexie turned, arms folded beneath her breasts. "You could have asked me not to go. You could have told me you wanted me to stay. But that's not the way you are. You just sit there and say, 'Yes, no, sure, okay, yeah.' What's that supposed to mean? I went to Philip's thinking it was perfectly fine with you."

I sat on Miggin's bed. "Lexie, you know how I am; I wasn't going to make a big deal."

Lexie stared at me, her eyes hard, face taut. "I know how you are, Jinx, and I'm tired of the way you are. I'm sick and tired of you. You're *screwed up!*" Her eyes were narrow, accusing. "If you totally reject me because I had two drinks on an empty stomach after the worst fight in my life, which *you* never asked about, which you never knew about, in which Philip told me I abused Eleanor, I abuse him, and that nobody in the fucking world loves me, if you reject me for ... for being a human being and having real, human *emotions* which you don't have, well, screw you. Screw your delicate little sense of decency, Jinx. Shove it up your ass."

I went to the door. "Lexie..."

"You know something, Jinx," she said softly, "I don't give a damn about your sensitivity and pain and self-consciousness. Friendship means nothing to you, loyalty means nothing to you. You let the stupid rules of this school tell you what to do. You're just..." She squinted, her eyes small, hard beads. "You're just a ... bitch." She opened the door. "You're a self-absorbed bitch."

I slammed the door shut and lunged for her. I caught her by the shoulder and I slapped her. I slapped her so hard my fingers hurt. Her hand went to her face and a sound, a deep hoarse sound, came out of her chest. "Lexie, I lied for you. I told the conductor and Oakie and Woodie that you had the flu. I got your coffee and wiped up your puke and found your suitcases. I could have been thrown out, and you didn't even..."

Lexie dropped onto my bed and clutched the pillow. She beat the mattress with hard, rapid strokes. I stood, watching, until my throat tightened and my head began to spin. I fell onto Miggin's bed, sad, frustrated, frightened. It was a nightmare; I couldn't move. I lay there frozen. Then there was silence. Lexie's body was stretched across my bed like a corpse. Her black dress had risen up her legs and both shoes were on the floor. She looked dead, face against the pillow. I shut the bathroom door and splashed my face with water. When I came out, she was gone.

On New Year's Eve I sat in front of my parents' television. My folks were at a party. Outside it was dark and bitter cold. I held a blanket around me and stared at the gray tube. Walter Cronkite announced that 1964 had been the Year of the Negro. Negroes were participating fully in American democracy. Martin Luther King, Jr., had received the Nobel Prize for Peace. Negro voters had put LBJ back in the White House. In 1965, said Walter, Marina Oswald would become a college coed. Just before midnight, the phone rang.

"Jinx?" said the voice.

"Hello?"

There was a silence. "It's Lexie."

My stomach slid. My hands turned cold. I had thought about Lexie every moment since vacation started.

"Jinx?" I heard Lexie's hand cover the receiver as she yelled, "I'll be right there." In the background were voices and the sound of laughter. Her voice was soft:

"I'm at this lousy party, Jinx, and I thought I'd call you."

"That's nice. Are you having fun?"

"Jinx, I've been thinking about you."

"I've been thinking about you." It was my small voice.

"Things will be better after vacation. We've got the Music Club show, and you'll do the sets. We'll have rehearsals and good things and then spring." She stopped.

"Yeah..."

"Jinx, we don't have much time left."

"I know."

Lexie paused. "What are you doing tonight?"

"I'm watching Guy Lombardo." I glanced at the television. "These weird couples in party hats are waving little pom-poms at the cameras."

"You're lucky you're not at a party. I hate New Year's Eve parties."

I took a breath. "Is ... is Philip there?"

Lexie was quiet. "Yes."

I didn't say anything.

"Jinx, I love you very much. Do you ... well, I wanted to wish you happy New Year."

"Happy New Year," I said, and went back to the TV.

JANUARY IS THE HARDEST MONTH, I THOUGHT TO myself as I pulled my suitcase out of the idling cab. The campus looked cold and bare — the trees gray, shivering in the damp wind, the buildings lifeless and worn without foliage surrounding them.

Miggin was in the room unpacking, her cinnamon smell already softening the empty, institutional odor of Senior House. Her red hair was braided in long pigtails tied with blue ribbons. Her face was tan and freckled from skiing. I snuck up behind her and tapped her on the shoulder.

"Tuckwell!" She turned and hugged me.

"You look good," I said. "Healthy."

The room was the same — the same twin beds, the same posters, the same bare floors. Outside, the pasture rolling up behind the house was brown, frozen. The horses were in for the winter.

Miggin watched me unpack. "Did you go to New York?"

I looked at her quizzically. "No. Why?"

"I don't know," she said quickly. "Anyway, we skied at Vail and Daddy didn't like the snow, so we flew to Squaw. He's like a spoiled kid if anything goes wrong." Miggin sat on my bed, chin resting on her knees. "Do you feel better, Jinx?"

"What do you mean?"

Miggin tapped a pencil on the bedspread. "You know. You were depressed or something before vacation."

I shrugged. "I'm okay." I heard laughter in the hall. "Who else is back?"

Miggin sat up. "You mean, is Lexie back?"

"Boy, you're Anna Freud today."

"Who's Anna Freud?"

"A lady doctor." I slid my suitcase onto the top shelf of the closet and closed the door.

That night, I wrote Lexie a note and slipped it under her door. "I'm back," it said. "How are you?" At breakfast the next day, Lexie handed me a note. *"Chère Jinx. J'espère que tu vas bien. Le samedi, viens avec moi au Huntington. Nous mangerons les hamburgers au Rexall. A bientôt. Attendrissement,* The Incomparable Rosalie."

The fluorescent lights at Rexall flickered above us. Lexie sat in the booth reading a movie magazine, absently twisting her fingers through her hair. I flicked through the jukebox listings, and pushed the plastic buttons for "Town without Pity," by Gene Pitney. I was nervous. I was going to tell Lexie about my feelings. I'd decided. It was after two; the fountain was just about empty. *"When you stop to gaze upon a star,"* began the song, *"people talk about how bad you are..."*

Lexie looked bloated in her green corduroy jumper and black turtleneck sweater. And tired.

I cleared my throat. "Who's the Incomparable Rosalie?"

Lexie looked up. "That's my part in *Carnival,* the Music Club show. Have you heard it?" Lexie's eyes brightened; she closed the magazine. "It's based on *Lili.* You know——" She began to sing softly, *"The song of love is a sad song, Hi lili, hi lili hi lo..."*

"I love that song."

Lexie leaned forward on her elbows. "It's gorgeous. And, of course, there's Leslie Caron, beautiful, petite, quivering with each syllable — *The song of love is a song of woe, don't ask me how I know."* Lexie spoke with a delicate French accent. *"The song of love is a sad song, for*

I have loved and I know..." She stopped and looked intently over my shoulder. Oakie and Laura Carr were buying candy at the checkout counter.

"Of course," she continued, "that song's not in *Carnival*, only in *Lili*. I've got the record of *Carnival*, Anna Maria Alberghetti, Kaye Ballard, Jerry Orbach. You know them?"

"I don't think so."

Lexie shook her head. "I don't think you'd recognize *Paul Newman* if you fell over him. What's the matter with you, Jinx? Don't you know your stars? Don't you know what's going on in the world, Tuckwell?"

I felt silly making small talk. I wanted to tell her. "My folks," I began, distracted, "never talk about show business. I wasn't exposed."

Lexie laughed. "Jesus, you blame everything on your folks. They're not responsible for everything. Do you ever read newspapers? Watch TV? Pay attention?"

"Suppose you had Eleanor for a mother? You'd appreciate Helen and Fred. At least they think about more than their next bridge game."

Lexie waved to the waitress and ordered a plate of french fries. "Anyway, *Carnival*'s going to be terrific. It's about this French girl, Lili, who joins the Grand Imperial Cirque de Paris and falls in love with Marco the Magnificent. But, there's a slight problem because Marco's mistress, the Incomparable Rosalie, that's me, is jealous and doesn't want Marco fooling around. But it all turns out in the end. *Tu comprends?*"

"*Oui.*"

"Doesn't it sound great?" Lexie dipped her french fries into a mound of ketchup.

Tell her, I thought. Tell her about the crush. "It sounds like a good show."

Lexie stopped eating. "May I bring up an unpleasant subject?"

"No." I smiled nervously.

Lexie poured salt onto the formica table and arranged it in little piles. "Jinx, why are you so distant?"

I held the edge of the table. "I'm not."

Lexie blew bubbles into her Coke. "I have a permanent picture of you in my mind. You're staring blankly ahead of you, in a fog."

"I ... I'm not distant." I took a breath. Lexie was closing in.

"I'll give you an example, dear heart." She sighed. "On New Year's Eve I called your house, right? I was at a party. I left the party to call you and what did I say to you? Since you've already forgotten, I'll—"

"No, I haven't—"

"I'll tell you what I said. I said, 'I love you very much.'"

I looked around quickly.

"You know what you answered? You said, 'Happy New Year.' Do you know how stupid I felt when I put down the phone? I felt ridiculous. What the hell did I call her for? She doesn't give a shit."

"I do." It was my constricted voice.

"Sometimes I wonder why we're friends at all. What do you want from me, Jinx? Are you still mad about the train ride? I know I was obnoxious, but it was only *one* time." She leaned forward.

My hands and feet were ice cubes.

Lexie stared at me. A kid in a windbreaker dropped a coin into the jukebox — *"Oh my heart went boom,"* sang the Beatles.

I looked down at the table and dumped a bowl of sugar packets on top of it. "You think I'm distant, right? I don't have feelings like you, right?"

Lexie frowned. "I didn't say you don't have feelings. I said you don't give a damn about me. I don't understand why you even like me. Sometimes I think you hate me."

Slowly, I separated the sugar packs into groups of three. I looked at Lexie. "Do you ever hide your feelings?"

"What?"

I cleared my throat. "Maybe sometimes you hide your feelings."

Lexie eyed me suspiciously. "Why would I hide my feelings?"

I picked at a callus on my thumb. "If you're embarrassed about something you feel, you might hide your feelings. Because you don't want people to think you're crazy."

"Jinx, are we talking about you or me? Because," she laughed, "I already know *you're* crazy. I've always known that."

I breathed slowly, grouping each sugar pack with other packs that matched — two little Model T Fords, two blue jays, two autumn leaves.

"Have you finished, Jinx?" Lexie was irritated. "Or is Socrates going to continue the little dialogue?"

I slumped down. "Suppose you like someone a whole lot. So much that when you're with them your palms get sweaty and your head feels like it could fly off." I swallowed. "Suppose," I said, staring at the Model T sugar pack, "you have such strong feelings that you think something's wrong with you, like you have a disease or something..."

"A disease?" Lexie looked puzzled.

"Because you want to..." The waitress sponged a counter near us. I lowered my voice. "Because you want to touch that person and be near them and..."

"It happens all the time, Tuck..."

"But it's not a *boy* you feel it about, it's a girl. You feel romantic and it's a girl. All gushy and mushy inside..."

Lexie stared at me.

I kept going. "I mean, if you felt that way you might stop showing your feelings and pretend not to feel anything because what you *did* feel was weird and embarrassing."

"Tuckwell..." Lexie touched my hand with hers. I released the sugar packets. "It doesn't necessarily mean anything. It's not weird. Jinx..." She stopped.

My voice trembled. "Lexie, suppose it means you're queer." The waitress was serving coffee to an old man.

Lexie's eyes were distant, unfocused. She pulled a strand of hair away from her face. "Jinx, don't be silly."

"You try not to feel anything," I whispered. "You try as hard as you can not to."

"Jinx..."

"You try not to feel what you feel," I said slowly. "Lexie..." She was looking at me strangely. "Lexie, it's not just friendship. It's ... sexual love."

Lexie's voice was cold. My words frightened her. "You sound like a ten-year-old."

Her words stung. I sat up. "Lexie, I told you in New York; I've never done anything. I don't know anything about sex. You—"

"I'm the whore and you're Miss Goody Two Shoes," she said, reaching into her pocketbook. "We've been through this before."

"Lexie..."

She held a tiny mirror to her face and pressed her lipstick against her tightened lips.

"Let's get the check," I said.

Lexie looked over the mirror. "Is that it? You've finished? You want to go now?"

"It's getting late." I stood up and pulled on my coat. "The bus will be leaving soon."

"That's it, Tuckwell?"

I looked at her, confused. I had tried to explain. What

more could I say? Then I walked toward the door. She followed after me.

"You mean Princess Jinx will not talk any more on the subject?"

The cold air hit my face. "I'll talk."

Lexie buttoned her coat slowly. "When, may I ask, does it please the Princess to continue this conversation? Next year? At our ... at our Fifteenth Alumnae Reunion as our babies run through our legs?"

Babies? I looked at Lexie. "We can't talk here." Ahead, on the Huntington road, the orange school bus waited for us like a patient dog.

"Then when?" Her heels clicked against the sidewalk.

"Today."

Lexie's voice was teasing. "And where? In your room, while Miggin paints her toenails? In my room, with Gibbs and Matthews rehearsing next door?"

I stopped just before we reached the bus. I looked at her hard. "We'll take a walk. We have time before study hall."

She seemed appeased.

The minute we climbed into the bus, Lexie changed. Suddenly she was charming, bright, animated. She sat down beside Laura Carr and raved over the new clothes Laura had bought in Huntington. Her laughter filled the bus; her face masked any signs of our discussion. As the bus moved off, she stood up and turned around. "I," she shouted, "am the Incomparable Rosalie. Beside me is Marco the Magnificent. Stand up, Marco." She pulled Laura Carr's arm. Laura stood beside her. Lexie threw her head back and laughed. "Sing, Marco; sing, everyone. This is the Grand Imperial Cirque de Paris."

Suddenly, everyone was singing — Oakie and Laura, Jeepers, Rachel Simpson, Susie Gibbs. Singing and laughing, and all because Lexie was leading. I felt a tight pain in my stomach and cold envy in my head — envy of Lexie's charm, envy of everyone whom Lexie bewitched.

It was almost dark. The ground was hard as we walked toward the stables. I dug my hands in my pockets.

"Well?" Lexie's voice was tense.

I looked at the thin, leafless trees and the red brick gym towering above us on the right. Winter made everything look dead.

Lexie grabbed my arm. "For Christ's sake, Jinx. Don't be cute with me. What's going on? I know it's difficult for you to be serious with me, but I wish you'd try."

We walked in silence past the stables, past the white clapboard house where Randolph Nicholson lived with his family, down to the lower hockey field. We sat on the circular bench at the base of the huge elm tree. From here, we could see only the lower pasture and the ridge of pines that bordered the Huntington road. We propped our backs against the trunk of the elm, which shielded us from the eyes of the school.

Lexie pulled her knees up under her dark fur coat. The vapor from our breath formed smoky clouds in front of us. Our shoulders touched.

"You want to know what's going on?" I said, looking at the ground.

"Yes." She held a finger against her lips. Lexie's cheeks were pink from the cold, her eyes dark, expectant; her black turtleneck covered her throat. My head seemed to be rising, my legs falling.

I pulled my hands up under my sleeves. "I'm in love with you." Lexie looked at me. She did not take her eyes away. It was almost fully dark. In the distance, cars whooshed by on the Huntington road, and house lights began to flicker on.

Lexie moved closer to me. I slid down her dark, wise eyes like a child on a sled. She took my hands in her lap.

"Do you feel it?" she whispered.

Tears formed in my eyes. I nodded. "Lexie?"

"Yes?"

"Are ... are you in love with me?"

Lexie squeezed my hands. "I love you, Jinx," she said deliberately.

"But..." I hesitated. "Are you *in love* with me?"

Slowly, she unfastened the buttons of my coat and slipped her arms around me. I moved closer, until I could feel her breasts next to my own. Her eyes brought me closer. I did not feel the cold.

"Jinx." Lexie's lips touched my cheek; her breath was warm. Her arms circled my waist. "So many clothes," said Lexie. "So many goddam clothes." I felt a dull ache in my legs. She pulled me closer, her mouth opening to mine, her tongue dancing on my lips, pushing them apart. Our lips, breasts, and legs were touching.

Lexie stared at me dreamily.

"We should go," I said.

"Time's winged chariot..."

I buttoned my coat. "Only five minutes till study hall."

Lexie laughed. "How can I study now? I'm so ... horny." She kissed me.

"Lexie?" I said in a small voice. "What ... Is there something wrong with us?"

She sat up and looked at me strangely. "There's nothing wrong with *me*," she said. "Not a goddam thing."

THE SHOW SUCKED US UP LIKE A GIANT HOOVER vacuum. I was the set designer, and I was in love with the leading lady. Day after day I sat in the theater, feet propped on the seat in front of me, watching Lexie move across stage, performing the role of the Incomparable Rosalie. I watched Lexie coach Dawson, the piano accompanist, on timing, teach the chorus their dance numbers, block scenes with Miss Jonas, plot lighting with the crew. In rehearsals, Lexie pulled her hair off her forehead with a red bandanna and wore a man's shirt over her skirt. Her concentration was complete. From the start, she knew everyone's lines better than they did, and if rehearsal went badly, she cracked jokes or offered suggestions for improvement.

"Love makes the world go 'round," the performers sang as they danced across the stage in rehearsal. *"Love makes the world go 'round."* As corny as it was, the song delighted me, like a field of bright spring flowers — so simple and romantic. Sometimes Lexie would look down from the stage and smile and I felt loved and appreciated and proud to be Lexie's friend. Even Miss Jonas, who was faculty director, grinned when the chorus sang that song and the tassels on her buckskin jacket shook in time to the music, as she kicked her leg.

It was hard leaving Lexie, even to work on the sets in the studio. The theater excited me — it seemed like a place where anything was possible. I saw that I wasn't the only one with a crush. *"Love makes the world go 'round,"* the girls sang, and the cast and crew believed it. Crushes were popping up everywhere, encouraged by the show's sentimental songs and story.

At Huntington Hill there weren't any boys to play the male roles, so all parts were played by girls. Lines and lyrics that were written for men were performed by girls. Laura Carr played the magician, Marco the Magnificent; Oakie was Dr. Schlegel, the carnival owner; Allison Henry played Paul, the Puppeteer; and Jeepers was Jacquot, Paul's assistant. No one thought twice about girls playing boys. It was a convention as old as the school. But all the romance in the script of *Carnival* seemed to make feelings that were always just under the surface at the school more intense and convoluted than usual.

Laura Carr was the principal object of the cast's devotion. She was irresistible in her tight black pants and black silk scarf twisted around her neck. Sometimes, when I sat with the chorus watching scenes, I heard them laughing about who would be chosen to give Laura her flowers on opening night and which member of the chorus Laura liked best. Something else was happening with Allison and Isabel Richards, who played Lili. Outside the theater, they were always together, and in the senior common room, they lounged around a lot, laughing and sitting on each other's laps.

Lexie and I began manically passing each other notes. In classes, I scribbled drawings and poems in my notebooks. She wrote funny letters in French and Latin and pig Latin, and we traded them in the halls. The notes were our substitute for time alone together. When there wasn't a rehearsal, one of us was making costumes or programs or sets or something. On weekends there was no longer the time for trips to Rexall or walks to the lower field. I tried not to feel hurt if Lexie was too busy to talk.

I'd had the idea that telling Lexie about the crush would make everything simpler and less confusing. All the mystery and ambiguity would be over, I thought, and

Lexie would either be horrified and drop me, or she'd understand and our friendship would continue on a sounder, surer footing. I'd even thought maybe the physical attraction would go away once the feelings were expressed.

But it hadn't worked that way. Things were as messed up and peculiar as ever. Lexie had said she loved me and we had kissed, but we never really talked about what it meant. She didn't want to talk about what it meant. I began to think that maybe there was some category of girls who were attracted to other girls and even did sex things with them without being queer. Or maybe everyone was partly queer and just didn't call it that. They called it having a crush. After all, Lexie still talked about Philip a lot. Oh, she always prefaced everything by saying how lousy he was, but whenever she got a letter from him, she got hysterical and told everybody in the dorm. It was hard to figure out, and I was jealous of Philip and confused about what Lexie felt about him. And did she really go all the way with him? I mean, as cousins, they shouldn't really be doing *any*thing. But knowing Lexie...

Another thing that bothered me was the fact that Lexie was always the center of attention these days. I mean, I could understand it in the theater; Lexie was going to be a professional performer someday. But lately she seemed to be performing all the time, even when she wasn't onstage.

At lunch, in the common room, even in the study hall, she hammed around all the time, talking loudly, showing off. Then she started bossing around everyone in the show. Miss Jonas didn't seem to mind. She was amused by Lexie, amazed by her energy and enthusiasm. Lexie could do no wrong. I guess that got me mad, too, because Lexie was getting the approval of *everyone* in the whole school.

Well, not everyone. Not Miggin. Miggin was in the chorus. Being a cheerleader, she was good at the dance numbers. She got tired of Lexie's always telling the dancers what to do. She thought Lexie was a busybody, should stick to being the Incomparable Rosalie and forget telling everybody else what to do. Especially me.

"Lexie bosses you around too much," Miggin said one day as we walked up to Senior House after rehearsal. We were tired. It was cold and dark. The smell of dinner in the kitchen was the only comfort.

"What?" I said, kicking a stone up the path.

Miggin shrugged. "Lexie bosses you around, Jinx. 'Get a chair for Marco, Jinx ... Hurry up with that staircase you're building ... Bring me a glass of water.' She's got you running around like her slave."

I pulled my coat closer to my body. "I'm ... those are things I'm *supposed* to do, Miggin. I don't mind."

Miggin stopped. Her blue eyes watched mine. "Jinx, you're the set designer, not a crew of ten. Let other people do some of the shitwork. It shouldn't always be you."

The fluorescent lights in study hall glowed ominously as we passed. "I should be studying."

"That's another thing." Miggin blew on her hands. "You spend so much time helping Lexie, you never study. She doesn't know you flunked the history midterm."

I winced. "I didn't flunk."

Miggin shrugged. "D minus. Sorry."

"That's better than flunking."

"Jinx..." Miggin slowed her steps as we approached Senior House. "I don't want to hurt your feelings. I just think Lexie might be taking advantage of you."

My face was hot and I felt the tears building. It was true, some of it, what Miggin said. Lexie did have me running around a lot. But I enjoyed it, didn't I? That was part of the fun, part of putting on a show, part of being in love. Maybe sometimes it was a drag — sometimes I said yes to Lexie when I wanted to say no. But most times, it was okay. "Miggin," I said finally, "I like the Music Club people. I like the theater."

Miggin opened the door for me. We walked to our room in silence.

"You've got a crush on Lexie, Tuckwell," she called from the bathroom.

"What?" The word *crush* made my hands sweat.

"You've got a crush." She came into the room holding a sneaker in one hand, shoe polish in the other. There was a basketball game tomorrow, and her sneakers had to be white.

"Why do you say that?" I said nervously. Miggin frowned. "You eat lunch with her. You talk about her, you follow her around like a puppy, you—"

"Miggin..."

"The whole *school* knows it. It's obvious." She dabbed polish onto her sneaker. I stared at her, terrified. How much did the *whole* school know? Did they know about the oak tree? Did they know that we'd touched?

Miggin sat down on my bed. "I don't care if you have a crush on her. Half the cast of *Carnival* has a crush on Lexie."

I sat leafing through my Ancient History notes. Athens, Rome, Antioch, Carthage... "Do they?" I said casually.

"Sure." Miggin wiped her shoe with a Kleenex.

"Who does?" I said, still cool.

Miggin unbuttoned her blouse. "Well, in addition to half the chorus, I would say that Laura Carr has gone berserk over Lexie."

"Laura Carr?" Beautiful Laura Carr. Tall, dark, silky, with boyfriends at every Ivy League college.

"Everyone knows about that one, Jinx. That's why Laura's been wearing a red carnation on her blazer. Lexie gave it to her."

"You mean that artificial thing?"

"Yes, idiot." Miggin stood up. "Jinx, all you think about these days is Lexie and the show. Do you know there's a whole world outside Huntington Hill? People are starving; crazy people go around with guns; there's a war in Southeast Asia..."

"Miggin..."

"Jinx, I don't mean to lecture you, but you used to care about other things, about injustice and suffering. Most people would love it if the only thing they had to worry about was a silly crush." Miggin turned. "Anyway, the point is, I miss you, Tuck. I never see you anymore. I wanted to know if you'd eat lunch with me at Rexall on Saturday."

"What?"

Miggin sat down beside me. "Are you listening? I said I'll take you to Rexall for lunch Saturday."

"I'm supposed to work on the puppet theater," I said, dazed. "Lexie wants it by Tuesday..."

Miggin slammed down her books. "That's what I mean. All you can say anymore is 'Lexie this, Lexie that.' You and your stupid cr—"

"I'll go!" I yelled, before she could finish the word. "I'd love to go, Miggin. It'll be good."

We walked to study hall. I was a mess.

The next morning, Lexie passed me a note between French and English. Her face was flushed, eyes bright. I took the note quickly and hurried on, pushing through the crowded hall to my next class. "Let's eat at Rexall tomorrow," said the note. When it rains, it pours.

I passed her a note between History and Biology. "I can't," it said. "I'm going with Miggin."

At recess, Lexie glared at me on the porch of Century House, where she stood, eating a stack of graham crackers.

"You said you'd work on the puppet theater Saturday," she sputtered. The crumbs stuck to her mouth.

I shrugged and looked at the Lower School kids tear around their playground. The day was cold, the February sun shining weakly through the clouds. Behind Lexie, I saw Jonas pass by, wave to us, and open the door of the faculty lounge. Lexie, following my eyes, turned and flashed Jonas a smile.

"Idiot teacher," she muttered, when Jonas was gone.

"Don't smile at Jonas if you don't like her," I said.

Lexie looked at me, surprised. "Is Goody Two Shoes coming to the rescue of her beloved teacher?"

"Lexie..."

Lexie hurried down the steps of Century. I followed after her, thinking of Miggin's words: "like a puppy."

"Why are you going to Rexall with Miggin?" Lexie looked ahead of her.

"She's upset because we never do things together."

Lexie brushed off her blazer. "What *things* does Miggin have in mind?"

"Lexie, don't be silly."

"Oh, Jinx, don't be silly," mimicked Lexie.

I took a deep breath. We were starting again.

"Miggin and I are roommates," I said as we climbed the stairs and walked down the hall to Lexie's room. "We haven't had lunch together since the show started."

Lexie riffled through her desk. Her room was a mess — books and clothes everywhere. "Can I come?"

"What?"

"I'll join you." She stood up. "I found my notebook. Let's go." We walked quickly out of Senior House.

"Well," she said, turning toward study hall. "Can I join you?"

I swallowed. "I think the idea is for just the two of us to do something together."

"That means I won't see you all weekend," she said, looking away.

"No, it doesn't. We've got the basketball game today." Lexie and I loved going to basketball games together, because we could sit beside each other and yell and cheer and hug whenever Huntington Hill scored.

"Laura and I are rehearsing a scene at three."

I stared at her. "There aren't any rehearsals today."

Lexie pulled a twig off the box bush by the path. "It's ... it's a private rehearsal. We're ... going over some lines."

I could feel the deep end rising, higher, up to my chin, up to my lips, to my mouth. "Poor, overworked starlet," I said as Lexie started to leave.

She turned and calmly gave me the finger. "Screw you," she said softly.

That night, after study hall, Lexie and I sat on the piano bench in the common room. The noise in the room had not yet reached its full Friday night level. Oakie had a new album by the Rolling Stones and she'd scheduled a sock hop at nine. It was eight-thirty now, and Lexie, in her blue-and-white Moroccan caftan, was waiting for it to begin. Girls drifted in and out, eating ice cream they scooped from half-gallon tubs in the kitchen.

"How was the game?" said Lexie, indifferently playing a chord on the piano.

"Okay," I said. Why am I with her again? I thought. Why do I keep coming back? Why don't I leave her alone?

Lexie kicked off her rubber flip-flops. "Laura's parents are getting divorced. She's not learning her lines."

"Are you rehearsing lines or giving her marriage counseling?"

Lexie took her hands from the keys and looked at me. In the far corner of the room, Elizabeth Knight, reading *Vogue* on the couch, glanced up at us. Lexie's eyes narrowed.

"Jinx, it's not funny. Laura's upset. You make a joke of everything."

I moved uncomfortably on the bench. Lexie was right, I guess. But I was mad at Laura Carr and that fake red carnation. "Play a song from *Carnival*," I said finally.

Lexie softened. "Which one?"

"'It Was Always You.'"

Lexie sat up straight, pulled the bench closer, and played the introduction slowly. Her music, clear and confident, drew others to the piano.

"*It was always, always you,*" began Lexie sweetly. Her knee moved close to mine.

> *Always, always you.*
> *Oh, my eyes do wander,*
> *To and fro and yonder,*
> *Still my heart's affection,*
> *Always beats in one direction.*

As she sang, I could feel the tingling in my legs and arms and a light feeling in my head like a helium balloon. Oakie stood behind us now, humming with Lexie, and several underclassmen stopped to listen too.

> *Every beat for you my sweet,*
> *All the love my beating heart can give.*
> *It shocks me so, you didn't know,*
> *That it was always you.*

Lexie looked at me, her eyes warm, cheeks pink, lips full. I wanted to touch her. I wanted the tension between us to stop.

"It's such a beautiful song," I said.

Lexie laughed. "It's not so beautiful onstage."

"What?"

Lexie stretched, her arm brushing the back of my neck. "That's the scene where Marco locks Rosalie in a box. It's a magic trick. She's locked in there and every

167

time he says he loves her, he's actually sticking knives in her."

I laughed. "That sounds profound. I think there's something to be learned from that."

"Good," said Lexie. "You can start learning right away because we need the box for rehearsal next week. Maybe you can start on it tomorrow. We should..."

I hesitated. People were listening. "I can't work on it tomorrow, remember? I'm going to Huntington."

Lexie twisted abruptly around toward the piano and began to play. It was happening again. Why couldn't things ever be peaceful with us?

"*You would cheat your mother,*" sang Lexie,

> *In your heart a thief dear,*
> *Still I want no other,*
> *Doctor, lawyer, Indian Chief, dear.*

"Maybe Sunday I can work on the trunk."
Lexie shrugged.

> *Life is strange,*
> *A girl can change,*
> *The years may find me*
> *Basking in the sun.*
> *But all the same,*
> *I'll dress for rain.*
> *It was always you.*

Everyone in the room clapped when Lexie stopped.
"Bravo," they yelled. "More, more!"
Lexie stood up and curtsied coyly.
"Play more."
"Play 'Love Makes the World Go 'Round.'"
Lexie laughed. "Time for an ice cream break. I can't sing without ice cream." She headed toward the kitchen, then stopped as Laura Carr, dressed in jeans and a Venetian gondolier's shirt, entered the room. Laura's

long black hair was twisted in a bun, her eyes dark and bright.

Laura looked at Lexie. "I heard you playing. Shall we sing our duet?"

"But, of course, my darlink Marco," smiled Lexie, in her French accent. She looked at the piano bench where I was sitting. "Mademoiselle Tuckwell," she said brusquely, *"levez-vous, toute de suite."* Laura settled down beside Lexie. I bounded upstairs and out of the common room. I could hear their voices, soprano and alto, soft and enchanting. Then I heard Lexie's laughter and the audience applause.

By Monday, I had almost finished the sketches for the knife box and the puppet theater. I had worked all day Sunday and in an hour it would be done. The studio door opened suddenly and Elizabeth Knight walked in. Elizabeth and I never spoke anymore. She worked in her corner; I worked in mine. Today, she was unexpectedly friendly.

"What are you making?" She leaned over the bench where I sat. She must have eaten peanut butter and jelly for lunch. I could smell the peanuts on her breath.

"The scale's wrong on this," she said, pointing to the drawing of the stage.

I sighed. "I can't change it again. Lexie's coming to look at it this afternoon."

Elizabeth straightened up and adjusted her beret. "When's she coming? I'll be sure not to be here."

I looked up. "Soon."

Elizabeth pulled out her easel and began to paint. "How do you like being a star?" she said abruptly.

"What?" She was squinting at her canvas.

"You're a star. You're Lexie's protégée."

I shrugged. If I stayed casual, maybe she'd leave me alone. "If I'm a star, where's my fan club?"

"Isn't Lexie enough?" Her voice was icy.

I turned on the radio by the sink and didn't answer. For an hour we worked in silence. When I'd finished, I looked at the clock.

"Where's Lexie?" said Elizabeth. "I thought she was coming soon."

"I thought so." My voice was small. "I guess she's in rehearsal now."

Elizabeth gloated. "You've been stood up."

"I guess so." I put away my supplies and stuffed the sketches in an envelope.

Elizabeth watched me. "Not very considerate of her. You worked all weekend to get the sketches ready."

I looked at my package. "Maybe I'll take them down to the theater."

"You don't have to ask *my* permission," said Elizabeth archly, as she rinsed her brushes in the sink.

The air had a stinky, putrid smell. For three days it had been warm — above freezing — and when that happened, strange smells seeped out of the ground near study hall. I walked slowly down to the theater trying not to breathe too deeply. I already had a headache. It had started in the studio when Elizabeth came in. Around some people, I tried not to breathe too deeply, as if their molecules would sneak into my body like poison.

I hadn't been feeling well for a while. Lexie was draining my energy. There was just no peace between us, just bickering and jealousy and bitchiness. Was she using Laura to *make* me jealous? Or did she have a crush on Laura? Maybe Laura was my replacement. Laura was certainly prettier than I, and she was popular with boys from Princeton and Dartmouth and Yale. So Laura was a natural for Lexie. Maybe I should just let the two of them carry on and be grateful that it was over with Lexie and me. If it was over, I wouldn't have to worry. I wouldn't feel so jealous. And I wouldn't be queer anymore. Being a queer was exhausting. It would be a good thing to get rid of. I'd just stop all this nervousness and self-consciousness.

Slowly, with a mushy feeling in the pit of my stomach, I opened the heavy door to the theater. A freshman, standing just inside the door, held her finger to her lips as I entered. Rehearsal was under way. On the stage, Paul, the Puppeteer, was telling Jacquot, his buddy, that he might leave the circus because nobody really liked him. Paul was upset because Lili had fallen for Marco, and Paul was secretly in love with Lili himself.

In the front row, Jonas watched intently, clipboard in her lap, hands in the pockets of her buckskin jacket. On either side of her were two freshmen, and just in front of them sat Dawson, back erect, at the piano. In the rows behind them, the chorus watched respectfully, while the crew tried to catch up on homework. In an aisle seat by the door sat Miggin, hair braided in pigtails, sneakers resting on the chair in front of her. She waved at me, patting the seat next to her.

"Where's Lexie?" I said, looking quickly around. The back of the theater was dark. They were trying out the new lights.

Miggin turned and pointed to the back of the theater. In the far left corner, underneath the lighting platform, sat Lexie and Laura, heads close together, deep in conversation. Lexie's hand was on Laura's shoulder. Laura's face looked pained, uncomfortable.

"They're having a lovers' quarrel," said Miggin softly.

"What?" The headache pounded in my forehead. Miggin's cinnamon smell drifted into my nose.

"Lexie claims Laura is blowing her lines. Laura claims Lexie's upstaging her."

On the stage, Paul began to sing.

Everybody hates me.
Everybody hates me...

"They've been rehearsing Laura's scene with Lili," continued Miggin. "When Marco invites Lili to join his act. I think Lexie's jealous."

Miss Jonas turned around and held her finger to her lips. "Shhh, girls."

"But that's not Laura's fault," I whispered. "That's how the play is written. Marco's *supposed* to fall for Lili."

Miggin shrugged. "A crush is a crush."

I sat back in my seat and watched rehearsal, trying not to think about Lexie and Laura sitting behind us. It's over, I thought. Lexie and I are over. Laura's replaced me.

"Okay," yelled Jonas, walking up the steps to the stage. "Cut! Stop! Ginny," she called to the lighting tech, "could we have the houselights?" Jonas squinted. "Where are Lexie and Laura?"

Everyone looked toward the back. Lexie and Laura stood up slowly. Whatever they'd been fighting over had been resolved. Lexie's arm was around Laura's waist. Laura was smiling.

As Lexie and Laura passed our seats, Miggin poked my arm. "Give her the sketches, Jinx."

I stood up. "You give them to her."

Miggin's smile disappeared. "Aren't you going to stay for my number?"

I shook my head. "I don't feel well. I feel weird." I could not get out of there fast enough.

That night I went up to Lexie's room. "It's over between us," I was going to tell her; "you have Laura as a friend now, and that's fine with me, because this whole thing is just too much of a strain. You have my blessings," I would tell her. "I'm dropping out of the competition."

But Lexie's door was closed. I lifted my arm to knock and heard Laura's voice inside. I turned away. I guess Lexie didn't need my blessings. She and Laura were thick as thieves.

The next day, I worked in the studio.

"Did Lexie like your sketches?" said Elizabeth, hanging over me. Her breath smelled of peanuts again.

"Why do you always smell like peanuts?" I said.

"Screw you."

We worked in silence.

"Did Lexie like your sketches?" she asked again, without looking up.

"I don't know."

"Hasn't she seen them?" Elizabeth's dark eyebrows rose unnaturally high.

"I don't know."

"You don't know?"

"I don't know," I said. "But why don't you mind your own business? Why don't you worry about something important? Worry about the B-52s dropping bombs on North Vietnam. Send a telegram to Queen Elizabeth and tell her you're sorry Winston Churchill died. Leave *me* alone." I picked up my coat and slammed out.

It was two-fifteen. Rehearsal wasn't till three. I had told Miggin I'd be there to see her dance number, but I felt sick and crazy and I just wanted to lie down on my bed and go to sleep. The room was empty, so I pulled down the shades, took off my uniform, lay down in my slip, and spread the quilt over me. If I just lay there and took deep breaths, maybe I would feel all right, not so nervous and afraid. I closed my eyes.

The door opened slowly. "Jesus, it's dark in here." Lexie stood in her jeans and work shirt. Her hair was pulled back in a stubby ponytail.

"What are you doing, Jinx?"

"I'm sleeping," I said in a monotone.

She laughed and sat down beside me, her legs against my arms. "It's two-fifteen. You can't be sleeping."

"I'm sleeping," I repeated.

Lexie put her hand on my forehead. "You don't have a fever," she said.

"I'm not sick," I said in my monotone.

Lexie sat up and looked brightly at me. "I came to tell you the sketches look great. Are you really going to use those colors?"

"If you like them."

"I love them." For a moment, she was quiet. I could hear her breathing and feel her legs against me. "God, you look cute in there. Can I cuddle up with you?"

I opened my eyes. "No."

"Jesus, you're touchy today."

I stared at the ceiling. "It's over," I said in my monotone.

Lexie tucked her feet under the quilt. "*What* is?"

"Our friendship." I could hear the Beatles far off in someone's room. The floorboards began to shake as some smart aleck upstairs started jumping rope.

Lexie touched my shoulder. "What are you talking about?"

Go ahead, I thought. Go ahead. You've done it now. Keep going.

"You have a crush on Laura. I think that's fine. But our friendship is over."

"Jinx, what's wrong with you?" Her hands gripped my shoulders. "Look at me. Stop talking in that monotone."

"I'm not talking in a monotone," I said in my monotone.

"Oh, for Christ's sake." Lexie leaned closer. "What do you mean, 'our friendship is over'?"

"You have a crush on Laura," I said slowly.

Lexie stood up and walked to my desk. "I won't answer you till you stop talking like a robot." She looked at Miggin's bureau. "Jesus, Miggin has more lipsticks than I do."

Lexie turned back to the bed and stroked my hair. Don't let her con you, I thought to myself. Don't let her change your mind.

"*Do* you have a crush on Laura?" I repeated, finally meeting her eyes.

Lexie looked at me teasingly. "Laura Carr is very sexy."

My feet and hands went cold. "I can't help it if I'm not sexy," I said in my monotone.

"Jinx! What is *wrong* with you today? You're crazy. What have I done to deserve this?" She looked at me quizzically.

"You never came to see the sketches and then when I came to the theater you were falling all over Laura. I saw you."

Lexie had been staring at the quilt. She looked up. "Jinx, Laura Carr is screwing up the whole show. She can't learn her lines, and if she doesn't she'll ruin it for all of us. I've been trying to work with her. I love your sketches. I came to tell you that. Now you say our friendship is over. What's wrong with you?"

I felt cold and trapped and stupid. "You've got a crush on Laura. The whole school knows it. That's why she wears a red carnation."

Lexie stared at me. "Jinx..."

"It's true..."

"Jinx." She touched my shoulder. "Have I ever told you that I won't be your friend because you have a crush on Miggin?"

"Miggin?"

"Yes, Miggin."

"She's my roommate. I don't have a crush on Miggin."

"Well, she certainly has one on you."

I closed my eyes again. Miggin has a crush on me? What time is it? I thought. It must be time for rehearsal. It must be time for Lexie to go.

"Jinx?" Lexie shook me gently. Her voice was soft. I opened my eyes. "You hurt me when you talk this way. Don't be jealous of Laura. I love you." She paused. "How can I make you believe me?" She held her head in her hands, then sat up. "Spend the night with me tonight." Her hand touched my hair.

"What?"

Lexie looked quickly at the door. "Come up to my room tonight. After lights. Spend the night with me."

My brain felt disconnected from my body. The thought of staying all night with Lexie, of holding her close to me, of touching her shoulders, her breasts, the way we'd done in New York, made me feel dizzy.

"It's too dangerous," I whispered.

"I'll take the chance." Lexie's eyes were bright. "Come up when everyone's asleep."

"Suppose they catch us? What would they do, if they caught us together? In the same——"

Lexie stood up stiffly. "Jinx, I want you to come to my room tonight."

I felt crazy. "Lexie?"

"Jinx," she said slowly, holding the doorknob, "I would like you to sleep with me. I love you." She stared at the drawn shade, then turned to me. "Come to my room after lights. I want to hold you."

Lexie opened the door slowly. "I'm going to rehearsal now, Jinx," she said strangely. "Are you coming?"

I slid deeper under the quilt. "I feel funny. I feel like going to sleep."

"See you tonight." She closed the door behind her.

That night, before bed, I sat at my desk staring at my calendar. Miggin was washing clothes in the sink. In two and a half weeks was the show, then three days later, spring vacation began, and we'd hear from colleges, and then, in seven weeks, graduation. Time was running out. In June, Lexie would leave for New York and it would be over. It wouldn't be over just because of Laura; it would be over because of geography, because of time, because we would never be together the way we had been at school. We would never live in the same house and pass in the halls and write notes in class. We would never work again on a musical and eat lunches at Rexall and take walks by the pasture. It would just be over and we would be college students and that would be that. Crush or no crush, love or no love, we'd grow apart.

Miggin stood beside me, toothbrush moving against her teeth. "What's the matter?"

"What?" I looked at her red hair in the big rollers. Her mouth was full of white foam. Her wrapper hung off one shoulder. I would never see Miggin either. She'd be in California. Lexie said Miggin had a crush on me. Did that mean she felt for me what I felt for Lexie? I didn't want to think about it.

"You're weird tonight," said Miggin. "Far away or something."

"I'm okay."

"I thought you were coming to rehearsal. I looked for you." Miggin went back to the bathroom.

"I felt sick. I'm sorry I missed your number. I'll come soon. I promise."

Miggin turned. "I thought you said you felt okay."

"Oh, I do. I do, now," I said, standing up. "Really."

Miggin shook her head. "Did you hear we're bombing North Vietnam?"

"Yeah."

"Johnson wants Congress to give him more money for the war."

"Yeah."

"Is that what you're worried about?"

"No."

"Well, you should be."

I lay in the darkness listening to the night sounds of Senior House — the final rush of flushing toilets, the last spurts of steam in the radiators, Woodie's footsteps at the front door, bolting the lock and turning out the hall lights. Finally, there was only the rattle of the wind against the windowpanes and the occasional creaking of the floorboards. I looked at the clock — twelve forty-five. Would Lexie be asleep now?

It was a crazy idea she had. Me going up there in the middle of the night. Of course, it would be nice to touch Lexie, to hold on to her and feel her warm skin beneath her nightgown. But risk four years of obeying all those tiny, silly rules — rules about clean sneakers and skirt length and signing out — just because my hormones or something were messed up and I wanted Lexie — wanted her physically, the way men desire women and women desire men. Jesus. Walk up there in the middle of the night and get in bed with Lexie? I mean, at any moment, Woodie could come creeping in with her flashlight and kick us both out for being queer. It would be crazy.

Besides, it was over with Lexie, wasn't it? She wasn't my friend. She was Laura's friend. She had a crush on Laura. Tomorrow night she'd probably be up there with Laura doing the same thing. Laura was on her floor and wouldn't even have to climb a flight of stairs.

I looked at the clock. One-thirty. They must all be asleep by now. I read in an article on crime that the best time to steal is between two and four a.m., because people's sleep is deepest then. Maybe if I walked up slowly and carefully, avoiding the creaky steps, I could get there safely. Miggin was asleep. I looked over at her bed. She was asleep. If I got up slowly...

My heart was pounding now; my hands were damp. If I didn't do it now, Lexie would be gone forever. I would lose her to Laura and Philip and all those men she knew. Lose her to Bennington and show business and her moods. How often did such a strong attraction happen? It must be special. It must be worth taking a risk.

I swung my feet slowly onto the floor and glanced at Miggin. Had her breathing changed? Had she moved under the covers? I stood up. If I could get out the door without her hearing, I was safe. There were no other rooms on our hall. No rooms to pass till the second floor. And most people on the second floor slept with their doors shut.

In the darkness, I found my robe and slippers. I tiptoed toward the door.

"Jinx?" My heart jumped out of my skin.

"Are you awake?" said Miggin softly.

My knees trembled like leaves in the wind. "I'm going to the bathroom," I whispered.

Miggin turned over. "You okay?"

"Oh yeah, I'm fine."

I took off my robe and lay down. It was crazy to try.

The next morning Miggin looked at me curiously. "Did you get out of bed last night?"

I squinted at her; my eyes were puffy with fatigue. "I didn't sleep well. I had to go to the bathroom."

"Why were you wearing your robe?"

Jesus, I thought. She can see in the dark. "I don't know," I said. "It was cold."

IT WAS COLD THE NEXT DAY. THE CLOUDS WERE LOW and gray and full of snow. Lexie stood on the pathway to study hall. She held a notebook under one arm. The weight of her body rested on her right hip. Her hair was wild and strayed from her head like straw. She wore only her blazer. The collar of her uniform was unbuttoned, leaving her neck exposed to the cold.

"Where the hell have you been?" She glared at me, her lips purple from the cold, her eyes small.

I shivered. Something was wrong. "I forgot my history book. I need it for class."

Lexie moved closer. Her knee socks had fallen down her calves. Students walked by us toward study hall.

"You idiot," hissed Lexie. "They've got your notes."

I squinted at her. "What notes?"

Lexie nodded to Oakie, who was just closing the door to study hall. "Your notes to *me*. Your letters. Somebody found them and turned them in."

The blood drained from my face. "You mean..."

"We've got to get our stories straight, Jinx. I have to see Nicholson right after assembly. He wants to know everything."

I stared at her. Lexie frightened me. What she was saying frightened me. My fingers were frozen stumps. "I don't understand."

She gripped the lapel of my coat. "Idiot, they think we're queer. *Queer,* " she whispered. "What are you going to tell them?"

I rocked back on my feet. The door to study hall opened and the senior proctor waved at us. "Get in here

180

fast, you two," she called. "Assembly's about to start."

Lexie tightened her grip on my coat. "Tuckwell, tell them you had a crush on me. Tell them it was one-sided. Do you understand? I don't want anything to do with it."

I stared at Lexie. What was she saying?

"Tuckwell," she said, "we graduate in three fucking months. Don't blow it. Tell them it was a joke."

Suddenly we were surrounded by a swarm of children from the Lower School. They were waiting to enter assembly. Lexie yanked me up the steps to study hall.

"Lexie..."

"Shut up, Jinx."

We sat down in our seats, and seconds later Randolph Nicholson strode into the study hall, the faculty following behind him. With greater severity than usual, he announced the morning hymn.

"*A mighty fortress is our God,*" we sang, "*a bulwark never failing; our helper He, amid the flood of mortal ills prevailing.*"

I had to speak to Lexie. I had to find out what had happened. How could I talk to Nicholson without knowing what she would tell him, without knowing how much they knew? But after assembly, she disappeared into McAllister before I could stop her. Between Biology and English I looked for her in the hall where we usually passed. She wasn't there, either. Maybe she was still with Nicholson. My knees had been shaking ever since the morning. I kept my eyes on the floor between classes. How many people already knew? What were they thinking?

When Nicholson's secretary knocked on the door of Ancient History, I knew she was coming for me. It seemed appropriate that my summons came in that class, the class that I was failing. The secretary whispered to Mrs. Kelbow, then asked me to come with her. Miggin looked at me sympathetically.

"What is it?" she whispered.

I couldn't speak. My face was white, my eyes wild like a child's. This was it. This was the sentence. This was humiliation. This was what happened when you went off the deep end.

Nicholson did not look up when I entered. He was staring out the window, watching the first flakes of snow fall to the ground. His sleeves were rolled above his wrists, his tie was loose. A blue shadow darkened his jowls. Out by the entry road, Woodie, clipboard in hand, walked briskly toward the gym. He knew I was there, because he got up slowly, walked to the door, and closed it. Finally he returned to his desk, leaned back in his swivel chair, and faced me.

"Sit down, Jinx."

I sat by his desk. I could see the gray sky, the swirling specks of snow, the empty goal cages on the hockey field.

"Do you know why you're here, Jinx?" Nicky's small black eyes froze on me.

"No," I said softly. It was a long time since we'd had snow. It was December when it last snowed.

Nicholson raised his eyebrows. The crescents of sweat underneath his armpits were growing. "You don't know why you're here?"

"No," I said again, fixing my eyes on the little baseball trophy by his desk.

Nicholson leaned forward. "You've had us in quite a tailspin, Jinx. I spoke to Lexie this morning. Now I want *your* explanation."

A clock on the table behind him ticked quietly. Upstairs, I could hear chairs moving in the Biology classroom.

"Jinx," said Nicholson, opening the top drawer of his desk, "somewhat by accident a disturbing matter has come to my attention." He cleared his throat and waved a packet of letters, held together by two rubber bands. "These notes were found yesterday by a student and given to me. Do you recognize them?"

The snowflakes were moving wildly now, sucked up, then pushed down by the wind. I looked at the packet. I recognized my handwriting.

"They're mine," I said mechanically.

Nicholson slipped off the rubber bands and pulled a letter out of the pack. *"Chère Lexie, ma très chère amie. Quand je te vois au théâtre mes pensées sont seulement de toi."* Nicholson dropped the note on his desk as if it carried a contagious disease. "Jinx," he said, "these notes to Lexie Yves have, have some specific ... references and connotations. Do you write letters like this to all your friends?" He forced a smile.

I stared at him, afraid to move or breathe.

"I hope you don't, young lady, because I don't think they'd be appreciated. They were certainly not appreciated by Lexie." Nicholson pinched his nostrils and looked at me expectantly. What had Lexie said? How much had she denied?

"Jinx? Did you realize that Lexie found these letters upsetting?"

If I said yes, I would seem like an idiot for sending them. "I don't know. I ... No," I said slowly.

Nicholson walked to the window. The snow was coming down steadily now — larger flakes. He picked up his phone. "Mrs. Grant, I think we'll let the day students go home early. Looks like the snow's going to stick."

How I wished I were a day student now ... to go home, to get away from this place.

Nicholson turned back to me. "Jinx, the notes imply that you ... you felt a physical attraction for Lexie. Is that so?"

"Can I have a dime to call my lawyer?" I mumbled.

Nicholson scowled. "Jinx, this is not a laughing matter. Lexie tells me you had a crush on her, that you imagined ... you wished for a deeper relationship than actually existed. Is that correct?"

I felt as if I were floating away. How could I say anything without knowing what Lexie had said? "Lexie and I are friends."

Nicholson stuck his hands in his pockets and unconsciously jingled some coins. "Jinx," he began, "do you know what homosexuality is?"

I stared at him, then looked outside. A thin white layer was now sticking to the hard ground. Nicholson sat down beside me and put his arm around the back of my chair. I leaned forward.

"Jinx, do you know what homosexuality is?"

I looked down at the floor. "Love between two people of the same sex."

Nicholson coughed. "If that's all it were, Jinx, it wouldn't be a problem. It's more than love, Jinx. It involves ... physical, sexual ... *contact*." This time Nicholson looked out the window. I could smell his sweat and the bitter smell of cigarettes on his breath.

"Jinx, are you homosexual?"

My stomach slid down my legs.

"Have you sought *contact* with girls at this school? With Lexie?" Nicholson tapped the packet of notes on his desk. "An episode like this can disrupt the entire student body. It can damage school morale, school admissions, alumnae support..."

Endowments, I thought.

"It is not," he said, pacing the floor, "a matter I take lightly." He turned to me. "Is that clear?"

I nodded.

"Are you homosexual?"

"What did Lexie say?" I said finally. Lexie's opinion seemed to rate higher than mine.

He rubbed his hand over his beard. "Lexie didn't understand your intentions. She thought you were simply being affectionate. When she ... realized ... the nature of your interest, she became frightened. She has assured me that she was not involved ... in a *damaging* way."

Nicholson lit a cigarette and returned to the chair behind his desk. "I am certain that Lexie is *not* the kind of girl who would seek this sort of ... contact. Lexie is more physically precocious than her classmates, and her ... her attraction to ... to the opposite sex is unquestionable."

I stared at him. What did he know about Lexie's attraction to the opposite sex? What did he know about anything?

"Jinx," said Nicholson, opening a manila file, "I am sorry to have to say that we are putting you on probation immediately."

Bam.

"You will be grounded through the end of the year." He paused. "You will, of course, terminate any further correspondence with Lexie and curb your ... your fantasies regarding her." He leafed through the folder, then looked up. "Woodie and I both feel that you should begin treatment with the school psychologist right away. We have made you an appointment for this afternoon."

Woodie knows, I thought to myself. Woodie knows about the letters. The thought of her stern, scowling face reading my little fragmented notes to Lexie made me tremble.

Nicholson coughed. "The very, very delicate nature of this matter, Jinx, requires the most careful, quiet handling. We are no more eager to make this affair public than you are, Jinx. For your own good, and the school's, no one on the faculty or the student government will be told. The ... *official* reason for this disciplinary action is your failure to obtain the proper permission for your visit to Huntington last weekend."

"But I got permission."

Nicholson scowled. "Wouldn't you prefer that reason to the real one?"

My voice stuck in my throat. I felt I was falling out of the realm of gravity.

"I spoke to your parents this morning."

I looked up quickly. The snow pelted against the windows. My parents. My parents. What had he told them?

"They expect to hear from you immediately. In fact, I suggest you call them from Senior House as soon as you leave here." He paused. "Jinx, do you have any questions?"

I looked past him, at the frozen landscape. "Who turned the letters in?"

Nicholson coughed. "That matter is not open for discussion."

"How did she find them?" I continued. "Did she steal them?"

"Jinx, that's not the point." He was standing now. He wanted me out. He wanted me to leave. "I can assure you that no one in the school besides you and a handful of others, know about the matter. The girl who turned them in did it in the best interest of the school."

Nicholson extended his hand. "We want you to recover quickly, Jinx. If you think you might ... if you think another crush is developing, then you'll speak to me or Miss Woodruff. Do you understand?" I walked to the door. "Today at one, Jinx. Dr. Philpot's office. In the infirmary."

I DIDN'T GO BACK TO CLASS. I WALKED ALONG THE path to Senior House, my feet slipping on the thin layer of new snow. Were the eyes of the school following me? Did they know? Nicky said only a few people knew about the letters, but whoever turned them in could have talked to someone and passed the word on. Jinx is queer, they were thinking. There was always something odd about her, something strange. So *that* is her secret. Tuckwell is a homo. It was dangerous to be a homo — disruptive, Nicholson had said. It was so dangerous he had invented a lie to cover it up.

I pulled open the door to Senior House and walked quietly back to our room. I didn't want to run into Woodie; I didn't want to see anyone. What had Lexie said? Had she used me to save herself? Had she denied having any affection for me? Who hated us enough to turn the letters in? Who would have sneaked through Lexie's bureau? I thought of the strange expression on Elizabeth's face the other day in the studio. Then of Laura Carr — Laura Carr and Lexie walking arm in arm in the theater. But would she really want to hurt me that badly?

The shoebox on the top shelf was still there and Lexie's letters to me were in it. Later, I would have to destroy them, get rid of them — stick them in a paper bag and throw them in the huge green garbage bin by the dining room. No one would look for love letters there. By tomorrow they would be deep in the bowels of a garbage truck. At least Lexie would be safe.

It was strange to make a call on the pay phone when the dorm was so empty, when the only sounds were the hum of the huge furnace and the wind whirling snow against the windows. There were no phonographs, no shrieks of laughter, no lines of people waiting to use the phone. Did the house have ears? Was it listening to my voice? Was there someone, studying in her room nearby, listening as I dialed my folks in Washington?

My mother answered. Her voice was worried. She knew. She'd been waiting for my call.

"Will you accept a collect call from Jinx?" said an operator with a twangy Virginia accent.

The tension in Mother's voice made me feel sleepy. "Jinx, are you all right?" I looked down the long hall at the rooms opening off either side. Outside, students moved quickly along the paths. The bell had rung; they were changing classes. For them, it was just another day, different only because it was snowing.

"I'm okay," I said finally. "Did Nicholson call you?"

Mother's southern accent was comforting, familiar. "We spoke to him this morning. What happened?"

Downstairs, I heard the front door open, but the footsteps faded off toward the common room. I spoke softly. The tears, which hadn't come before, now choked my throat. "They think I'm homosexual. I'm on probation."

There was a silence. When Mother spoke, her voice was calm. "Wait a minute, let me call Daddy."

The snow was sticking to the trees by the driveway. The school looked gray, unearthly — like the moon or outer space.

My father's voice was artificially cheerful. "Hello there, Jinx. How are you?"

"I..." The tears, the months of fear...

"We're very concerned about what's happened."

"Fred," Mother snapped, "let's find out what *has* happened first. Jinx, Nicky mentioned some letters."

I could see them in the house in Georgetown. My father was speaking from his study, surrounded by his books, comforted by their seasoned leather bindings, by his diplomas and awards and prizes; their presence reassured him, certified his worth and importance in the world. Mother was in the kitchen, standing by the wall phone, tracing and retracing the letters of Nicholson's name with a stubby golf pencil left from summer vacation.

"I had ... a ... a crush on Lexie. We wrote these notes."

"What kind of notes?" Mother's voice was tight.

I glanced down the long hallway. No one had come in, no one had gone out. "They were just little notes, sort of silly, things that you write when you have a crush."

"Are you getting enough sleep, Jinx?" said my father.

"Fred, let her finish." My mother would yell at him when the call was over.

"Someone found the notes in Lexie's room," I said. "They turned them in and Nicky says I'm queer."

"Is Lexie on probation too?" Mother asked cautiously.

I thought of Lexie, sitting in Nicky's office, arguing her way out of the crush. "No," I said. "She's not in trouble."

"Why not?" Mother sounded cool.

My father cleared his throat. "Jinx, would you like to come home this weekend? Is there something—"

"Jinx," interrupted Mother. She would get to the point now. "I think you're much too serious for your age. You need to have more fun, to relax. I think being a debutante will be great for you. You'll have parties to go to..."

"Helen," began my father, "perhaps we should take it one step at a time. Jinx is upset..."

"Well, of course she's upset. She's been accused of something she never did."

"Mother..."

"She's been put on probation and given the brunt of the punishment. I never thought Lexie Yves was dependable. There's something too grown-up about her. She's too sophisticated for Jinx. Too..."

Father said, "Mr. Nicholson mentioned the school psychologist. When do you see him?"

"This afternoon." I could see Dr. Philpot's tiny office in the infirmary.

"Jinx." Mother must have been pacing the kitchen floor now. "I think you should come home this weekend. We'll talk things over. I'll fix roast beef and you'll relax. Fred, do you have the train schedule at your desk? What time—"

"Mother, I'm on probation. I can't take weekends. Not for the rest of the year."

"Well, we'll come see you. We'll take you to dinner. We—"

"No, Ma, really. I'll be okay."

"Jinx—" Mother's voice cracked — "I think Mr. Nicholson has handled the whole thing very badly. He's overreacting. Girls in high school get crushes. It's normal. You haven't done anything wrong. You're just a child. You didn't know." Her face must be red now; she would cry when she hung up. "I've never liked the man; he's got no gumption, no—"

"Are you sure you don't want us to come see you?"

"No, Daddy. It's okay."

"Helen," said my father, "I'm going to get off now. Jinxie, we ... love you..." I could feel the tears.

"Fred, I don't see why you have to rush when Jinx is going through a difficult time. Can't you slow down long enough to talk to your own daughter?"

"Ma," I said, "I've got to go to class."

"Well, Jinx..." She paused. "We love you. We want you to be happy. We'd do anything..."

"I better go. I'm..." I stopped. "I'm sorry about all this. I know it's embarrassing. Maybe Grandmother—"

"Grandmother will never know. No one will ever know. You've done nothing wrong," whispered Mother.

When I put down the phone, the tears began.

Where they found Dr. Philpot, I don't know. He was six feet tall and weighed about three hundred and fifty pounds. He was the palest, fattest man I have ever seen. He always wore a gray suit, a gray tie, and small rimless glasses that left two red marks on either side of his nose. I had been to him once in tenth grade when the whole class had to take this personality test to show if you were crazy. Only one person had to go back to him for a follow-up — Marsi Jackson — and everyone already knew Marsi Jackson was crazy. One day she had just started to limp when there was nothing wrong with her, and she was always giggling at things that weren't funny.

Dr. Philpot's office was on the second floor of Clayton, in the infirmary, which was the worst place to go when you were sick because the smell made you feel sicker — a combination of mentholated vaporizers, alcohol, and rubber. When I knocked on the door, Mrs. McDune, the white-haired, pink-skinned nurse, smiled, and, after tucking her handkerchief under the sleeve of her white uniform, she escorted me to Dr. Philpot's windowless, pine-paneled cubicle, recently decorated with three Swissair posters and a Huntington Hill banner placed at a jaunty angle just above Dr. Philpot's head.

Dr. Philpot was drinking coffee from a Styrofoam cup and eating a jelly doughnut. He sat up, pushed his glasses up on his nose, pointed to a wooden chair beside his desk, and shook my hand.

"My, your hand's cold, Jean," he said, looking curiously at me. "Perhaps we're a little nervous."

I stared at him. I wanted to get it over with. I wanted it all to be over.

"We needn't feel nervous, dear," he said, tapping on the pine paneling. "What we say here won't go beyond these walls." He looked down at the file in front of him and cleared his throat.

"Well, now, let's see, Jean, I saw you once in 1963 when you took the TAT. You..." He paused. "You had a fairly typical score." He glanced up at me, his pale eyes examining my face. Was he looking to see if he could *see* it, see the queer blood?

"You've been put on probation over a matter of some letters to Alexis Yves." He opened another file, Lexie's, I guess. "Now, she's the very *pretty* girl, isn't she? She was in the show you girls put on last year?"

"I guess." There were lots of *pretty* girls in that show.

"Very pretty girl indeed. And very talented." He clucked admiringly at Lexie's record. "Very, very bright." He looked at me and smiled. I held tight to the arms of the wooden chair.

"Now, Jean, Mr. Nicholson is concerned about your rather strong affection for Alexis."

I stared at him. He smiled.

"Once again, Jean, let me remind you that what we say here won't go beyond these walls." I didn't know what he was going to say, but I wasn't planning to say anything that mattered beyond these walls.

"Now, Jean, would you say you had a pretty deep attachment to Alexis?" He looked at me encouragingly. "I can see it would be easy to *admire* someone so bright and attractive."

My face felt hot. I focused on the cold, snowcapped peaks of Zermatt on the wall poster behind him. Still, tears began to roll silently down my cheeks. Dr. Philpot pushed a box of Kleenex toward me.

"Go ahead, Jean," he said. "Have a cry."

I looked down at the floor.

"Jean, I know this isn't easy to discuss." His voice was tightening. "The important thing is for us to feel comfortable here." He was waiting for the confession.

"You don't *have* to say anything you don't wish to, Jean. But I think, frankly, if you *can* talk about it, it's in your own best interest to do so." He tapped a pencil on his blotter. "I should tell you that Mr. Nicholson has requested a complete psychological profile be sent to the colleges you've applied to."

I looked up at him. "He's going to tell the colleges?"

Dr. Philpot smiled, pleased to be getting a reaction. "You've no reason to be frightened. It's ... it's a formality. I'm sure we can give you a very good report. You've never had disciplinary action before, have you?"

I paused. Downstairs, the door to the infirmary slammed and heavy feet plodded up the stairs. "No," I said.

"Now, Jean, I would like to know whether there was any physical ... involvement between the two of you. And what *kind* of involvement was it?" He smiled. "Was it kissing, holding hands, something more?"

I looked him in the eyes. They were going to tell art school that I was kissing Lexie? I took a deep breath. "I've never had physical contact with Lexie."

Dr. Philpot nodded approvingly. "We're *sure* about that?"

"Yes."

"Was it ... was it what you girls call a 'crush,' or was it something *different?*" He leaned back in his swivel chair, which squeaked unexpectedly, like a hurt animal. He reddened. "Awful noise, isn't it? Was it a crush?" he repeated, when he'd collected himself.

He seemed to think it was okay if it was a crush. He seemed to want me to say it was a crush.

"It was a crush," I said.

He looked at me closely. "And there was no physical involvement?"

I stared at the gondola car suspended in the air over Zermatt. "No."

"Good," he said, scribbling something in my file. "Now..." He looked up and took a brown cough drop from a box in his pocket. "Have one? Jean," he said, sucking the cough drop loudly, "there's something that's troubling me." He smiled. "'Jinx' is your nickname, is it not?"

"Yes."

"Does your *family* call you Jinx?"

"They ... that's where I got the name."

He nodded and cleared his throat. "And your chums and so forth call you Jinx?"

"Yes."

Dr. Philpot shook his head sadly. "Too bad." He leaned back in his chair. "Now, Jean — and I'm always going to call you Jean — how do you *feel* about your nickname?"

"What?"

Dr. Philpot's nose twitched, like a rabbit's. "Jean, I ask you this because I think it may bear upon your ... situation." He paused. "Does it ... has it ever occurred to you that *Jinx* is not a very positive, very *happy* name for a pretty young girl?"

"What?"

He leaned forward; little beads of sweat popped out of his forehead. "Jinx means a curse ... bad luck. It's ... rather a *negative* word, don't you think?"

I could feel the tears again. I had never thought about the name Jinx. It was just my name. What was he getting at? What did it have to do with anything?

"Jean is a very pretty name, I think. But Jinx" — he laughed nervously — "might be a burden for a pretty young girl. I wonder why our parents let us keep that nickname? I wonder why our parents don't call us Jean? Jean is a prettier, a more *feminine* name."

The tears were coming down again. "I don't feel well." Dr. Philpot pushed the Kleenex toward me. Suddenly, the lunch bell blared through the little room. I jumped up.

"Take your time, Jean," he said in a soothing voice. "We don't have to hurry."

I picked up my books. "I'm on probation. I might get kicked out if I'm late."

He stood up. "That's up to you, dear. I'm sure, under the circumstances, Mr. Nicholson would understand."

"Good-bye," I said. I hurried down the steps of the infirmary and banged out the door, a soggy Kleenex wadded in my hand.

A SILENCE SEEMED TO FALL ON THE DINING ROOM as I approached the sea of faces looking up from the rows of tables. I spotted Lexie. There was still a place at her table. But when she looked up at me, her face was blank and unrevealing.

"That seat's saved for Laura," she said quickly, turning to talk to her neighbor. "I told him," she babbled, "that I wouldn't go unless..." I stood, confused, scanning the room. I wanted to leave, to run out the side door, but I could get demerits for leaving the dining room before lunch was over.

"Jinx!" Miggin stood beside me and tugged my arm. "There's a seat at my table. Come on." There really wasn't a place, but Miggin found a chair and made everybody move over. They were so quiet that I guess they all knew I was on probation. But did they know why?

"Want some stewed apples?" asked Miggin cheerfully, passing me the bowl. "Alice," she said to the girl next to her, "did you hear Van Cliburn at the Civic Center?" She was diverting their attention. Slowly, conversations began again. But toward the end of the meal, Sophie James, a junior, looked up and said, "What happened, Jinx?" The table was suddenly quiet.

"Don't you think," started Miggin quickly, "that—"

"I'm on probation," I said.

"Jinx," Miggin continued, "don't you—"

"I forgot to sign out for Huntington last weekend. I didn't get the right permission form."

"Jeez," said Sophie, sympathetically. "That's rough. Just for not signing out?"

I nodded. A chorus of sympathetic sighs went around the table. Miggin looked at me strangely. She knew I'd gotten the right permission.

When lunch was over, I tried to find Lexie. She was gone.

Miggin closed the door of our room and sat cross-legged on her bed. Outside, the pasture was covered with snow; more flakes were still coming down.

"What's going on?" Miggin's mouth formed a quizzical smile. I sat on my own bed, back propped against the headboard; I pulled the quilt over me.

"Jinx, I *know* you signed out. I was *with* you."

I looked at Miggin's soft red hair and freckled face. The way she was sitting, it looked like Steve McQueen was about to jump off the poster behind her onto her head. She was such a kind, honest person; I didn't want to lie to her.

"I had a crush on Lexie."

Miggin's eyes narrowed. "So what?"

I took a breath. "I wrote Lexie these notes and somebody turned them in. They thought the letters were weird."

Miggin stared at me. "They were weird?"

I nodded.

"They put you on probation because you wrote weird letters?" Her eyes were wide, incredulous.

I could lose Miggin now. I could lose everyone. "They thought that Lexie and I had touched or something." I looked down at the patchwork quilt. "I ... they think I'm queer."

Miggin was quiet for a long time. She looked out at the snow.

"Is Lexie on probation?" she said at last.

"Nicky ... Nicky doesn't think Lexie's queer."

Miggin moved to my bed. I could smell her sweet soap. I waited for her loathing and disgust.

"Jinx, I'm sorry," she said softly. "I'm really sorry."

I looked at Miggin's eyes. She was crying. She put her face in her hands.

"I'm the one who's sorry, Miggin. Maybe you should get another roommate. You have a right to."

"Jinx, I don't want another roommate. I love you." She was crying harder. I put my hand on her shoulder. "Don't cry. It's okay.

"School will be over in two months," I said finally. "Then it'll seem funny."

"It's *not* funny," she whispered. "I hate this school," she said. "I hate this goddam school."

I would have cracked up if it hadn't been for Miggin. There was so much for me to do that last week before the play, and I needed her near me. She helped me make lists of things I had to do.

1. Check the pulley on the puppet theater.
2. Finish painting the wrought-iron rail on Dr. Schlegel's circus wagon.
3. Fix the bottom step of the staircase up to the circus platform.

Miggin wrote me out a schedule telling me when I had to be in the theater — full rehearsals Tuesday afternoon and Tuesday night; full dress rehearsal Wednesday afternoon and Wednesday night; ditto Thursday. Friday and Saturday nights, of course, were the performances. The following Wednesday was spring vacation.

In a way, the show made my scandal less important. My probation and the mystery surrounding it got swallowed up in the excitement of the play. It wasn't just the performers and crew; the whole school was looking forward to it. People were so caught up with the show that no one seemed to notice that I was in a state of shock. In fact, they didn't notice that Malcolm X had been slain or that the Reverend James Reeb, a white civil rights worker, was murdered in Selma by three white men as he left a black restaurant. "You want to know what it's like to be a *real* nigger," they said as they beat him to death.

I still hadn't talked to Lexie. She was always busy. On Tuesday night, the cast and crew gathered in the theater. Jonas and Lexie sat on the edge of the stage giving a last-minute pep talk. Jonas wore blue jeans instead of her shirtwaist dress, and, as always, her buckskin jacket. Lexie was in her work shirt, and a red bandanna. It had stopped snowing, but there were six inches on the ground, and the theater was cold and drafty. The houselights were on and the theater looked worn and shabby.

Emily Jonas talked about concentration and relaxation, while we watched her nervously, eager to start rehearsal. Then Lexie had her turn. The room was silent. She stood up, slowly, and squinted out at us. There were dark shadows under her eyes. Her bandanna concealed her wild, unmanaged hair. She paced the stage.

"Girls," she said, stopping just left of center, "we have three more days, and five more rehearsals to work on the show. Can you do it?" She stared silently at her audience. She was in a nasty mood. "You have three days to stop farting around and get this show together." She looked at Miggin, next to me, but she didn't look at me. I didn't exist anymore. "I don't think any of you wants the show to be an embarrassment. Do you? I want you to be *on time*, in your place at every rehearsal. I don't want anyone to study in the wings or joke around backstage. Do you understand?"

Lexie seated herself on the right side of the stage, a few feet from Jonas. "There's one particular group I want to speak to." Lexie looked at each of the seniors in the cast. "Seniors, I think we'd all like to be remembered by this school as a class who dared." Miggin looked at me and rolled her eyes. "I think we all want the class of 'sixty-five to be considered a *great* class. A class with talent and flair. Not a bunch of boring half-wits."

Jonas pulled Lexie's arm. "Lexie, I think that's——"

Lexie shook her off. "Do you want to be remembered as idiot slobs who were too scared to get up onstage and give a knockout performance?"

"Lexie, we're running out of time." Jonas looked at her watch. "I think——"

"Just a minute." Lexie stared down at us. "Some of you," she said, "are pretty good. Most of you stink——"

"Lexie..."

The audience laughed nervously.

"I want all of you, for the sake of 'sixty-five, to overcome your pitiful, dull natures and make this the best Music Club show in history. Do you *understand?*" Lexie walked off the stage. The audience was frozen.

"Places, please," said Jonas quietly. "Places, please, let's get started."

I found Lexie backstage, in the chorus's dressing room.

"I want to talk to you," I said, as she stood staring in the mirror.

"I can't talk now."

"You've got to." I moved closer.

"There's a show starting." She turned away. "I don't want to be seen with you."

I shivered. Laura Carr entered the dressing room, smiling.

"Lexie," she said, "I have a question about my entrance in the first scene."

"Make it snappy, darling. We're starting in five minutes." Lexie led her out of the dressing room.

I pushed open the stage door. Lexie turned. "You'll be at *all* the rehearsals, won't you, Jinx," she called. Then she turned back to Laura. "Now, what's your problem, honey?"

I sat down next to Jonas in the front row. She looked up from her clipboard.

"Shouldn't you be backstage?"

I shook my head. "Somebody else better do it."

Jonas looked at me curiously. "I want to talk to you after rehearsal."

It was ten p.m. Jonas and I sat in the front row of the empty theater. She touched my arm.

"How do you think it went?"

"Good," I said. "Good.

The theater was dark. I shivered. A pencil poked out from behind Jonas's ear. Her curly black hair was rumpled.

"Jinx, I'm sorry about what's happened. I'll understand if you can't crew."

I looked at her. What did she understand? What was she sorry about?

She looked down at her clipboard. "I'm very sorry you're on probation. I know you must be upset."

"I forgot to sign out," I said without inflection.

Jonas twisted the woolen cord of her shoulder bag. "Jinx, Mr. Nicholson told me about the letters."

"What?"

"He suggested I talk to you. I like you and because I'm directing the play and you and Lexie spend so much time here..."

"He said no one knew." My small voice. Who else had he told?

Jonas pulled a pack of cigarettes from her bag. She put one in her mouth, but didn't light it. You weren't supposed to smoke in the theater.

"Jinx, I told him I didn't approve of disciplinary action. I..." She looked sadly at me, her mouth twisting down at the corners. "I suggested psychological counseling, some kind of—"

"I'm getting psychological counseling. With Dr. Philpot." My feet were disconnecting from my legs.

Jonas frowned. "I'm sorry to hear that. I ... had suggested an outside therapist, someone not connected with the school. You need someone on the outside, someone to give you support, guidance."

"Like you're giving me now?"

Jonas was startled. "Jinx..." She struck a match, then blew it out. "Let's go outside. I want to smoke this."

The cold wind tossed the snow against the trees. We walked slowly toward Senior House.

"Jinx, I've always been very fond of you. Huntington Hill is a small school," she said, choosing each word carefully. "We all know each other's business." She stopped and looked at me; a floodlight from the parking lot lit her face. I walked on, feet squeaking on the snow.

"Jinx." She held my arm. "What can I do to help? I would like to help. I'm afraid I should have asked much sooner."

I looked at her. "Nicholson's sending a psychological report to Cooper Union and Parsons." Monotone.

Jonas smiled. "*I* could write the schools, Jinx. I'd be happy to tell them you were one of my best students, that whatever has happened should not affect your admission. Would you ... how would that be?"

"Fine." I let out a long breath.

Jonas squished her cigarette in the snow. "Listen, Jinx. I care a lot about you. So do a lot of others here. Do you understand? You are well liked." She glanced at her watch. "You'd better get to Senior House."

I opened the door slowly. Lexie sat at her desk, rollers in her hair. There were papers and books all over her room. Someone's radio blared rock and roll. And a farting contest was under way downstairs.

"Why won't you talk to me?" I said.

Lexie squinted. She stood up and closed the door. "You shouldn't be here. We shouldn't be seen together."

I stared at her. "*I'm* the one on probation."

Lexie riffled through a drawer. "Jinx, we've got a show in three days. I'm very busy. I'm exhausted. You may have noticed that I've got things to do."

I pushed some books off a chair and sat down. "*You* may have noticed *I've* been called a queer, put on probation, and sent to Dr. Philpot for the rest of the year. Nicholson's also writing a psychological *report* to the art schools."

Lexie looked at me for the first time since yesterday morning, when she'd told me. "He didn't mention that."

"I'm glad he's so comfortable talking to you, Lexie. What'd you tell Nicky? Why did you say the letters upset you?"

Lexie sat down on her bed, crunching a paper. "I did it for both of us," she said slowly.

"What?"

Lexie stood up. "Would you stop feeling sorry for yourself. At least you're still in school. You'll graduate in June like everybody else."

"Thanks."

"What was I supposed to say?" Her voice rose. She looked at the door. "Would you feel better if we'd both been kicked out? Jinx, I saved your ass."

"I don't see how."

"Oh, for Christ's sake." Lexie picked up a pencil and began to write on the paper she'd been sitting on.

"If you hadn't said the notes upset you, maybe he'd have dropped the whole thing." I moved to the bed. "Lexie, listen to me."

"You'd better go." She opened the door.

"Lexie..."

"The vice squad is probably watching. Get out, Jinx."

"Lexie." I was desperate. She was pulling away from me. She was leaving me, just dropping me, writing me off, after everything we'd been through. After the love and the closeness.

"Lexie, don't throw me out."

"Jinx..."

"Did you really lie to protect me?" I wanted to believe her. I wanted to believe that she'd protected me.

"Of course I did," she said quickly. "Why would I want to hurt you?"

"I don't know why."

"Well, I didn't want to hurt you."

Maybe I was being paranoid. Maybe everything she'd said, whatever she'd said, had been necessary. Lexie had a better sense of survival than I did. Her instincts in danger were more finely tuned. She did what she had to. She wouldn't hurt me intentionally. Her involvement was as deep as mine. Her feelings were just as strong.

"Jinx..." Her voice was cold.

"Lexie, stay with me in Washington over spring vacation," I said quickly. "We'll talk. We'll go sightseeing — to the Botanical Gardens. Have you ever seen the Botanical Gardens? They're beautiful."

Lexie sneered. "Your folks wouldn't let me in your house."

"They would, Lexie. They like you. Please…"

"They'll blame me, Tuckwell. I'm sure they think it's my fault." Was she reconsidering?

I reached for Lexie's hand. "Really, it's okay. They'll understand. Especially if I want it. Lexie—"

"Don't, Jinx." She pulled her hand away. "Really, I can't."

I felt the water, the deep, freezing water, rising up to my chin, splashing against my throat. She was finished with me.

"When will we talk? When can we be together?"

"We have two months after vacation," she said flatly. "I'd be uncomfortable at your parents'."

I looked at her in disbelief. Lexie had never been afraid to do anything she wanted to do. She would never give up something she wanted. "Lexie, I can't believe you're afraid. It's not like you."

"I'm not afraid," she said quietly. She was scribbling on her paper again.

"Then come. Please."

Lexie looked up and smiled. "Jinx, I'm going to Bermuda."

I stared at her. "With Eleanor?"

"With Laura."

Laura. Laura. The lights-out bell roared through the dorm. My knees were shaking. My hand was frozen on the doorknob.

"Can I tell you something, Jinx?"

"I've got to go," I said mechanically.

Lexie put her hands on my shoulders. "Jinx."

I stepped back.

"I know who turned in the letters."

"You what?"

"I know who turned the letters in," she repeated.

"Who?" I said hoarsely.

She squeezed me tighter. A strange smile appeared on her face. I opened the door. It was better not to hear. Just go to bed, sleep.

"Jinx," Lexie said flatly. "Maddy Hansen turned them in. She stole them from my desk."

I looked at her one last time and slammed the door. I was going crazy. I knew I was going crazy.

I SAT THROUGH BOTH SHOWS IN THE DRESSING ROOM backstage, helping people put on their costumes. I was supposed to be stage manager, but I just handed my list of scenes, set changes, and props to Ginny Turkington, who'd been doing it with me all along, and I stayed in the dressing room. There was no point in my trying to do anything else. I was a mess. At the last two rehearsals, I'd gotten panic spells, and I'd just blanked out while cold waves passed through me. Somebody would ask me for a prop — a whip, juggling balls, the puppets — and I'd just stare at them, unable to remember where anything was.

I just sat in the dressing room, like an old grandmother in her rocker, helping people with their costume changes. Occasionally, Emily Jonas would pop in to see how I was doing. I tapped my foot to the singing, listened to the songs I had heard so many times before, and imagined the scenes that went with them. Sometimes I thought about the letters, about Maddy Hansen turning them in. I wondered why she did it and why Lexie had pretended the crush was all my invention. I worried about art school and New York and my parents. I wondered why I always felt so weird and separate from everything.

After all the months of work, the show never really happened for me. Even if I'd watched it from out front, as Jonas had suggested, I wouldn't have seen it. I was numb. I was behind some kind of Gardol Shield, like the Colgate toothpaste ad; nothing reached me.

When it was over, they made all the crew come out and take a bow. I looked out at the audience in a daze;

I watched the cast to be sure I bowed when they did.

They said the show was a real success. They said Lexie was terrific as Rosalie, that she had almost stolen the show from Isabel and Laura. Laura, Miggin told me, was wonderful as Marco, in her tight black pants, black vest, and derby hat. The dance numbers were spectacular and the Friday night audience was so impressed that half of them came back Saturday. There was hardly room to breathe, the theater was so crowded. Everyone said the sets were the best they had ever seen in a Music Club show. They especially liked Schlegel's circus wagon and the puppet theater. On Saturday night there were twelve curtain calls, and behind stage, people were running around screaming and yelling and hugging each other.

I stayed in the dressing room until all of that was over and the theater was quiet, and the cast and crew had left for their party in Clayton. Then I smelled cinnamon.

"Jinx?" It was Miggin.

She stood in the doorway, her red hair still twisted behind her head. She wore her beret. "Are you okay, Jinx? Are you ready to go to the party?"

"Don't wait for me."

Miggin frowned. "Come on, idiot!"

She pulled me up and out and through the slush. The basement of Clayton was hung with crepe paper streamers — pink, yellow, and green — and someone's stereo was blaring music from *Carnival*. The cast sang along, gulping ginger ale and Cokes, eating the pretzels and chocolate cake Miss Jonas had provided.

I sat down on the couch by the wall. Someone put on the Beach Boys and everyone began to dance. I just sat. I didn't want to dance.

Emily Jonas sat beside me on the couch. Her face was radiant. She wore a fancy red dress and a gardenia corsage that the cast had given her.

"It's over, Jinx," she said, her voice exuberant.

"Yep."

"Funny, isn't it? We work for three months and after two nights, it's over." She tapped her foot to the music: *"The East Coast girls are hip, I really dig those styles they wear..."*

"I'm sort of crazy," I said.

"You need your vacation, Jinx. You need to be away. I'm worried about you." Jonas sat up. Laura and Lexie stood over us, smiling.

"Come on, dance, you two," laughed Lexie. She was wearing a black skirt and an emerald green sweater. Her eyes were dark with mascara and eye shadow. She was high from the show and the applause. She was a star. She tried to drag me from the couch. Laura pulled on Miss Jonas, who was giggling. "No, girls, please." But finally she got up.

Lexie leaned close to me. "Come on, Tuckwell. It's all over. You survived. We don't have much time left," she whispered.

I looked helplessly at Jonas, who was watching me from the dance floor.

"Jinx isn't feeling well, Lexie," she called.

"Oh, shit." Lexie dropped my arm. "Call off your dogs, Tuckwell. I'm not going to hurt you—"

"You okay, Tuck?" Miggin handed me a glass of ginger ale.

"I'm okay."

The crepe paper streamers shimmered as the music shook the room.

It was twelve midnight when Laura, Lexie, Miggin, and I walked up to Senior House, arms linked together in a chain. We all had special late passes because we were in the show. Lexie was still high. She wanted to sing and laugh and wake up the whole school. The cold air was beginning to wake me up.

Lexie stopped us all near McAllister. "Let's have a reunion this time next year. One year from today exactly. Wherever we are, we'll get together."

Miggin laughed. "I'll be in California if I get into Mills."

"Come anyway. We'll meet in New York, since Jinx will be in school there, and we can stay at Eleanor's. Right, Jinx?"

"I'll be living in New York?"

"Art school, dummy."

"I've applied to art school," I said slowly.

"God, what's wrong with you?" Lexie stared at me. "You should call those schools and tell them to come look at your sets before we take them down."

"My sets?"

"Jinx is tired," said Miggin quietly.

"Me, too," said Laura.

Lexie stopped, hands on hips. "Shit, what a group. We just set the world on fire and you're all tired."

"I've got to rest up for Bermuda," said Laura, scooping up some snow and throwing a snowball at Lexie's ass.

Lexie's laughter filled the night as she chased Laura back to Senior House.

Miggin had to leave the night before spring vacation began. It was the only time she could get a flight to Vail. Before she left, she packed my suitcase and wrote me a reminder list for the next day.

> Put suitcase on Century House porch at recess
> Get pocketbook and coat from room after classes
> Board bus for station at 2 p.m. in faculty parking
>   lot
> Be sure Woodie gives you your ticket
> At station, take southbound train for Washington
> Your parents will meet you in Washington

Lexie was seated on the bus. "I saved you a seat," she said as I walked by.

What did she want? Why did she keep coming back? I sat down.

"How was your second appointment with Herr Doktor?"

The big bus smelled of cigarettes. It was the kind of bus that took football fans to Steelers' games in Pittsburgh.

I looked at Lexie. "It was okay."

The bus rolled down the front driveway and turned onto the Huntington road. It was good to be going away from the school. I needed to be away. It was a gray day, but not as cold as it had been. Most of the snow had melted and now there were just dirty clumps of ice on the side of the road. I could smell Lexie's perfume.

"Christ, what a semester," she said, staring out the window. "There's the Holiday Inn," she said. "Remember that?"

I shivered. "Yeah."

"Just think, in two months we'll be out of school. I'll be in Easthampton, in the sun. And no more shitty rules." She looked quickly at me. "You can come visit. We'll get that white skin of yours all dark and tan."

Why did she still talk as if we were friends? Why did she pretend nothing had happened?

"I don't get tan. I burn and peel."

Lexie laughed. Then her smile disappeared. She stared out of the bus the rest of the trip. I listened to two sophomores talk about Princeton boys in Hobe Sound.

"S'long," I said to Lexie at the station. She was westbound, I was southbound.

"Take a good look at me," she called. "Next time you see me I'll be three shades darker and sexier than Sophia Loren." She blew me a kiss.

TWO WEEKS LATER THE CAB SWISHED THROUGH the puddles in the school driveway like a Chris Craft riding the waves. It was still raining hard. Rain had collected on the tennis courts; the lower corner of the hockey field looked like a frog pond. The ground was so wet that my high heels sank deep into the grass. I lugged my suitcase up to Senior House. More rain, spurting out of a broken gutter, splashed down over the door. The white clapboard was slick and shiny as fresh paint.

The dorm was quiet. Nobody was back. Our room was the same, but hot. The furnace must have been set for winter, and the radiators gurgled and hissed and steamed as if it were an old people's home. I turned on Miggin's radio and unpacked. It was going to be okay, I told myself. In less than two months I'd be out and finished, and I'd never have to return to this sad, bare room again. Outside, in the pasture, rain pelted the high grass and the wind whistled through it like a giant hair dryer.

Miggin's face was wet and radiant when she came in from the airport. It was already dark — the rain had delayed her flight. She looked like a Raggedy Ann doll. "Guess what?"

"Your father bought you a giraffe?"

Miggin laughed and threw her arms around me. "I got into Mills."

"That's terrific." We hugged and danced around the room. "Of course, you'll turn into a surfer and you'll never come back east again."

"Oh, shut up." She tore open her suitcase looking for the acceptance letter. "Who's back? Who shall we tell first?" She waved the letter in her hand. "Come on," she said, and burst through the door.

The common room was a madhouse. A lot of people had heard from colleges over spring vacation and they were waving acceptance letters like one-hundred-dollar bills. On one wall of the room was a bulletin board — one side for acceptance letters, one for rejections. Posting rejections made the whole college thing into sort of a joke. I sighed. I wouldn't hear from art school till the end of April.

In one corner of the room, a bunch of people were gathered around the couch laughing. Lexie and Laura sat in the center, like royalty. Lexie was beautiful — her face dark, cheeks pink from the sun. She looked like a cross between Sophia Loren and Elizabeth Taylor. Laura was more like Rudolph Valentino in her panama hat and white slacks. Her hair was pulled off her face, and her eyes were smoky and watchful. They were telling stories about their trip to Bermuda. Lexie gesticulated wildly.

"So, the tall one," she said, brushing her hair off her face, "went with Laura. I didn't mind, because, dear girls, the shorter one was by *far* the more attractive of the two — *totally* suave. A junior from Princeton." Oakie giggled enthusiastically while the others fired questions.

"Was he fast?"

"How far did you go?"

"Did he invite you to Princeton?"

Why did she always have to be the center of attention? Why did she always have to talk about her conquests? How did I fit into her crazy, fast world?

Lexie stood on the couch. "Darlings, wait. Don't be impatient." She shook her chest suggestively. "You'll get the details, but let's not be crude about it."

"I bet you didn't do anything," yelled Oakie, slapping her knee.

"Please, dear," said Lexie, puckering her lips. "Don't damage my reputation. I'll tell all in a minute."

Miggin broke in and waved her letter. "Guess what, everybody? I got into Mills!" A cry of approval went up. Miggin was now the center of attention. Lexie jumped down off the couch.

"How are you, Tuckwell?" She winked. "How was your vacation?" She squeezed my arm. I could smell her perfume; I could feel the heat from her body.

"I spent most of it in a doctor's office."

Lexie rolled her eyes. "Another one?"

I shrugged. "How was Bermuda?"

Lexie glanced at Laura, who sat silently on the couch listening to Miggin. "She can be a bitch," whispered Lexie. "She's so gorgeous she treats everybody like shit. She didn't like the guy she met, so she took mine."

I shrugged. "Too bad."

"I was so glad when she got sick." Lexie smirked.

I looked at Laura. She didn't look sick. She looked tan and healthy. Suddenly the room was quiet. Lexie looked around quickly and dropped my arm.

"Now, girls," she said, returning to the couch, "before you disperse, you must hear the story of Raymond, my second love."

"Another one?" cried Oakie.

"My dears, you don't think *one* is enough for the Incomparable Rosalie?"

I studied the rejection board, while Lexie detailed her afternoon on a Bermuda beach with Raymond.

By the next afternoon, the rain had stopped and the gray ceiling opened. The sky was a clear, crystal blue. The air was cool, but the icy bite of winter was gone. After lunch, Miggin and I walked down the back drive. The bark of the elm trees was still dark from the rain, and the branches were pale green with buds ready to burst.

Miggin wore only her blazer. I was wrapped in my winter coat. I didn't trust the unexpected warmth of the afternoon.

"What was the doctor like?" said Miggin tentatively.

I kicked a stone up the road. "He was okay. I may have to go back this summer. He's a psychiatrist."

Miggin looked puzzled. "Was he like Dr. Philpot?"

"More or less. They both ask a lot of questions."

We walked on in silence. On our left was Adair, the huge clapboard sophomore dorm. Girls sat on the front steps, faces lifted to the sun.

Miggin looked at them pensively. "Did you talk about ... homosexuality?"

She pronounced the word carefully, without expression, as if it might bite her if she said it too quickly. I kept walking. For the first time in ages, the horses were grazing in the pasture. Up by the stables, I could see a rider walking her horse around the paddock.

"Jinx?" Miggin touched my arm. "Did he say that if you're a girl, and you love another girl, then you're ... a lesbian?"

I looked at her, surprised. Her red hair was braided in her Heidi pigtails. Her blue eyes seemed to darken, to match the color of her blazer. The cool air pinkened her cheeks.

"It has to do with sexual feelings," I said slowly. "If you have *sexual* feelings for a girl, then it's more like being lesbian."

We continued to walk. I could smell Miggin's shampoo. We reached the end of the driveway. Without permissions, that was as far as we could go.

"I don't know, Jinx," said Miggin shyly. "But I love *you* a lot."

A shiver ran through my legs. I held my coat close to me.

"Jinx, if loving you means I'm a lesbian" — she paused — "then I'm glad I'm a lesbian, because I like loving you."

Miggin had stopped and was facing me directly, searching my face for a reaction. I could feel the dampness sneaking through my shoes. I thought of all the times Miggin had helped me and defended me, all the times she'd listened to my stories about Lexie, all the times we'd laughed together and joked about our insecurities. All that time I'd been thinking of Lexie, loving Lexie, wanting Lexie to love me, and never paying attention to Miggin, who had been kind and loyal and tender all along.

"Oh, Miggin," I said, pressing my cheek against her shining red braids, "I love you too. I love you so much. You're so precious to me." We hugged, right in the driveway, right by the elegant, tasteful, hand-lettered sign saying, "Huntington Hill for Girls."

I took her hand and we walked back to Senior House, in front of all the sophomores sunbathing, in front of the Lower School girls playing tag, in front of Randolph Nicholson's office and the entire administration staff. And it didn't seem weird and strange, it didn't seem like a crush, it seemed like two friends who are so close, who love each other so much, they're ... they're like sisters.

WE HAD SIX WEEKS TO GO AND IT WAS GOING to be okay. The May sun grew slowly warmer, and small, pale leaves unfolded each new day. Spring had come and the sun was thawing all of us. It was going to be okay. "Our quarrel with America is a lover's quarrel," said William Sloane Coffin to reporters asking him why he supported the giant march on Washington to protest Johnson's war in Vietnam. Maybe that was how I felt about Huntington Hill. I hated the school because I loved the school. At least I loved my friends — Miggin, Oakie, and my teammates.

Lacrosse season began, and I was back outside again, running around the lower field, stretching with the awkward excitement of an animal awakening after hibernation. Fortunately, Maddy Hansen didn't play lacrosse in spring. She played tennis. I didn't have to see her at practice every day and think about her turning in the letters. Being grounded meant that I couldn't play away games with the team. That was disappointing; but when we lost the first away game we played, Nicky decided that I *could* leave the campus after all. They put it on a week-to-week basis; I guess as long as I was behaving normally, they didn't mind my leaving. The day before each away game Woodie would take me aside and tell me whether I would be able to play. In her own gruff way, she seemed friendlier. I had never been one of her favorites; deep down, I knew she thought I was a troublemaker. But at least we got along.

After the Music Club show, Jonas and I became friends. She sent the letter she'd promised to write the art

schools and she gave me a copy. The letter was good —
it said that I was a "conscientious" student and an important "contributor" to the school community. In the halls,
Jonas would stop me to see if I'd heard from art schools,
and a couple of times she dropped in the studio to look at
my work.

For the first time in months, I was painting my own
things again. *Carnival* had taken up most of my time, and
during the show I never had enough energy left over to
work on my own stuff. Now, every afternoon, between
lunch and lacrosse, I went to the studio. The pasture
stretched before us like a lush green carpet. The horses
were back now, grazing, chewing the grass.

I wasn't painting from photographs anymore. They
had lost their appeal. Something to do with Dr. Philpot
and Dr. Matthews, the other psychiatrist. I felt as if my
life had been exposed and hacked at, and I needed to
protect myself. The photographs were too personal and
revealing. I was losing interest in analyzing the past. I
mean, that's what the doctors were always doing and it
didn't make me happier or help me understand my feelings about Lexie any better.

So now I was painting impersonal things — like ash-
trays full of cigarette butts and attaché cases. A lot of
times I felt angry when I painted. I could hear my mother
saying, "What does it *mean*, Jinx?" But I kept on painting
these impersonal objects. I didn't understand it myself.

Miggin and I were together a lot. She was very considerate and thoughtful. Whenever she went to Huntington she'd bring me back candy or flowers, because I
couldn't go. I felt like one of her little hospital charges she
visited each week. She never mentioned homosexuality,
being a lesbian, again. I didn't either, because it made me
nervous.

With Lexie, things were strange. We had sort of an
understanding that our friendship was over. We never

talked about the letters or probation, and when we did talk, there were usually other people around, so we never got personal. She was spending most of her time with Laura now. But I don't think Laura and Lexie were as close as Lexie and I had been. I think Lexie was always jealous of Laura's boyfriends and her self-confidence and poise. Lexie seemed more subdued now. She wasn't as reckless and loud as she'd been. She kept her uniform neater. She didn't pass notes in study hall and she went to all her classes on time.

The whole thing about the letters never really leaked out. I guess Maddy Hansen had been afraid to tell anybody about the letters in case someone asked her how *she* knew so much about it. They might figure out that she had stolen them from Lexie, and then Maddy would get kicked out. Every time I saw her, I avoided her. I didn't want to be reminded of the whole thing. I wanted it *behind* me. I was trying to keep the lid on till graduation.

On April 30, I got a letter from Cooper Union. It was a thin envelope, the kind they always said rejections came in. I took it back to the room to open it alone. I didn't want anyone to see me cry. I wanted to absorb the pain and disappointment by myself, with no one watching. After that, I would pin it on the bulletin board with the other rejections. But first, I had to lick my wounds alone.

"Dear Miss Tuckwell," it read. "We are pleased..." I stared at the words. "We are *pleased*..." I felt the excitement rise from my feet to my head. *We are pleased*. I was in. I was in. I was in. I was going to live in New York. I was going to be a painter. I was going to get out of Huntington Hill and society and the thin, narrow band of acceptable behavior forever. Cooper Union had accepted me. I was in. In that moment, the nightmare and sadness of the letters, of probation, of Dr. Philpot and Dr. Matthews, of Nicholson, of Woodie, of Lexie, of the crush, lifted.

I had to tell Miggin. I had to tell her I had been accepted by Cooper Union in New York City. Cooper Union, where there were real, serious artists. Not people who posed in berets, but real artists. And I would be one of them. I would be a real painter someday. Cooper had let me in.

Someone said Miggin was sunbathing on the terrace. I raced down the steps of the common room and opened the door. Sun poured down on the hot flagstones and baked the ground, but Miggin wasn't there. No one was there. I stood in the sun and read every word of the letter. They were letting me in and if I wanted to go, I should let them know immediately. My stomach was floating. I went back inside.

In the kitchen adjoining the common room, I heard a cabinet door shut. I went in. There was Maddy Hansen, alone, spreading jam on a piece of Wonder Bread.

"Have you seen Miggin?" I said. I was so happy I even smiled at Maddy.

She turned around quickly. "Why would I have seen Miggin?" she snapped.

I shrugged. I remembered a rejection letter I had seen recently on the board. Holyoke had turned her down last week. Holyoke was her first choice. "Someone said she was down here."

"She's not." Maddy looked at the letter in my hand. "What's that?"

"Cooper accepted me. Do you believe it?"

Maddy turned and spread more jam on her sandwich. "I'm surprised. Cooper's such a *prestige* place."

I watched her, conscious of the slow drip in the kitchen sink. "Are you sorry I got in?"

Maddy put down the knife and turned. "That's a very strange thing to say, Tuckwell. Why would I be sorry?"

She held her arms close to her sides and stared at me. Could she really say that with a straight face? Could she really steal the letters, turn them in, and then, with complete equanimity pretend she was happy for me? I felt my chest tighten.

"Don't you know, really?"

Her eyes widened. "What are you talking about?"

"I'm on probation."

Maddy laughed artificially. "Of course, Tuckwell, how could I *not* know that? That's your claim to fame. 'Poor Tuckwell,' everybody says. 'Put on probation so close to graduation. So unjust.'" Her eyes narrowed. "Jesus, Jinx, I'd have to be deaf, dumb, and blind not to know about your ... *sentence.*"

I listened for footsteps in the common room. But there was only silence, and the drip of the faucet. It was safe to talk. "Maddy, I would have preferred not to have my *'claim to fame.'* But, thanks to you, I have it."

Her scowl deepened. "What are you talking about?"

"Oh, come on, Maddy. You can't fool me."

She stepped back. "I don't know what you're talking about."

"Don't you?" I could feel the anger rising in my throat. I could feel a scream pushing to get out. "*You* turned in the letters."

Maddy frowned. "You've been painting too much, Jinx. You should get out of the studio more. It's rotting your brain."

I moved closer. "Maddy, I'm on probation because you turned in my notes to Lexie. You know that's why I'm on probation." She backed into the counter, hitting the plate behind her. My eyes fell on the knife, still covered in jam. I grabbed it and held it to her side. "I could kill you, Maddy. I could—"

Maddy's face went white. "Get that away from me. Stop it!"

"Just admit it," I whispered. "Just admit you turned the letters in to Nicky. Just tell the truth. Just say to my face, 'Yes, Jinx, I did it.'"

Her voice was unnaturally calm. "I don't know what you're talking about."

"Just admit it. You turned them in." I pushed the knife into her ribs. The jam smeared on her sweater.

"Who told you I turned the letters in?" she said.

"Admit it."

"Jinx, listen to me. Who told you I turned them in?"

"Lexie," I hissed. "Nicky told Lexie, and Lexie told me."

Maddy's lip curled. "Did it ever occur to you that Lexie might be lying? I don't know what letters you're talking about, but it's possible that your beloved Lexie lied."

I looked at her in disbelief. She was *still* denying it.

"You're a liar," I said.

"Jinx, I never, ever *saw* any letters. I don't know what you're talking about and if you don't put that knife down I'm going to scream—"

"Lexie's not a liar," I said, leaning backward.

Maddy jolted my arm quickly. The knife fell. She rushed by me. "Lexie's a bitch and a liar," she yelled. "And so are you." She leaped up the steps and did not look back.

That night I knocked on Lexie's door. She was sitting at her desk, hair in rollers, a mirror in front of her. She was plucking her eyebrows.

"Come on in, Jinx," she said in a cheerful, artificial voice.

I sat down on the bed, pushing her half-packed suitcase out of the way. "You going away this weekend?"

She looked up. "New York. Eleanor and I are shopping for clothes. I need dresses for the deb parties."

I looked at what she'd packed. Undies, a nightgown — the salmon-colored one — a huge bag of cosmetics. "I guess that will be fun."

Her voice was unrevealing. "A weekend with Eleanor? Torture. You know that."

I took a breath and fingered the paper clip in my pocket. "I talked to Maddy today."

"Oh?" she said calmly, carefully extracting a hair. "She's such a pain."

"I talked to her about the letters."

For the first time, Lexie looked up. Her forehead was shiny from a bath. "Jinx, I told you not to discuss it with Maddy. If it gets back to Nicky, we could all get screwed."

I stared down at the floor. "I didn't mean to bring it up. I was looking for Miggin. You know, I got into Cooper Union today, I got..."

"I know." She sat beside me on the bed. "What did you tell Maddy?"

"Lexie, I got into Cooper."

"What did you say to Maddy?" Her voice was cold.

"I told her about Cooper, and then we talked." I looked at the big curlers in her hair. "She said she didn't know anything about the letters."

Lexie's face reddened. She stood up. "She's lying."

"She said she never saw any letters. She said you must be lying."

Lexie glared at me. "You told her I said she turned them in?"

I nodded.

"Well, screw you, Tuckwell."

"But, Lexie, why *would* Maddy turn them in? I never did anything to her."

Lexie gripped my arm. Even now, after all the mess, her touch gave me goose bumps. "Listen to me, Jinx. Maddy *hates* you. You took her place on the hockey team.

223

The one game she played, you took her out at halftime. You have more friends; you're smarter. Maddy *hates* you, Jinx," growled Lexie. "Do you understand?"

I looked at her. It was screwed up.

Lexie's nails were gouging my arm. "Don't you believe me, Tuck?"

"Lexie, I'm confused. I'm ... I..."

"Because, if you believe Maddy and not me, you're more of a bitch than I thought." Her eyes were small, hard daggers.

"I'm not saying you lied; I..."

Lexie released my arm. "You believe her," she said with disgust. "You believe her and you doubt me." Her nostrils flared. "That is an unforgivable sin. Do you understand?" Her mouth turned down, her lips pushed forward. "Now get out of here. Get the hell out!" She opened the door.

"Lexie..."

"Get out."

IN THREE WEEKS, SCHOOL WOULD BE OVER, BUT I had a cold, sinking feeling there was going to be trouble. I wasn't sure where the danger would come from, but it wasn't over yet. Somewhere, a stick of dynamite was burning, and the pungent smell of smoke already filled the air. In Selma, the Ku Klux Klan was burning crosses. At Huntington Hill, something else would go up in flames. Take it easy, I told myself. Just hold on and take it easy. In three weeks, you'll graduate. But I was scared. It wasn't over yet.

On Friday night, after the lacrosse game, I started studying for exams. If I studied very hard, if I kept out of the dorm, maybe the evil could be warded off. Occasionally the image of Lexie, standing by the door in her rollers, eyes narrow, angry, flashed through my mind. But Lexie is away, I told myself — she's in New York with Eleanor. She's far away. Then I'd try harder to memorize the rulers of the Roman Empire. I sat four hours in study hall Saturday morning, poring over my books. Concentrate, I told myself. If you concentrate, you can't think about the danger. I went back to study hall after lunch on Saturday, and back again Saturday night. Sunday, after chapel, I went to the library. Just study, just hold on. It will be over soon. Just don't think about Lexie. Study. The books will protect you, the books will ward off danger. Study.

It was five p.m. Sunday afternoon when Scottie Ellis knocked on my door. "Telephone, Tuckwell," said Scottie. "It's a man."

I looked at her. She was wearing jeans and a t-shirt from WHAR Radio that said, "The Rainbow Sound."

"My father?" I sat up.

"He's young." She turned. "Don't talk too long. Oakie and I are waiting for calls."

I got up slowly. I didn't know many boys.

Outside, it was warm. A bunch of seniors were playing Frisbee on the lawn.

As I picked up the phone in the second-floor hallway, Oakie tapped my arm. "Don't talk long," she whispered. "I'm waiting for a call."

I nodded. "Hello?" Oakie stood watching me.

I heard the receiver change hands.

"Tuckwell?" It was a familiar voice. I could almost smell the danger. Lexie.

Oakie watched me and mouthed the words "Who is it?"

"My cousin," I said softly. Satisfied, Oakie walked away.

"Jinx, listen carefully." Lexie breathed heavily into the phone. "Can you listen carefully? Is anyone near you? Listen, Jinxie, I need a little favor." She was drunk. She sounded the way she sounded the day she was drunk on the train.

"Are you there, Jinx?"

"Yes." My palms were cold against the receiver. Elizabeth Knight walked slowly down the hall, then stopped when she saw me.

"Listen, Jinx, I need a favor. I didn't go to New York with Eleanor. I went to Fisher's Island ... with Philip."

This was it.

"Are you there?"

"Yes."

"See, Jinxie, Philip has a house there, so I decided it would be more fun to go there. It's a beautiful day. Is it beautiful there?"

226

"Lexie..."

"Don't say my name, Jinx."

Outside, the Frisbee players still spun the plastic discs on the front lawn. Woodie, clipboard in hand, stopped on the stone steps to watch them.

"Jinx?"

"Yes."

"What's wrong, honey?" Lexie was eating something now.

"Nothing."

"Jinxie, we missed the ferry and there's not another one till seven."

"You've got to sign in by nine," I said. It was coming. The explosion was coming.

"Idiot, that's why I'm calling you."

I sat down on the little stool by the phone. "You should call Woodie."

Lexie laughed. "She thinks I'm in New York."

Scottie Ellis walked down the hall and pointed to her watch. "Hurry up," she mouthed.

"You better call Woodie," I repeated.

"Lissen, honey. Here's what you do. Sign me in around eight, after dinner. Turn on my light, and when I get back, I'll climb in through your window. They'll never know."

I took a breath. "They'll know. They'll know you're not back. Call Woodie, now. I'll go get her, I'll—"

"Jinx! You're not listening. Go to my room, turn on my light..."

"Lexie..."

"Don't say my name. They'll hear." She hiccupped, then laughed.

"Listen," I whispered, "even if they think you're back, Miggin will hear you come in. She'll know. Call Woodie. She'll understand. We graduate in three weeks. They won't kick you out."

"Listen, Jinx, I can't talk much longer..."

I glanced down the hall. "Why are you calling *me*? Why aren't you calling Laura? She's your friend."

"Laura's a bitch, Jinx. I don't trust her."

"Call Nicky. He'll—"

"He's a bastard. Listen, I've got to get off. Jinx, I'm counting on you..."

"Lexie, I'm on probation." Oakie was coming up the steps.

Lexie started to cry. "Jinx, you're my best friend. I've always counted on you."

"I can't."

"You can." Her voice was desperate. "Please, for me. It was always you, Jinx, always you..."

"Lexie, don't..."

"See you tonight." She slammed down the phone.

"Who was that?" said Oakie quizzically, as she picked up the receiver.

"My cousin."

Oakie laughed. "What cousin? I bet you've got a honey somewhere."

"Right." I tried to laugh. It sounded more like choking.

I went out the back door of Senior House and looked up at the pasture. This was it. This was Lexie's final request. Fake her handwriting, turn her light on, help her enter the dorm through the window. It would never work. There was no way it would work. Even if I faked her handwriting, they'd know she wasn't back. No suitcase in her room, nobody who'd seen her. It was stupid to consider it. Even if it worked *that* far, she still had to get in through the window and up the stairs. It was crazy. Lexie, drunk, climbing the stairs in the dark? There was no way I could do it. I didn't want her to get in trouble. I didn't want her kicked out. But there was no principle involved here, no higher cause, just Lexie's selfish impulse. Was it worth taking the risk because she couldn't wait three weeks to see Philip? Why didn't Philip call and make up some story? Why didn't she get Mrs. Dennis to? Mrs. Dennis always did what Lexie asked. Why me? Why me again?

The dinner bell jarred my thoughts. I ran into Senior House and put on my dinner uniform. And all through dinner I thought about it. What was I going to do? Why did she ask *me* when two days ago she'd called me a bitch?

It was the crush. The crush. The crush allowed Lexie to ask favors of me she would never ask anyone else. If you loved Lexie, she made you pay the price, initiated you into her ways. She wouldn't settle for less. Because I had loved her, I had to agree. But what if I didn't? What if I refused? Could she hurt me? How would she get back at me? She could tell Nicky everything — about the crush, about our touching, but then she'd be getting herself in as much trouble as me.

Hadn't I tried to help her by telling her to call Woodie? Wasn't that better advice? Woodie *would* understand. A lot of things were overlooked when you were going to graduate in three weeks. They'd invent some excuse for Lexie the way they had for me — she forgot to get the proper permission, took the wrong ferry, train broke down. For Lexie, Nicky would think of a good one.

After dinner, I stood in the front hall and leafed through the sign-out book. I found Lexie's name. "Destination: New York. Time of Departure: 5/20/65. Time of Return: *blank.*"

I looked around. The hallway was empty, the door to Woodie's room was closed. It wouldn't be hard. I could do it. I *could*.

But for the plan to work, I'd have to wait a few more minutes, wait till eight, when more people were in study hall. So close to exams, everyone was studying hard. No one would go looking for Lexie.

I went to study hall. I tried to memorize the nitrogen cycle. I reviewed the process of photosynthesis. In three weeks, I would graduate. I would go to Cooper Union in New York. It would all be over. No more school, no more Lexie, no more crush. Keep the lid on. Don't touch the sign-out book.

At ten p.m., Oakie knocked on our door. Miggin was rolling her hair in the bathroom. I was lying on my bed.

Oakie's face was tense. "Have you seen Lexie?"

Miggin looked at me. I shook my head.

"She's not back," said Oakie. "And she hasn't called."

"Jesus," said Miggin.

"She hasn't signed in?" I said in a whisper.

Oakie shook her head. "Let me know if you hear anything." She closed the door.

Woodie called a dorm meeting at eleven p.m. Lexie had not returned. Woodie had phoned Mrs. Dennis, and Mrs. Dennis said she had never signed a weekend permission form, nor had she planned to see Lexie until graduation. Woodie stood grimly by the piano. Nicky stood beside her, arms folded, jaw dark. They had called the meeting, he said, because they wanted to still the rumors going around the dorm. People were saying Lexie had disappeared, that the police were after her. There were three more weeks to go, said Nicky. Let's stay calm. Let's not react emotionally.

Laura Carr raised her hand. She sat in the front, on the floor, legs crossed like an Indian. "What's going to happen to Lexie when she comes back? Will she, is..."

Nicky scowled. "We'll cross that bridge when we come to it. Meantime, if anyone has any idea where Lexie might be, please tell me immediately. She ... she may be in trouble."

When the room emptied, I approached Woodie. Her face looked tired. The tiny wrinkles around her mouth and eyes were deeper. "Woodie, I spoke to Lexie today."

Woodie's eyes widened. "What?"

"Lexie called me this afternoon."

Woodie glanced at the kitchen, where Nicky stood talking to Laura Carr.

"What time did she call?"

"Around five." I looked down at the floor.

"Where was she?" Woodie's hands closed tightly around her clipboard.

"Fisher's Island."

"Where?"

"Fisher's Island. She's with Philip."

Woodie ground out her cigarette. "What are you saying?"

"She was with her cousin Philip. He has a house there. Lexie missed the ferry. She was going to take a later one."

Woodie's hands were on her hips. "Why didn't she call in?"

I looked over at Nicky. "She was afraid."

Woodie wrote something on her pad. "I'll call her guardian." She turned away. "Nicky..."

"Woodie?" I said quietly.

"Yes?"

"Lexie wants to come in through my window tonight."

"Tonight?"

I nodded.

"What did you tell her?"

I could feel it in my knees. I could feel the fear. "I told her not to. I said she'd get caught."

Woodie frowned. "She certainly will."

"Woodie, what should I do if she comes?"

Woodie looked at me impatiently. "Let her in."

MIGGIN AND I LAY IN OUR BEDS LOOKING UP AT the plastic glow-stars on the ceiling. The dorm was quiet now, the calm returning. Miggin was talkative. When school was over, she wondered, should we take the stars down, or leave them for the girls who had our room next year. Maybe they'd even think of us when they saw them. Or would the stars have lost their glow? Already, their radiance was fading. It was depressing, I said, when you thought about it. Year after year, students came and went, and except for a few photographs in the Trophy Room or a name stitched in a varsity tunic, all evidence of us would be gone. Our plastic stars, even glowing weakly, would be remembered longer than we would.

Then Miggin asked about Lexie. Strange, she said, that Lexie would do such a crazy thing with only three more weeks till graduation. In three weeks we'd be out, and now she'd screwed things up completely. Where had she gone? What was she doing? After four years, three weeks wasn't much time to wait. We'd all go off in different directions anyway, and next time we got together we'd probably be married, with kids hanging off us, and we'd be stuffy and silly, the way alumnae always are.

It seemed like a lot of life was saying good-bye, I said. Getting to know someone, then saying good-bye. It would be nice, I said, if friendships were somehow guaranteed to last, to hold up whatever happened. But even the deep ones can fall apart, or you change — your feelings change, something, and what held you together can disappear. Miggin said maybe it was a good thing that you had to fight to keep up friendships, that you had to write and visit and care, because those things made you realize how important friends were and how they couldn't be taken for granted. If you really love someone, Miggin said, you have to stick by them.

I shivered when she said that. I wanted to tell Miggin that Lexie had called. I wanted to tell her that Lexie might be knocking on our window any minute. I wanted to tell her how bad I felt about telling Woodie, how guilty I felt for not signing Lexie in. I mean, sometimes, even if you love someone, you *can't* stick by them. Would Miggin understand that? Would she agree that this time Lexie had asked too much, exceeded the limits? Do you have to stick by friends if they ask you to risk your own safety, your own future? Do you have to stick by them when their demands are outrageous?

If you really love someone, Miggin had said, you have to stick by them. But what *was* love? Maybe I didn't love Lexie. Maybe I never had. I wanted to talk to Miggin about it. I thought she would understand. But I didn't want her stuck in the mess with Lexie. I didn't want her in trouble too.

Anyway, I had made my decision. Talking probably wouldn't do much good. I was going to go to art school. I was going to graduate. I was going to be a painter. I wouldn't risk it all for Lexie and a half-baked plan that would never work. This time, Lexie had gone too far. She could mess with her own life, but she wouldn't mess with mine.

I don't remember falling asleep, but I remember waking, suddenly. Something scratched on the screen. It scratched through my sleep, and slowly, I opened my eyes. Fingernails on the screen, outside the window.

I looked at the clock. Three a.m. I got up and put on my robe. Lexie had come. Without turning on the light,

I opened the window, then the screen. In the darkness, I could see Lexie's wild, pale face.

"Let me in," she said hoarsely.

Miggin sat up. Her eyes were wide. "Who is it?" she whispered.

"It's Lexie," I said. "Go to sleep."

She pulled off her covers. "Don't get in trouble, Jinx. Get Woodie. Please."

"Hurry up." Lexie's voice was loud, too loud. She tried to lift herself onto the window ledge. Her breath reeked of alcohol. She had no coordination.

"Hand me your suitcase first," I whispered. Slowly, she inched her stomach up the ledge. I gripped her arms and pulled her through. Her green suit was covered in mud. Her eyes were red, her hair disheveled.

"Here I am," she giggled, collapsing onto my bed.

I stood beside her in the dark. Just touching her, pulling her through the window, had brought the feelings back. There was something soft inside me. But when I spoke, my voice was flat.

"I told you not to do this, Lexie."

"Of course you did," she laughed.

"How could you, Lexie?"

Lexie stood up. "Well, for Christ's sake, let's not argue about it. I'm here and I'm going to my room."

"Lexie?" Miggin sat up again. "What's going on?"

Lexie scowled. "This is none of your goddam business, Miggin."

Miggin looked at me. "Jinx?"

"Go to sleep," I said. "Put your pillow over your ears. Don't listen." I didn't want her dragged into this. I didn't want her in trouble, whatever happened.

Lexie supported herself on the night table, then wobbled toward the door.

"Lexie, they know," I whispered.

Silence. Outside, the crickets chirped peacefully.

"What do you mean?" hissed Lexie.

"I didn't sign you in. I told Woodie."

Lexie didn't move. "You mean, I could have come in the front door? I've spent the last twelve hours sneaking around and I could have come in the front door?"

I shrugged. "You could have tried."

Lexie stumbled toward the door, then slipped as she reached for the knob. Her legs stretched out in front of her, her head was tilted to one side — a broken doll.

I listened for footsteps. No one.

Lexie groaned. She had hurt something. She was in pain. Again, I felt the softening. I reached under her arms and lifted her slowly.

"Jinx, don't," said Miggin. "Get Woodie."

Lexie's body was soft, malleable. She was helpless. Suddenly, I forgot about Woodie and the rules, about the fact that they all knew, that they were all waiting somewhere. If we hurried, maybe it would be okay. Maybe they'd forgive her. Maybe things would work out.

"Come on, Lexie. Get up."

Slowly, we tottered down the hallway, Lexie's arm slung over my shoulder for support. At the steps, we paused — still no footsteps, and slowly, step by step, we ascended. We were halfway up when Lexie stumbled. She stumbled and one of her high heels fell off and banged insanely down the steps. We waited. Silence. No one came out. No doors opened. No lights went on. We continued up the last few steps, limped down the hall, then around the corner to Lexie's room. Lexie fell onto her bed.

"Get undressed," I whispered. "Hurry."

"What?" She squinted up at me. Her eyes were bloodshot. She looked crazy, like one of those paper-bag ladies who carries her life around in a sack.

"Get undressed," I said, turning quickly. The door clicked open. Long and ghostlike in her gray robe, hair curled in bobby pins, stood Woodie, flashlight in hand, scowling.

25

THE MORNING SUN BURST BRILLIANTLY THROUGH the windows of Nicholson's office. On the playing field, a lacrosse class drilled backhand shots into the goal.

I sat by Nicky's desk. He was already in shirtsleeves, cuffs rolled, tie loosened, face damp with perspiration. Beside him, on his desk, his silver baseball trophy sparkled — it was no longer brown and tarnished. Someone had polished it. Woodie sat grimly on the couch, arms folded, feet on the floor. They had just seen Lexie. Now it was my turn. Nicky leaned forward on his elbows and rubbed his chin. I held my hands folded in my lap. My throat was dry. I was exhausted. We had been up late.

"Jinx," began Nicky, "why didn't you tell Woodie or me that Lexie Yves called you yesterday at five?" His voice was calm, well modulated.

"Lexie asked me not to."

"And at ten p.m.," he continued in his soothing voice, "when Oakie asked you if you'd heard from Lexie, you said you hadn't." He brushed his hand against his darkened armpit. "Why, Jinx?"

Outside, the grass was green, the campus quiet. In the classrooms above us, teachers stood at blackboards preparing students for exams, reviewing the great themes of literature — good *versus* evil, light *versus* dark. In History class, somewhere, they taught the fall of empires, the corruption of leaders.

"I hoped Lexie would call herself." I paused, keeping my eyes on the silver trophy. "I didn't want to turn her in."

Nicholson lit a cigarette and followed the smoke's ascent with his eyes. "Jinx, I wish you hadn't waited so long to tell us, the whole thing might have been cleared up, might—"

"Lexie asked me not to tell you," I repeated. Nicholson leaned back in his chair and glanced at Woodie. Was the room getting hotter? It seemed very hot. But Woodie still wore her wool cardigan, buttoned under the collar.

Nicholson coughed. "What about the honor code, Jinx? If you know that someone has broken a rule, you must report them. By not doing so, you are, in effect, breaking the code yourself. You ... you did know that?"

I looked down at my shoes. It was lucky school was almost over. The brown leather was beginning to crack, the seams to split. I could get demerits for wearing such old shoes.

"There was an honor code for Lexie, too," I said.

Nicholson frowned and pushed his horn-rimmed glasses up on his nose. Then he nodded to Woodie. "Miss Woodruff?"

Woodie sighed. Almost imperceptibly, her head trembled. She braced her jaw with her right hand, to still the shaking. "Jinx, Lexie's explanation is very different from yours. We're ... frankly, we're confused."

A small muscle in my eyelid twitched. What had Lexie told them? Had she lied again? After all this, was she still lying? Did she expect anything less than expulsion? Was she hoping for a lighter sentence? A wave of fatigue passed over me. It was falling apart. Things were failing apart. And graduation was so close. So close.

Woodie sat up. "Lexie says that you told her *not* to call me or Mr. Nicholson. She says you insisted she try to sneak in later. She says she wanted to call and explain everything, but you convinced her not to."

I lifted my eyes and searched their faces for sympathy. Surely they must know how silly that was, what a desperate, last-ditch lie Lexie had told them. But the two of them watched me silently, like scientists observing a lab rat under stress. Nicky spoke first.

"Jinx, Lexie feels you wanted her to get in trouble. She claims you deliberately set her up."

I remembered how my cousin in Tennessee had once invented a torture to use on me. He put a laundry tub over my head, held the tub down with cinder blocks, and banged a hammer against it. This was Lexie's torture; this was her farewell.

I gripped the chair. "Lexie's not telling the truth."

Woodie crossed her legs. Her Weejun loafers had been polished this morning. For the first time, I noticed the dogs, the little brown puppies printed on her shirt. I looked at her wrinkled face. There was honesty in her face, pride in the way she held her head. She must believe me, she must know, that after all these years, I wouldn't lie. There was too much at stake, too much to lose. In three weeks I would graduate. Why would I do it? But Woodie's face did not soften.

"Jinx," she said, "that's a serious accusation."

Nicky tapped a pencil on his blotter. "We can only guess why you might have wanted to hurt Lexie. Perhaps you were still upset by her ... rejection of you. Perhaps you still felt some of the ... attachment you felt in the past. Perhaps you don't even know yourself why."

Upstairs, feet moved on the floor. The bell had rung, classes changed. Out on the grass, the lacrosse players ambled up to the locker room.

Nicholson cleared his throat. "Jinx, we're trying to make sense of what's happened. We..." He trailed off. "Perhaps," he said slowly, studying me, "you wanted revenge."

I stared at him. "Revenge?"

His face reddened. The veins in his neck bulged. Quickly, he stood up, rattled the change in his pocket, and paced to the window. Then he turned. "Jinx, let's not beat around the bush. You were very fond of Lexie. You expressed certain feelings for her last winter and she wasn't the least bit interested."

They were crazy. Everybody had gone crazy. They had taken bits and pieces of the story and built a whole, fabulous plot around them. "How do you know?" I said, my voice cracking. "How do you know Lexie wasn't *interested?*"

Nicky and Woodie both looked at me curiously. I heard the rapid tick of Nicky's clock and the voices of two teachers passing near the window. Then Nicholson sat down.

"Jinx, we know because in March Lexie sat right where you're sitting, handed me your letters, and said, 'Please, Mr. Nicholson, do something about this. Please stop her.'"

I dropped my head into my hands. I hadn't eaten breakfast this morning. If I could just lie down, just rest...

Woodie's hand touched my shoulder. "Are you all right?"

I whispered. I could only whisper. "Maddy Hansen gave you the letters."

Nicholson raised his eyebrows. "Maddy Hansen had nothing to do with it."

I shook my head. Lexie had lied to me. All this time Lexie had been lying. She had given Nicholson the letters herself. The walls of the office seemed to be moving, bending in toward me.

"You believe Lexie?" I said hoarsely.

Nicholson's eyes flashed. He stood up again, a hungry wolf pacing. "Jinx, is there any reason why I shouldn't believe her?" He jingled his change. "Perhaps you know something we don't. Can you give us any ... proof that Lexie was lying? Either about her call to you or ... about her ... feelings for you?" He pinched his nose with his fingers. He was excited. "Is there any evidence at all that, say, Lexie Yves might be ... homosexual? Perhaps, if there were more information, we could ... reconsider the matter of disciplinary action, in your case, at least."

I looked at him, amazed. He wanted to know if Lexie was queer. He didn't care if she had lied, if she had betrayed me, if I was telling the truth. He wanted to know if Lexie was queer. If she was queer, everything would be all right. I thought of the letters I had thrown into the garbage bin, the notes in which Lexie had said she loved me, in which she talked about touching me. They were gone; I had thrown them away to protect Lexie. But there were other things — poems, a drawing, a letter she had written me at Christmas. All hidden in drawers and secret places where I thought no one would find them. I could *prove* Lexie loved me. I could prove it. That's what he wanted. *Proof.* What did I want?

"Well, Jinx?"

When I finally spoke, my voice was clear. "I don't have any proof," I said.

Nicholson sat down. "Then we have no choice." He talked to Woodie as if I were already gone. "Call a meeting of the student government. I'll speak to the school at one. Contact Jinx's parents..." His voice droned on. Perhaps he was talking to me. "Jinx won't be graduating with the class. She may take exams this summer and we can certify completion of course work. Cooper Union *may* consider that satisfactory. Her parents should take her home tomorrow."

Woodie was on her feet, Nicholson was conferring with his secretary. And that was it.

26

EXIE'S BED WAS UNMADE, HER SUITCASES sprawled across the room. Piles of clothes covered the floor. Every drawer was pulled open, socks and underwear falling out of them. In the midst of the mess, Lexie leaned over a mirror carefully painting her eyes with mascara. Laura Carr sat at the foot of the bed.

I stood in the doorway. "Lexie, I'd like to talk to you."

Lexie did not look up. She was dressed in black — black suit, black stockings, black heels. "Go ahead," she said flatly.

I stepped farther into the room and glanced at Laura. Lexie saw me in the mirror.

"Laura can stay. She's my friend."

I looked out the window. In the distance, mowers rolled over the lawns and fields. Getting ready for graduation. The school must look proper for parents, for alumnae.

"Why did you give Nicholson my letters? Why did you tell him your escapade was my idea?"

Lexie's eyes narrowed. Laura Carr stood up. "I'll see you later, Lexie."

"You can stay," said Lexie.

Laura shut the door behind her. Lexie clicked open a compact. I sat on the bed, inches from her.

"Lexie, don't deny it. Nicholson just told me." My voice rose.

Lexie laughed artificially. "Take a breath, sweetheart. Then repeat after me, 'Do you know May?'"

"Lexie, we were friends. Why?"

She laughed again, this time throwing her head back dramatically. "Listen to her. She says we were friends."

I winced. "Was it because I wouldn't stay with you that night? Because I wouldn't go cruising around the dorm in the middle of the night?"

"Jinx, I don't have time to talk to you." Lexie began throwing clothes into her suitcase. "I don't have time for this. I'm leaving. I've been expelled."

"So have I."

For the first time, she looked at me. She stepped back. Her brown eyes, swollen, smeared with black makeup, met mine. She sat down slowly, on a mound of clothes.

"I didn't know that."

I stared at her. She was next to me now. "That's what you wanted, isn't it? You wanted me out."

She shook her head. Tears, black from the makeup, streaked her cheeks. "That's not what I wanted."

I touched the back of the chair. "What *did* you want, Lexie?"

She didn't answer. She blew her nose loudly into a Kleenex, then she began searching for something. She kicked clothes across the room, pushed her hair dryer off the bed, and dumped her desk drawer onto the floor. Finally, she found what she was looking for — a small, gray box.

"Here." She threw the box at me. It fell at my feet.

"Pick it up, stupid." She watched me closely. "Go ahead. Open it. It's ... a graduation present." Her tone became light, mimicking. "Please understand that, under the circumstances, I could not wait for the ... appropriate moment."

I stared at the box. It was from Cartier's. It was wrapped with a white ribbon.

"Open it." Her voice was menacing.

I untied the bow. Inside, beneath a layer of cotton, was something folded up in tissue paper. I opened it slowly. It was a small gold disc, attached to a tiny gold chain. The disc was engraved. On one side it said: "To JT, With love, LY." On the other side, it said: "Always, always you."

I shivered. "What's this?"

She laughed. "Your graduation present, stupid." She came toward me.

I looked at her. I couldn't believe it. "Is this supposed to explain something?"

She closed her eyes. She wanted me to understand. She wanted me to know something.

"Lexie, I don't want this. I want you to tell me why you turned in the letters. Why did you tell Nicky I set you up?" I stood up.

Lexie looked out the window. Her voice was superficial, playful. She squinted. "Well, you *did*, didn't you?"

"What?"

Lexie squeezed my arm. "You did set me up. You tried to trap me. You wanted..." Her face tightened; her mouth turned down. "You wanted me to be ... like you. I'm not like you."

It hit me the way a dentist's drill hits a nerve. I stood up. "What do you mean — 'I am not like you'?"

"You know." Lexie began piling all her clothes into one corner of the room.

"No, I don't."

Lexie folded up her French whore's bra and put it in her suitcase. "You're a lesbian, Jinx. You wanted me to be one too." Black mascara smudged her chin like soot. "I prefer men, you know. I fucked Philip's brains out this weekend."

"Lexie, *you* were the one who got in bed with me in New York. You were the one who wanted me to spend the night with you in Senior House. You wrote *me* as many letters as I wrote *you*." I moved closer to her. I wanted her to hear what I was saying.

She stopped packing and squinted at me. "You wanted it, Jinx."

I stared at her. "I'm not saying I didn't want 'it,' but you wanted '*it*' too. How can you say you are not like me? Just because Philip fucked your brains out this weekend. Maybe I'll fuck my brains out too one of these days."

"Right." Lexie laughed.

"Lexie, you're crazy. Don't you know *why* you do anything? Do you ever think before you do something? Do you ever consider that you might be hurting someone? Do you—"

"Jinx, you can leave now." Lexie's hands were on her hips.

"Did you ever stop to think what would happen to me if I let you into the dorm in the middle of the night, if—"

"None of this would be happening if you'd let me in. If you'd loved me, if you were a friend, you'd have let me in."

I looked at her in disbelief. "Loving you means only doing what you want. It means being your servant. That's not love, Lexie, that's using people. That's—"

"Get out." Lexie's hands grasped my wrist.

"Great, now you don't want to talk about it." I pulled my wrist away.

"There's no point in talking, Jinx. We're two different people. You're a—"

"Lexie..."

"A lot of people really *love* me, Jinx. They're not afraid of me. Philip loves me; Laura—"

"Philip loves you?" This time I laughed. "Philip loves you so much he got you kicked out of school three weeks before graduation. Ah, true love, it's—"

"Jinx..." Lexie looked at me strangely, almost pleadingly. And then she tried to hug me; she pressed her body against mine.

"Get away from me, Lexie."

"Jinx..."

"And you can take this gold disc from Cartier's and shove it up your ass."

"Jinx, it's a present for you."

"Make it into a cuff link for Philip, or a wedding ring." I tossed the box onto her bed. Lexie picked it up and stuffed it in my pocket. "Take it, Jinx. Please. I want you to have it, even though you used me."

"I used you? What the hell are you talking about?" I reached for the doorknob. I had to get away from her. "Good-bye, Lexie."

"You used me to make yourself feel alive. To get you out of your narrow, tight, repressed little world."

I laughed. I stood at the door and laughed, astounded. "Well, I didn't use you too well, did I? First you get me suspended, now you get me expelled. Know something, Lexie? I'm going to stop using you right now." I stepped through the door. "I never, ever, want to see you again."

I<small>T WAS NOT AN EASY SUMMER.</small> T<small>HERE WERE DEBU</small>-tante parties and doctors and exams. In July, I went back to school for exams. I stayed at my grandmother's and drove the car there each day. The school was empty. Woodie was there, of course, and so was Nicky, but I didn't speak to them. Nicky's secretary, Mrs. Gaylord Grant, "administered" the exams. The funny thing was, even with the whole school gone, the mowers still kept cutting the grass, cutting the grass. That whole week I took exams, I heard the sound of mowers on the lawn and playing fields.

I passed the exams and Cooper Union said I could go there after all. They wouldn't let me live in a dorm, what with my record and all. They wouldn't go that far. But they did let me in.

My folks were good. They believed me. They believed that I'd been falsely accused and that Nicholson had been unfair. Of course, my mother was sorry that I hadn't reported Lexie's call at five p.m., the way the honor code required, but she understood my reluctance and the fact that I hadn't wanted to get Lexie in trouble. My father was more shocked. Rules were rules. If they had to be broken, the consequences had to be accepted.

Jonas wrote me all summer. She was leaving the school. She was going to teach in Washington next year. She wrote and told me not to give up my dream of being a painter. She believed I would be an artist. Keep working, she said, keep working.

Miggin came east in August. My expulsion had shaken her. She hated the school for it, and she almost refused to graduate with the rest of the class because of it. I had told her it was okay for her to graduate, to stand up on the platform with the others, white dress and all. But I told her, just don't sing the school anthem, the alma mater that was all about the importance of truth and honor and loyalty. So she didn't sing the song. And she wrote Lexie a letter, which she showed me. She wrote Lexie saying how horrible and thoughtless and cruel she'd been. She hated Lexie.

For a while, I hated Lexie too. Especially when it looked as if Cooper wasn't going to let me in because of the trouble. More than anything I wanted to go to Cooper and live in New York and be a painter. And when I thought the whole thing would be impossible, I really hated her.

But when Cooper wrote and said it was okay, I stopped hating her as much. Of course, even while I hated her, I thought about her a lot. I still think about her a lot. I think about the fact that one day she'll probably get married and have kids. In fact, she'll probably have about ten kids and ten marriages. She'll do crazy, wild things and live in Europe and Paris and Italy. And she'll speak ten languages and have a villa on the Côte d'Azur. But the thing about Lexie is that if she doesn't slow down and try to figure things out, if she doesn't ever stop running, then one day she'll probably do something *really* crazy, and irrevocable. I know that one day she'll drive her Jaguar off a cliff or swallow a fistful of Darvon. And that'll be it.

I still have the gold disc. I never wear it. But I look at it sometimes.

Other books of interest from
ALYSON PUBLICATIONS

ACT WELL YOUR PART, by Don Sakers, $6.00. When Keith Graff moves with his mother to a new town, he feels like the new kid who doesn't fit in. He hates his new high school and wants only to move back to where his old friends still live. Then he joins the school's drama club, meets the boyishly cute Bran Davenport ... and falls in love. This gay young adult romance will appeal both to teenagers and to adult gay men who want a glimpse of what their adolescent years might have been.

ALL-AMERICAN BOYS, by Frank Mosca, $6.00. "I've known I was gay since I was thirteen. Does that surprise you? It didn't me. Actually, it was the most natural thing in the world. I thought everyone was. At least until I hit high school. That's when I finally realized all those faggot and dyke stories referred to people like me..." So begins this story of a teenage love affair that should have been simple — but wasn't.

AS WE ARE, by Don Clark, $8.00. This book, from the author of *Loving Someone Gay* and *Living Gay*, examines our gay identity in the AIDS era. Clark explores the growth and maturation of the gay community in recent years. By breaking down our ability to love and care for one another into its components, Clark creates a clear picture of where we have been, where we are going, and he emphasizes the importance of being *As We Are*.

BECOMING VISIBLE: A READER IN GAY AND LESBIAN HISTORY FOR HIGH SCHOOL AND COLLEGE STUDENTS, edited by Kevin Jennings, $10.00. Explore the history that has been hidden from gays and lesbians until now, rendering us invisible to the rest of the world. Drawing from both primary and secondary sources, this reader covers over two thousand years of history and a diverse range of cultures. This book will be welcomed by general readers seeking insight into gay and lesbian history.

BETTER ANGEL, by Forman Brown, $9.00. Written in 1933, this classic, touching story focuses on a young man's gay awakening in the years between the World Wars. Kurt Gray is a shy, bookish boy growing up in small-town Michigan. Even at the age of thirteen he knows that somehow he is different. Gradually he recognizes his desire for a man's companionship and love. As a talented composer, breaking into New York's musical world, he finds the love he's sought. This new edition contains an updated epilogue and black-and-white photographs from the author's life.

CHANGING PITCHES, by Steve Kluger, $8.00. Scotty Mackay is an American League pitcher who, at thirty-six, has to hit the comeback trail to save his all-star career. All goes well until he gets teamed up with a young catcher he detests: pretty-boy Jason Cornell. Jason has lots of teeth, poses for underwear ads, and has blue eyes ... and Scotty's favorite color is blue. By August, Scotty's got a major-league problem on his hands.

CHOICES, by Nancy Toder, $9.00. Lesbian love can bring joy and passion; it can also bring conflicts. In this straightforward, sensitive novel, Nancy Toder conveys the fear and confusion of a woman coming to terms with her sexual and emotional attraction to other women.

CODY, by Keith Hale, $6.00. Steven Trottingham Taylor, "Trotsky" to his friends, is new in Little Rock. Washington Damon Cody has lived there all his life. Yet, when they meet, there's a familiarity, a sense that they've known each other before. Their friendship grows and develops a rare intensity, although one of them is gay and the other is straight.

COMING OUT RIGHT: A HANDBOOK FOR THE GAY MALE, by Wes Muchmore and William Hanson, $8.00. Every gay man can recall the first time he stepped into a gay bar. That difficult step often represents the transition from a life of secrecy and isolation into a world of unknowns. The transition will be easier for men who have this recently updated book. Here, many facets of gay life are spelled out for the newcomer, including: coming out at work; gay health and the AIDS crisis; and the unique problems faced by men who are coming out when they're under eighteen or over thirty.

GAY MEN AND WOMEN WHO ENRICHED THE WORLD, by Thomas Cowan, $9.00. Growing up gay or lesbian in a straight culture, writes Thomas Cowan, challenges the individual in special ways. Cowan has written lively accounts of forty men and women who offered outstanding contributions in different fields, ranging from mathematics and military strategy to art, philosophy, and economics. Each chapter is amusingly illustrated with a caricature by Michael Willhoite.

HAPPY ENDINGS ARE ALL ALIKE, by Sandra Scoppettone, $7.00. It was their last summer before college, and Jaret and Peggy were in love. But as Jaret said, "It always seems as if when something great happens, then something lousy happens soon after." Soon her worst fears turned into brute reality.

NOT THE ONLY ONE: LESBIAN AND GAY FICTION FOR TEENS, edited by Tony Grima, $8.00. Many lesbians and gay men remember their teen years as a time of isolation and anxiety, when exploring sexuality meant facing possible rejection by family and friends. But it can also be a time of exciting discovery, and of hope for the future. These stories capture all the fears, joys, confusion, and energy of teenagers coming face-to-face with gay issues, either as they themselves come out, or as they learn that a friend or family member is gay.

REFLECTIONS OF A ROCK LOBSTER, by Aaron Fricke, $6.00. Guess who's coming to the prom! Aaron Fricke made national news by taking a male date to his high school prom. Yet for the first sixteen years of his life, Fricke had closely guarded the secret of his homosexuality. Here, told with insight and humor, is his story about growing up gay, about realizing that he was different, and about how he ultimately developed a positive gay identity in spite of the prejudice around him.

REVELATIONS: GAY MEN'S COMING-OUT STORIES, edited by Adrien Saks and Wayne Curtis, $8.00. For most gay men, one critical moment stands out as a special time in the coming-out process. It may be a special friendship, or a sexual episode, or a book or movie that communicates the right message at the right time. In *Revelations,* twenty-two men of varying ages and backgrounds give an account of this moment of truth. These tales of self-discovery will strike a chord of recognition in every gay reader.

SOCIETY AND THE HEALTHY HOMOSEXUAL, by George Weinberg, $8.00. Rarely has anyone communicated so much, in a single word, as Dr. George Weinberg did when he introduced the term homophobia. With a single stroke of the pen, he turned the tables on centuries of prejudice. Homosexuality is healthy, said Weinberg: homophobia is a sickness. In this pioneering book, Weinberg examines the causes of homophobia. He shows how gay people can overcome its pervasive influence, to lead happy and fulfilling lives.

TESTIMONIES: LESBIAN COMING-OUT STORIES, edited by Karen Barber and Sarah Holmes, $8.00. More than twenty women of widely varying backgrounds and ages give accounts of their journeys toward self-discovery. The stories portray the women's efforts to develop a lesbian identity, explore their sexuality, and build a community with other lesbians.

WORLDS APART: An anthology of lesbian and gay science fiction and fantasy, edited by Camilla Decarnin, Eric Garber, and Lyn Paleo, $6.00. Adventure, romance, excitement — and perhaps some genuine alternatives for our future — highlight this startling collection of lesbian and gay science-fiction writing. The authors of these stories explore issues of sexuality and gender relations in the context of futuristic societies. *Worlds Apart* challenges us by showing us our possible alternatives. The results are sometimes hilarious and sometimes disturbing.

SUPPORT YOUR LOCAL BOOKSTORE

Most of the books described here are available at your nearest gay or feminist bookstore, and many of them will be available at other bookstores. If you can't get these books locally, order by mail using this form.

Enclosed is $_____ for the following books. (Add $1.00 postage if ordering just one book. If you order two or more, we'll pay the postage.)

1._____

2._____

3._____

name:_____

address:_____

city:_____state:_____zip:_____

ALYSON PUBLICATIONS
Dept. J-54, 40 Plympton St., Boston, MA 02118

After June 30, 1996, please write for current catalog.